Readers everywhere love the novels of Susan Meissner.
Here's what they're saying about *Why the Sky Is Blue*...

"I just finished reading *Why the Sky Is Blue*...wow. Thanks for such a great read...I am a worship minister, artist (I paint murals), wife, mom of two girls, daughter of two great parents who live on my block...but I'm also a woman with deep wounds and a sad past that has made it difficult for me to trust in anyone or in my God very deeply...your book gave me a lot to ponder and muse upon, and I wanted to say thanks."

A reader in Texas

"I just finished reading your book *Why the Sky Is Blue,* and I wanted to tell you that I thoroughly enjoyed it...I have to have to say that I have never been a big fiction reader, but I think your book may have influenced me to change my ways!"

A college student in Missouri

"Bring out the Kleenex—you are certain to need them....*Why the Sky Is Blue* is an impressive debut and one that leaves me hungry for more. I hope Ms. Meissner can write quickly. I am anxious to see what else she has in store for her readers."

Tracy Farnsworth, reviewer for roundtablereviews.com

"Thank you so much for your book *Why the Sky Is Blue*...I found the characters and situations so real and true to life....I shall look forward to reading other books of yours in the future."

A reader in Georgia

"What we choose to believe about God is probably not even close to what God truly is. For this reason, we are constantly amazed and surprised when God shows us the way during our darkest moments. This book made me think about the hedge that's been growing around my 51-year-old heart—and that needs trimming."

A reader in Florida

"THANK YOU...for *Why the Sky Is Blue*. I just finished reading it and find it hard to express my response. This book touched my heart...it is one of the best novels I have read. I'm looking forward to your next book. Keep writing!"

A reader in Iowa

"Wow! What a brutally honest, beautifully expressed, compelling book! I simply could not put it down. I will definitely recommend it to many, since I work in my local public library. This book is so personal that I thought I was reading a diary or personal letter."

A reader in Minnesota

"Meissner crafts a gripping novel of lives torn apart by tragedy but healed by sacrificial love. The characters are sensitively portrayed through the first-person voices of Claire and, later, her grown-up oldest daughter."

Jill Elizabeth Nelson, Romantictimes.com

...and about *A Window to the World*

[Meissner's] characters are vivid creations, and there are good intergenerational moments between Megan and an elderly furniture upholsterer. Megan's early platonic relationship with the home-schooled and ultra-polite David Christopoulos will play well with conservative Christian readers, as will Megan's assertion, "I don't want to live in a world like this one without God."

Publisher's Weekly

"What a wonderful story and written with such ease and flow. I read lots of books—mostly Christian fiction—and this one is such a delight. "

A reader in North Carolina

"I just finished *A Window to the World*—it was amazing! I could hardly put it down...You really made each character come to life and filled the events with meaning at every turn. Thank you for writing one of the most entertaining and thought-provoking books I have ever read."

A high school teacher in Minnesota

"Thank you so very much for using your God-given talents to write a book which God has used to help me better understand my own life.I am eager to read another book from you. Please let me know the minute it hits the press!"

A reader in Washington

"Realistic characters make this novel one that could come from today's headlines, which is what inspired this book to begin with. If you enjoy Christian contemporary novels with a touch of romance, be sure to check out this wonderful novel."

Sherri Meyers Romancejunkies.com

"This gripping page-turner will tempt readers to devour it in one sitting. Well-developed characters and an original story-line create a masterful novel with a valuable message: God can use heartache to shape His people."

CBA Marketplace

The Remedy for Regret

Susan Meissner

HARVEST HOUSE PUBLISHERS

EUGENE, OREGON

Cover by Left Coast Design, Portland, Oregon

Cover image © Condé Nast Archive / CORBIS

THE REMEDY FOR REGRET
Copyright © 2005 by Susan Meissner
Published by Harvest House Publishers
Eugene, Oregon 97402
www.harvesthousepublishers.com

Library of Congress Cataloging-in-Publication Data
Meissner, Susan, 1961-
  The remedy for regret / Susan Meissner.
    p. cm.
  ISBN-13: 978-0-7369-1664-6 (pbk.)
  ISBN-10: 0-7369-1664-4 (pbk.)
  1. Single women—Fiction. 2. Female friendship—Fiction. 3. Mothers—Death—
Fiction. I. Title.
 PS3613.E435R46 2005   2005001901

Printed in the United States of America.

05 06 07 08 09 10 11 12 13 / BP-MS / 10 9 8 7 6 5 4 3 2 1

*For my parents, Bill and Judy Horning, who
—unlike the parents in this story—
ably and willingly met my every childish need*

Acknowledgments

Caroldene and Oran Jones warmly welcomed my husband, our infant daughter, and me when we moved to Blytheville, Arkansas, in the winter of 1986. I was a new Air Force wife, a new mother, and 2000 miles away from home for the first time in my life. Their many kindnesses back then have been matched only by their sweet hospitality again in the summer of 2004, when I revisited Arkansas in preparation for writing *The Remedy for Regret*. I am in their debt.

Brian and Carol Finley, Air Force friends from our shared tour of duty at RAF Upper Heyford, lived on the Azores while stationed at Lajes Field. They kindly read with a discerning eye the first few chapters. Brian, a medical doctor, also checked the accuracy of the events in this book that are of a medical nature. I extend my thanks to them both.

First Lieutenant Yvonne Levardi, Chief of Public Affairs at Lajes Field, kindly answered all my questions about the Azores and the American base located there.

The remarkable staff at Harvest House Publishers has encouraged me in countless ways, giving me the confidence every writer needs to attempt new things. Nick Harrison and Carolyn McCready in particular are wonderful editors whose insights make me want to be a better writer.

My husband, Bob, and our children, Stephanie, Joshua, Justin, and Eric, never doubted for a moment that I could write books that people would want to read. They began sentences with, "When the book gets published," long before I did, long before there *was* a publisher. I am privileged to call them my family.

My young friend Tess Emmert graciously allowed me the use of her beautiful first name.

God has gifted everyone with talents and abilities that can honor Him. I hope I have done that with this story, and if I have, I am grateful for having had the privilege.

Author's Note

Although this novel is a work of fiction, most of the places that appear within its pages are real and therefore subject to change. Of particular note, Blytheville Air Force Base, mentioned in this book, was renamed Eaker Air Force Base in 1988. I do not allude to this in the story because it bears no weight on the story's telling. Eaker Air Force Base closed in 1992. RAF Upper Heyford, also mentioned in this book, was home to several squadrons of American aircraft until 1992, when this Tactical Fighter Wing and its aircraft were relocated to Shaw Air Force Base in South Carolina. The base itself was turned back over to Great Britain's Ministry of Defense in 1994. Lajes Field, located on the Azores Islands and mentioned in the first chapter, is still home to American servicemen and women of the 65th Air Base Wing.

"It may be a terrible thing to fall into the living God's hands. But oh, Roxanna, imagine falling *out*. He's the only hand there is."

Reynolds Price, *Roxanna Slade*

"Come to me, all you who are weary and burdened, and I will give you rest."

Matthew 11:28

CHAPTER 1

Last Breath, First Breath

Chicago, Illinois

Thoughts of my mother and the island where I was born are heavy on my mind as I get ready to leave the boutique after a long day at work. I have finished redecorating the main window displays at *Linee Belle,* and I must say I am proud of how they look. I doubt if even Antonia, who owns the boutique, could have done a better job. I can almost hear Antonia saying, "*Lavoro eccellente,* Tess!" Excellent work. I love the way she says my name. It sounds like *Tezz* when she says it.

Summer fashions are in, though it is only early April, and my primary mannequins are now lounging in breezy beach attire, stretched out on and atop sand Antonia had shipped from Myrtle Beach. She told me that once your toes have sifted through the sand of an ocean beach, no other kind of sand will do. A beach needs beach sand. I don't think she even bothered to consider the cost. Money to her is wonderfully relative.

The gauzy dresses and linen capris, in shades of the warmest yellows and corals, nearly give off their own heat, and I feel an island breeze as I take one last look before calling it a day, though the only movement above my head is the chilly indoor air from exhaust fans in the ceiling. Nevertheless, the island is near me and so is my mother's face as I turn and walk away.

Tourists, shoppers, and business owners call where I work Chicago's Miracle Mile because if you can walk the length of it without spending any money, it's—you guessed it—a miracle. But it's really just an ordinary commercial district, brimming with the usual upscale shops and restaurants. Antonia's boutique is one of nearly one hundred stores in the Water Tower Place mall at the mile's north end. I spend my weekdays there waiting on women who have too much money in their wallets and dressing anorexic mannequins in fashions with price tags that make me shudder, even after four years of looking at them. Even so, I like what I do. I like making these tired, rich women look good. And I love dressing the mannequins. It's like never having to give up playing with dolls.

They all have names, my mannequins. Madeline, the one I have named after my mother, is the only one who carries a purse. It's our private little joke, Madeline's and mine. Madeline always gets the purse no matter which display I put her in because all mothers carry purses. It's part of their mystique. Kids long to look in their mother's purses, to play with their contents, to discover where all those hidden scents come from.

I take a quick peek over my shoulder at Madeline as I start to head for the tiny office in the back of the store. Madeline's purse is sunshine yellow and made of soft Moroccan leather. It perfectly matches her strapless, lemon chiffon dress. The mannequin I have named Blair, after my childhood friend Blair Devere, would look better in the dress, but Blair doesn't get to carry the purse, Madeline does. And it's a perfect match.

The store and the little office at the back are quiet. I am the last to leave *Linee Belle* for the day; Antonia left several hours ago and Elena, our main part-time worker and a busy single mother, left ten minutes ago when the mall closed at seven.

I like finishing the window displays when no one else is around, when no one can hear me whisper to the mannequins. If they had minds and could be interviewed, you'd find that they know literally all there is to know about me. I tell them everything.

I grab my jacket and my canvas bag and switch off the lights, winding my way through the darkened displays. There is almost an eerie sense of unease within me as I lower the grinding metal cage door over my island tableau. I should be hearing the call of gulls, not the heavy sound of steel hitting marble tile. Madeline is looking at me with her painted, unmoving eyes as I turn the lock. I wink at her to convince myself that I am not bothered by her stare.

The drive home will be slow going as usual but I don't care. I'm not entirely thrilled with the idea of going home to Simon and his demons. The remnants of rush hour traffic will give me time to unwind.

Simon is my fiancé. Sort of. He wants to marry me. And I want to marry him. I'm just not able to set a date at the moment. It's hard to explain so I usually don't. Besides, people aren't asking about us as much anymore. And especially not right now since everyone seems to understand Simon is in no condition to pledge anything to anyone.

I spend the next twenty minutes in sporadic stop-and-go traffic, wondering if I will go to the baby shower I have been invited to, as well as wondering if Simon needs professional help. I am undecided on both as I turn onto my street. I prepare myself for the worst as I park my car in our apartment's underground garage.

Simon is sitting in the chair we bought at an estate sale for fifty dollars as I open the door to our apartment. His back is to me but I can see what is etched on his face. He is sitting there just the way I left him this morning. I don't even bother to ask him how he's doing. It would be a dumb question. He is not *doing* anything. He is just letting things be done.

"Hi," I say simply as I make my way in.

The tiniest nod of his head communicates to me that he heard me.

It has been nearly two weeks since his accident. Physically, all traces of that horrible night are gone. But I know what is happening to Simon on the inside: He can't forgive himself for what happened, even if it really was just an accident. He never meant to hurt anyone but it happened anyway.

He had been driving home from a guys' night out with fellow O'Hare air traffic controllers and it was raining. He was making a call on his cell phone, which he had dropped, when he decided to pass a truck. Simon didn't see another car coming up from behind when he leaned down to pick up the phone. He didn't see that the little Mazda was in the fast lane next to him when he started to pass the slow-moving semi. He didn't look over his shoulder; he relied solely on his rearview mirror. Simon sideswiped the Mazda, sending it careening off into the median, where it rolled into oncoming traffic. Simon swerved too when he saw what was happening, following the Mazda into the median. His car only rolled twice and then came to a stop in wet grass and soft, muddy earth. The toddler in the back seat of the Mazda died on impact when the car collided with two other vehicles. The child's mother—the driver—died on the way to a hospital.

I remember thinking, when the call came that night, that I was so lucky Simon was okay. That he had walked away from the crunched metal of his car with just some scratches and a bruised shoulder. A few days afterward, no one could tell he had been hurt at all. His supervisor expected him back at work. So did all his coworkers. But he didn't go back. He still hasn't.

Now Simon spends the better part of each day hoping someone will finally decide to come to the apartment and arrest him. He wants the handcuffs, the guilty verdict. He doesn't want the "inattentive driving" ticket that he got instead. And it doesn't matter to him that the Mazda had only one working headlight that night. All that matters is that he dropped his cell phone and made a careless decision to retrieve it while passing a slow-moving truck.

I look at him now, sitting there with just his wounded conscience for company, and I understand perfectly. I have understood from the moment I picked him up at the hospital. I try to tell him so.

"I know what you are going through," I say, kneeling down by him, draping an arm across his shoulder. I have wanted to say this for days. I know the pain of living with something you did that you wish with all your heart you could undo. I have always known it.

"No, you don't," he says coolly, in reply.

I am momentarily taken aback, but I quickly recover. I try to make eye contact.

"Yes, I do," I say softly. "Simon, I know what it is like to feel like you are responsible for someone's death."

He looks away with disgust.

"Give it a rest," he growls. "You *didn't* kill your mother, Tess."

I am speechless for several moments. Simon is one of the few people who knows what happened in the delivery room the night I was born. He is also the only person who knows that I too am aware of what happened that night, though no one else knows I know.

"But," I start to protest, when I am able.

"You didn't kill anyone," he continues.

"But Simon, if I hadn't been born..." I try again.

"Tess, that's like saying, 'Oh, if only the *Titanic* hadn't been built!'" he says, mocking me.

"Simon, I do know what you are feeling right now," I say, my voice shaking. I have never heard him talk this way. To anyone.

"You are so in love with your pain," he whispers, his eyes glassy with emotion, but he is not looking at me.

I can feel anger welling inside me and I know I should just walk away. But I fall easily into his misery. I am familiar with it.

"Well, look who's falling in love with his," I snap back. I rise to my feet and make my way to the kitchen. He says nothing as I leave the room.

I get myself a glass of water and drink it though I am not aware that I am thirsty. In the four years I have known Simon, he has never made me feel this way. I am searching for the word that describes it. *Foolish.* He has never made me feel foolish for my thoughts about the night I was born. As I hold the glass tighter in my hand, I am starting to sense that fear is getting mixed in with my apparent silliness. If I don't have Simon on my side, I don't have anyone. I know this. He is the only one I have ever felt comfortable telling what I know, what I feel, what I envision happened the night my mother died.

He is the only one who knows how I have always imagined it—the night that defines me but that I cannot remember. He knows I see a waiting room that is library-quiet, that smells somewhat like a mixture of Listerine, furniture polish, and scrambled eggs. He knows I see a pale moon outside a row of windows, a moon losing its radiance as the brighter light of the sun begins a slow ascent over the island where I was born.

I recall it now, though I don't particularly want to. With the empty glass in my hand, I see it as I have always seen it. In a waiting room chair that squeaks at the slightest movement is the doctor who sits with his head in his hands. The doctor is my father. He hasn't sat in a waiting room chair since he was a child. He had forgotten what it was like, but he remembers it slowly now. It was boring. It was stiflingly quiet. There was nothing to do but wonder if there would be pain. Will he get a shot? Will the doctor hurt him? Will he be able to keep from crying out? He doesn't want to shed tears in front of his mother.

Then the image of himself as a little boy suddenly vanishes as an Air Force medic brushes past him, and he can't help but imagine that pain indeed awaits him. He is no longer the little boy who knows nothing. He is a doctor who knows too much.

The doctor's gaze travels to the windows and he can see that the night is just beginning to give way to dawn. The island called

Terceira is slowly coming to life, as are the rest of the Azores, a group of tiny islands off the coast of Portugal. He has forgotten that the day will mark the beginning of the Sanjoaninas Festival. Thousands of Azoreans will attend, along with a handful of mainlanders and Air Force personnel like himself stationed on Terceira. Tomorrow there will be a bullfight in the street. There will be music and drinking and laughter. The air outside is charged with expectancy. Inside the Lajes Field base hospital, however, where the doctor waits, the air seems to have lost its ability to sustain life. He can feel it.

My father can't keep his hands from shaking as he waits for the doors behind him to open. He wants to get up and pace the room, but he can feel no strength in his legs.

This fear is new to him. Everything about this night is new to him. He has been a father for about six hours. He has not yet been told that he has been a widower for about six minutes.

He knows nothing about how to be either one.

I should say right now that my father doesn't like to talk about the night I was born and my mother died. I know what I know because his friend Joey was in the waiting room with him that night. Joey told me ages ago what it was like but only after I begged him. He was visiting us in Omaha before we left for my father's new assignment in Arkansas. I was twelve then. Joey took me out for ice cream when my father went to sign out two days before we left SAC headquarters.

I could tell Joey didn't want to tell me anything. He was thinking my dad should be the one to tell me, that I shouldn't have to beg old friends to describe what it was like the night my mother died. Maybe my dad should have been the one to tell me, but I didn't care then who did the telling. I just wanted to know how it happened.

Joey told me that my father found out just before morning broke and that the waiting seemed to take forever. Joey said my dad had called him in the middle of the night and asked him to come down to the hospital, that I had been born but that something was wrong with my mother. I have always had to imagine the rest.

Not the bullfights, though. Not the festival.

Hours after my mother died, Terceira Island celebrated its annual festival with typical reckless abandon. The islanders didn't know a young Air Force wife had died after giving birth. Had they known, the festival would have gone on as planned anyway. What happened at the Americans' airbase wasn't of much local interest unless it involved a search and rescue within the Azorean territorial waters.

Joey didn't actually tell me this part. I imagined it. I imagined it because when my father was making arrangements for my mother's body to be flown back to England where she was born, the streets of our island were crowded with spectators watching the blood of bulls spill onto the ground.

I don't know why exactly, but when I picture that waiting room in my head, I picture my father waiting there alone. I know Joey was there. But I just don't see him in the room until later, when the waiting is over and the grieving begins. I picture the doors opening behind my dad. I picture him reluctantly raising his head to meet the eyes of the one who has entered the room with the sole purpose of delivering horrible news. This person is probably a friend like Joey. The 1605th Air Base Wing at this base wasn't huge. The USAF hospital at Lajes was made up of a small company of average Americans: doctors, nurses, corpsmen—officers and enlisted—from average places like Des Moines, Amarillo, and Cleveland. My father worked behind those doors he now waited in front of. As a family practitioner, he hardly ever had to be the giver of bad news. No doctor at Lajes Field had to do it very often. In the year and a half he and my mother were stationed there, it never came up. He stitched torn skin, set broken bones, delivered babies, gave the hated shots. But at a small base like Lajes Field, a mini world within a world, death would come only on rare occasions. Like that night.

So I picture his coworker, another doctor I like to call Eddie, coming through those double doors with a weight on his shoulders that you can actually see. He walks over to my father and says those words movie doctors say when a patient dies.

"We tried everything," Eddie says softly, laying a hand on my dad's shoulder.

Joey, who has been standing the whole time, walks quickly over to my dad and sits down next to him. He wraps his arm around my father's bent shoulders.

My dad doesn't ask about me. But he probably thinks I am fine. I had been born several hours earlier, three weeks early, but with no complications. The trouble for my mother didn't start until the very end of labor when she started to feel strange. For a long time I didn't know what it was that had made her feel so sick. I tried asking my father about it—many times— but he would just smile a weak grin that had no sincerity in it and say, "It just happens sometimes." I remember asking him when I was ten and him saying something like, "Tess, sometimes there are complications when a woman gives birth and no matter how hard you try, you just can't do anything about them."

"What kind of complications?" I had asked.

"It's complicated, Tess," he said after a long pause, not even realizing he was telling me the complications were complicated, nor that he was giving me the answer a doctor would give, not a father.

I tried asking Joey too that day we went out for ice cream. I knew he knew how it happened. He was a dentist on base. All the medical personnel had to know how my mother died. Stuff like that didn't happen very often. It had to have been discussed at every watercooler, coffeemaker, and cluttered desk in the hospital.

At first he wouldn't tell me. He wouldn't confirm that he knew what it was that killed her, but I knew he knew because he wouldn't look at me when he told me I should just leave it.

"She died in childbirth, Tess," Joey said. "It happens sometimes."

"You sound just like my dad," I told him, and I stopped eating my ice cream.

"And she didn't die in childbirth," I continued, like I was desperate for someone to acknowledge I was not responsible for what happened to her. "She died afterward."

Joey had sighed then. He stopped eating his ice cream too.

"You can't change the past," he said gently.

I just sat there and said nothing. I didn't know how to tell him I wasn't trying to change the past. I was trying to understand it.

Then Joey sighed and said very quietly, "It was an embolism, Tess."

The word struck me to the bone and I didn't even know what it meant.

"What's an embolism?" I whispered.

I could tell Joey was wishing he had said nothing. He picked up his napkin and spoon like it was time to go.

"It's when something that doesn't belong in the lungs gets in the lungs, Tess," he said, not looking at me. "Promise me you will drop this. Promise me you will not mention this to your dad. I don't know why he hasn't told you, but he hasn't. So I want you to promise me."

When he asked me to promise him those two things, that's when he lifted his head and looked at me.

At first I said nothing. That word just kept swirling around in my head. *Embolism. Embolism.* It made absolutely no sense to me. What did a woman's lungs have to do with giving birth? My father had already told me everything about having babies. We had had the sex talk. I knew which body parts produced a child and which didn't. It was like telling me she gave birth and then died of a gunshot wound.

But the more I thought about it the more I decided it couldn't possibly have anything to do with me at all, and I could live with that. And I did. For about five months. But that day at the ice cream parlor I thought I knew everything, so I promised

Joey I would drop it and that I wouldn't mention to my dad that Joey had told me anything.

So for a little while longer, the black night ended in my mind with the man I have named Eddie standing by a weeping man, my father. Next to my father is Joey with his strong arm around him. Joey is trying to be brave for my father, but the tears are streaming down his face too.

This is where it stops. I have never been able to adequately imagine the next minute, the next hour, the next day.

My father doesn't ask about me. He thinks I am fine.

CHAPTER 2

Imagining Magnolias

If I close my eyes I can almost feel the ocean breeze and hear the sounds of island birds and the melodic pull of the Portuguese language. Even on the coldest and windiest of Chicago days, I can taste the salt in the air if I close my eyes and imagine it. Sometimes I wish my dad had taken more pictures when he lived in the Azores. Other times I am glad he didn't.

About a year ago, Simon told me that he would take me back to Terceira if I wanted to go. We were cuddled on the couch, enjoying expensive coffee while an early spring thunderstorm raged outside our apartment building. It was a rather tender moment, really. Up to that point Simon had not shown much personal interest in my private little world of sorrows, not even when he finally understood how much I had contributed to my mother's death. I surprised him by telling him after just a moment's thought that I really didn't want to visit Terceira, that I was happy with the pictures I had in my head. If I were to go to the Azores and see the islands for myself, I might realize that the pictures in my head are all wrong. I would rather believe that the way I envision my island is exactly the way it is than to actually see it and discover it is not that way at all.

Simon brought it up again this past Christmas, but that was the last time. I doubt it even crosses his mind these days. Now that he is locked within his own little world of sorrows, he has forgotten he had ever asked. And that he even thought of asking.

There are only a few photographs among my mother's things, none of the island itself. I carry a photo of her, taken on the island, in the canvas bag I bring to work every day. She is pregnant with me, but it is early into the pregnancy and the photo doesn't show that nestled under her skin and muscle is my tiny, forming body. She is sitting on a cement step at the entrance to the little duplex my parents shared with two married lieutenants. I can imagine that behind my mother—behind the house—is the sandy coastline and beyond that, an endless expanse of ocean. But all you can see past her head is a door.

Dad stayed at Terceira after her funeral. He was expected to ask for a reassignment for humanitarian reasons. Joey told me he would have gotten one too. But he came back, bringing my grandmother—his mother—with him. She stayed for six months. I was too young and new to go to England with him for the funeral. At least that's what he told me when I was older. I think he was simply too anguished to care for me himself. Joey and his wife, Marlys, watched over me the four days he was gone.

Just a few months after I met Simon, we were at a restaurant, eating clams and linguini, and he asked me if I had family in England. Did my mother have parents who lived there? Did she have siblings? I spoke the answer quickly so that I didn't have to dwell on the names or imagine the faces.

"Her father died when she was fifteen and her mother passed away a couple of years after I was born," I said. "She has a brother who still lives in England. His name is Martin. We've never met. So, do you want to split some dessert?"

One of the things I have always liked about Simon is he never complains when I want to change the subject.

Now as I stand in the kitchen with our angry, hurtful words filling my head, I am wondering what are some of the things Simon has always liked about *me*. At the moment nothing comes to mind. I look at the glass I am clenching in my hand. My fingers are turning white around it. I am inwardly glad I have not thrown it against the wall. I set it carefully down on the kitchen counter.

I should make Simon and myself something to eat, but I have no appetite. I start to wonder if Simon has eaten anything at all today, when I see two bowls in the sink. One with severely dehydrated Cheerios stuck to the side, another with slightly less dehydrated Cheerios stuck to the side. Simon had a bowl of Cheerios for breakfast and one for lunch. A tired smile crosses my face as I imagine myself calling out to the other room, "Hey, Simon! How about Cheerios for dinner! Whaddya say?" But then I hear the front door open and close. He has left.

I walk back into the living room and blink at the empty chair, then at the little table by our front door. Simon has not taken my car keys, though it didn't really cross my mind that he would. He hasn't driven since the night of the accident. I am trying to decide if it is good that he has left the apartment for a little while—even if only on foot—or if I should follow him to make sure he doesn't try to find a way to hurl himself off the John Hancock building. I honestly don't know what to do.

I ease myself into the fifty-dollar chair, warm from Simon's body, wondering how to call out to God. Wondering if I can. Wondering if there is any point.

I think of the little church in Arkansas that sat on the corner of my street where I lived when I was twelve, and I immediately see my friend Jewel's father, the pastor, swaying as he prays to the God he loves. I remember being in awe while Blair, sitting next to me, whispered "He's nuts!" in my ear. I am reminded of how I envied his faith.

God seems very far away right now.

Now that I am home, away from the boutique and my lovely beach scene, my mother and my island are floating away too, being replaced with thoughts of Jewel's dad as I sit in the chair. No, not Jewel's dad. Jewel's mother.

Spontaneous thoughts of Corinthia Mayhew unnerve me in a way that is difficult to put in plain words. Of all the people I have ever met, she is the one who, at the very thought of her, makes me want to step back and see if I have accomplished anything worthwhile with my life.

Corinthia is the first person I met when Dad and I moved into our rented, two-story brick house in Blytheville, Arkansas. It had only been a matter of days since Joey had breathed the word *embolism* and it was still swirling around in my twelve-year-old head. I didn't want to move to Arkansas, especially in the middle of the school year. I had made friends in Omaha the three years we were there, and like any twelve-year-old, I believed friends were more life sustaining than air and water.

Dad and I had made the drive to his new base in two days, dragging a little U-Haul with the bare essentials behind our Volvo station wagon. We lived in a cheerless temporary living facility that everybody called the TLF, for the first eight days. The only good thing about the TLF was that I met Blair there, a twelve-year-old cynic like me who was brought kicking and screaming to Blytheville from a base in New York.

It was the first week in January and everything was gray, including my mood. Dad pretended not to notice. Or maybe he was too preoccupied getting settled onto a new base *to* notice. He brought me to see the brick house after my third day at my new middle school, which thankfully Blair was attending even though she was going to be living on base. Blair watched us leave the temporary living facility to go look at the house with contempt written all over her face. Her father, a B-52 pilot, was required to live on base in one of the dozens upon dozens of look-alike duplexes behind the TLF.

I liked the house well enough. Without our things inside, it was hard to imagine it being my home. Dad liked the fireplace and the built-in bookshelves. I liked the wood floors and glass doorknobs.

As Dad signed the rental agreement and talked over the utilities with the owner, I stepped outside into the barren backyard. It was gray and dreary. *Is there any place that looks good in January?* I was wondering.

I was gazing toward the edge of our backyard at a large tree whose branches fanned out far into the adjoining yard.

A waist-high picket fence separated the two yards and I went and stood by it, leaned on it. I didn't see or hear Corinthia Mayhew approach me from behind.

"In the spring it will be covered with white blossoms the size of dinner plates," said a voice behind me.

I had jumped and then turned around quickly.

Behind me on the other side of the fence stood a tall, slender woman with creamy, chocolate-colored skin. She had deep brown eyes, and her wiry black hair was swept up into a clip on the back of her head.

"I'm sorry. I didn't mean to startle you," she said, smiling. She was wearing a flowery skirt, even though it wasn't much above thirty degrees outside, and a purple, woolly jacket. Over one arm she carried a black leather purse by its handle. It was nearly bursting with its contents.

"I'm Corinthia Mayhew," she continued, extending her free hand.

Everything about her had me mesmerized. Her voice with its heavy Southern accent, her deep brown eyes, her height, her bulging purse. And her name.

I shook her hand but could not say anything.

"And you are?" she asked gently.

I blushed.

"Tess Longren," I said.

"It's a pleasure to meet you, Tess," she replied. "Y'all movin' in next door?"

She motioned with her head to the brick house.

I nodded.

"Well, we'll be neighbors then!" she said, genuinely pleased. "That's my house," she said, using the arm that carried the purse to point toward a white house next door.

"I have a girl who must be about your age," she continued. "You twelve? Thirteen?"

"I'm twelve. I'll be thirteen in May," I said, captivated by her purse. It has always been a thing with me. I have always been drawn to purses carried by mothers. I never told anyone about it. It seemed silly. It still does. I could see a wallet sticking out of the top of Corinthia's purse. It was fat with pictures.

"Well, my Jewel is twelve too!" Corinthia said, beaming. "When are y'all movin' in? Y'all with the air base, then?"

"The movers are coming tomorrow," I said, already wondering what Jewel would be like and if I had already seen her at school and didn't know it. I had never had a friend with such an unusual first name before.

"My dad's a major in the Air Force. He's a doctor," I added.

"Well, isn't that just fine," she said. "We love having neighbors from the air base. We love to hear y'all's stories of all the places you've lived. Me and the pastor—that'd be Samuel Mayhew, my husband; he's pastor of the church on the other side of our house—we never lived anywhere but right here. We love to hear about where y'all have been. The last family that lived in your house moved here from Spain! Imagine that!"

I glanced over at the church on the other side of Corinthia's house. It was on the corner of the street. It was simple and white with a tall, pointed steeple. I couldn't see the sign that gave its name.

"You have other kids?" I asked. I'm not sure why I asked this at this point. Maybe it was because, being an only child back then, I was overly curious about families with more than one child. I tended to be a little envious of friends who had brothers and sisters.

"I've got *five*," Corinthia said proudly. "They are my whole world, they are."

Corinthia looked back to her house like she expected to see five dark faces smiling back at her through the windows.

"How about you, Tess?" she said, turning back to me. "You got brothers and sisters?"

"No," I said, looking back at the tree towering over our heads. "It's just me and my dad."

Out of the corner of my eye I could see her nodding her head, putting things together. *Would she ask it?* I remember thinking. *Would she ask about my mom?* I hated it when I could tell people wanted to know about my mother but were too chicken to ask.

Corinthia wasn't too chicken.

"Where's your momma, Tess?" she asked gently. Simply.

With my eyes still on the tree I told her.

"She died right after I was born."

For a moment, Corinthia said and did nothing. Then she reached out her arm and touched me on the shoulder. It was a gentle touch but I could tell there was strength there.

"I'm sorry to hear that," she said. "But I am glad your daddy has you to look out for him."

I turned to look at her. No one had ever said anything like that to me before, that it would have been far, far worse for my dad to have lost us both that night.

"Tess, it would be my pleasure when the movers are done tomorrow if you and your daddy would join my family and me for supper," she said. Her hand was still on my shoulder.

"Well, I'll have to ask my dad," I stammered, wondering if Corinthia was this nice to everyone. I was already figuring she probably was.

"Of course, of course," she said. "Tell him sixish, but we'll wait for y'all if things are runnin' late for you." She dropped her arm.

"Okay," I said, not sure what to say next. It seemed like our conversation was winding down. I turned back to the tree we shared between us.

"You ever seen a magnolia tree in bloom, Tess?" Corinthia asked.

"No, I don't think so," I answered.

"The blossoms are as big as dinner plates. *Dinner* plates," she said smiling up at the enormous tree. "Just you wait and see. When spring comes, you'll see how beautiful the world can be after a long winter."

Then she turned to me.

"Things will be beautiful again, Tess. After a time," she said, and her eyes were bright with a message she was trying to convey to me.

Corinthia did not know then, nor did I, that my life would take several unexpected and defining turns within months of meeting her, turns that would call to mind this message about holding on to hope when you can't see what lies ahead. We had no way of knowing that five months later I would stumble across my mother's medical records while looking for summer clothes, nor that my dad would meet Shelley that June, nor that Jewel, Blair, and I would find an abandoned, crippled infant on the steps of Jewel's church in July, nor that all these things would happen to me within the span of three months. Nor did I know that these three separate events were like strands of a common thread, tangled and indistinguishable as being connected, but joined at the middle nonetheless. I was unaware, even for years afterward, that the thread began and ended with three mothers and their children: my mother and me, the crippled infant and the mother who had abandoned him, and Shelley, the woman who would become my stepmother and who would, in time, bear my father's child and live. But all I knew then was that I was already troubled by many things, and Corinthia had sensed it.

The back door opened at that moment and I heard my dad call out my name.

"Guess I'd better go," I said, and I started to walk away.

"See you tomorrow, then?" Corinthia said.

I turned my head back but kept walking.

"Um, yeah," I said. Then I suddenly remembered my manners. "Oh, it was nice meeting you, Cor...I mean, Mrs. Mayhew."

She laughed.

"You can call me Corinthia," she said. "I can tell you want to."

I grinned back at her.

"And it was nice meeting *you*, Tess," she called out to me as she started to walk toward her own house, looking straight into my eyes and into my heart.

I am aware of just the clock ticking as the unbidden memory of Corinthia starts to slip away and I realize twenty minutes have passed since Simon left the apartment without a word and I sank into this chair. If I were a braver woman I would pick up the phone and call Corinthia right now. I know I could pour out my heart and soul to her and she would not even think to ask why I haven't called or written her in thirteen years. I know she still lives in Blytheville, that she and Samuel still live in the same white house. Jewel and I write each other every Christmas. I know Corinthia still thinks of me from time to time. Jewel has told me so.

But I am not a brave woman.

I walk into the kitchen and pour myself a bowl of Cheerios. Surely there will be munchies at the baby shower. A small bowl of cereal will suffice until the refreshments are served. When I am done, I put my bowl in the sink next to Simon's other two and grab the gift I had bought at the mall a couple of days ago.

I will be a little late, but that's okay. Small talk will have given way to the opening of the gifts, which is fine with me. I am not in the mood for a great deal of small talk, but neither do I want to sit in this empty apartment all evening.

And I can handle the basic questions.

How are things with you, Tess?

Great. And you?

Very well. Oh, I've been meaning to tell you how glad I am that Simon wasn't hurt in that accident.

Yes, yes. We're so very lucky.

So, how are things at the boutique?

Splendid. You should come and see our new summer line.

Oh, I'd love to.

That's the danger and the beauty of wounds that are invisible. Everyone thinks you are fine.

CHAPTER 3

On the Steps of a Church

I am a little more than fashionably late to the shower but, as I had guessed, Monica—a friend from the jewelry store next to *Linee Belle*—is just starting to open her gifts. I have missed the games, I am told, and there is much laughter as I am shown the booties the other women tried to tear out—from behind their backs—of pink paper.

"Looks a little like Texas," I say to a woman named Phoebe whom I barely know as she holds up one of her booties.

Laughter erupts around the room.

The hostess, Yvette, hands me a cup of punch and tells me how glad she is that I came. She is Monica's neighbor and I don't know her at all.

I take a seat by a few women I recognize from Monica's store and notice as I sit that one of them is holding a pink bundle. Monica's baby.

Tracy, the one holding the baby, and Caroline, just on her other side, are cooing and gushing; their faces are wide-eyed and silly looking.

"Look, Tess," Tracy says to me, shifting the infant in her arms so that I can see the baby's face. "Isn't she adorable?"

I nod and make a silly face myself. It is expected. The baby is asleep and sees none of this.

"Let's see the rest of her!" Caroline whispers.

Giggling, Tracy pulls the pink receiving blanket away from the baby's body. The infant is wearing a soft, white gown that is gathered at the bottom with a satiny pink ribbon.

"I want to see her toes!" Caroline says softly as if we were conspiring to commit a crime.

The crazy thing is, I want to see the baby's toes too.

We all lean in as Tracy loosens the ribbon and reveals the tiny legs inside. The two women gasp in delight. I gasp too. I can't help it.

Monica's baby has two perfect tiny feet. It's normal, of course, for a baby to have two perfect feet, but it still amazes me. On these rare occasions when I see a newborn's legs, my first response is always surprise. I can't help but remember how it was when Blair, Jewel, and I found that baby on the steps of Jewel's church. How it was when we pulled away the sweat-shirt that was covering that baby and saw one perfect foot and one misshapen one.

I am still contemplating the visual differences when Caroline asks about Simon.

Caroline is just an acquaintance, someone I see regularly at Water Tower Place but with whom I have never spent more than a minute in real conversation.

"He's coming along well," I say and then I add, "Thanks for asking."

That's the nice way of saying, *We're done talking about this.* She gets it.

"Let me hold her now," Caroline says to Tracy, reaching for the baby and taking her eyes and attention off me.

I spend the next twenty minutes as a spectator. The only person I know well enough to initiate a dialogue with is Monica. And she is busy opening gifts. Watching the other women engaged in riveting conversation, I can't help but feel a tad left out. I wish Antonia had been invited. But then again, Antonia wouldn't have come. Everything is business to her. Business and romance. She never does fun stuff with just a bunch of other women. She occupies herself with buying designer clothes and accessories for the boutique and chasing down eligible men who are richer than she is. I smile, thinking how much she reminds me of Blair.

Sometimes I wonder if Blair and I would have stayed friends if we had not found that baby on that lazy July morning. That one, daylong experience sort of bound us together in a strange kind of way, as if we were both survivors of the same plane crash or something. Jewel was bound to me after that experience too, in the same kind of way, but because Jewel and Blair never hit it off well, it has always seemed different somehow. It still surprises me that Blair continued to want my friendship long after she rose to the ranks of popular girls in our middle school, as well as long after we both moved from Arkansas to other bases.

In the beginning, when Blair and I first met, we were both so hungry for companionship because of our just-moved misery, we didn't realize that was the only thing we truly had in common. Well, that's not entirely true. She was starving for a mother's love just as I was even though she still had her mother. Aside from that, we were about as different as we could be.

When we met, she was already "boy crazy" as my dad liked to describe her, and she wore a face full of makeup everywhere we went, even to the pool on base. I liked boys, but I was too afraid to approach one or even let Blair know which ones I liked best. She had a figure well before her thirteenth birthday and deep, wide eyes that looked even bigger when lined with mascara and eye shadow. Blair also had perfect hair, nice clothes, and straight teeth, and she was never at a loss for words. Dad thought she was pushy and disrespectful and that she was falsely polite to him whenever she came over to the house. I used to defend her right and left but the truth was, he was right.

I liked classical music and looking at maps and working jigsaw puzzles, and Blair liked none of these things. My auburn hair, unlike her honey-blonde curls, was nondescript other than its color. People, especially women, commented that it was a very nice shade. But I didn't know what to do with it and Dad never thought there was something to be done. I don't blame him really. It just didn't occur to him to think I might look good with a stylish haircut. That's something a mom would have thought of. It wasn't that Dad couldn't buy me nice clothes either or didn't; we just didn't shop together very often. His parents would fly out from Wisconsin to see us every Christmas and summer, no matter where we were, and Grandma would always buy me new clothes. But Grandma's idea of shopping for clothes was paging through the JCPenney catalog or maybe making a trip to Sears. Antonia would die if she knew how deprived I was of fashion sense before I met Blair. And Blair's mother. Veronica Devere, Blair's mom, spent very little time at home, and I hardly said more than a sentence to her a month, but whenever I did see her, she was always impeccably dressed. Most of the time when I was at Blair's, Veronica was running out the house, late for something but dressed in a beautifully coordinated outfit. I have a mannequin named after her too.

It's funny; I didn't have much in common with Jewel either, but she remains one of the few friends, including Simon, whom I feel I could trust completely. And it's kind of odd that I should feel that way because I hardly ever see her, and neither one of us is very good about writing or calling. She lives in Memphis, is a pastor's wife like her mother, and has three little boys. The admiration I still feel for Jewel is partly because she reminds me of Corinthia, of course. But she also reminds me—more so than Blair—of that time in my life when everything changed for me, like a strong wind in the sail changes a ship's direction—and its destination.

Monica is done opening her presents, and as she finishes, I am feeling a little awkward. Her baby ended up in my arms when Tracy and Caroline went to help Yvette in the kitchen. The baby is starting to tense up as Monica makes her way to me. She's going to start wailing at any second. I smile with relief as Monica sits in the chair Tracy has vacated. All around us the other women are laughing, talking, and making their way to the dining room, where Yvette has laid out the refreshments.

"You're a natural, Tess," Monica says, winking at me.

"Oh, not really," I say nervously. I am anxious to hand the baby over.

"How long has she been awake?" Monica continues.

"Oh, the last three or four presents, I'd say," I answer, minimizing the feat as best I can.

"See?" Monica says with a smile. "You *are* a natural. It's way past the time for her next feeding."

As if on cue, the baby thrusts a tiny arm out from underneath the blanket and begins to cry. Her perfect rosebud lips part, revealing a tiny red mouth that is all gums. Monica laughs and I hand her her daughter.

At that same moment, in my mind, I see myself handing over another crying baby, this one to Jewel, who being the oldest of five, knows what to do.

"We should have my momma call the police," Jewel is saying in my memory, shaking her head but taking the baby anyway. It was nine o'clock in the morning on the Fourth of July. I had been living in Arkansas for just seven months. The three of us —Blair, Jewel, and I—had all just recently turned thirteen. Blair had spent the night at my house, and we had come outside that morning with plans to sit in my tree house and paint our toenails. I had decided to ask Jewel to join us, though Blair hadn't been too thrilled with this, and the three of us were on our way to my backyard when we heard the faint mewling sound of a baby. Or something. We really weren't sure what it was. But the sound had caught our attention, and we had followed it to the side door of Jewel's church. There on the steps was a wooden box that had pictures of peaches stamped on it. Inside, wrapped in a dirty sweatshirt, was a newborn baby. The moist, purple-gray stub of an umbilical cord was still attached to its belly, and a row of mosquito bites lined its forehead. No one else was around.

We had initially been speechless. Then Blair reached down and lifted the sweatshirt, revealing the perfect leg and the imperfect one. The shock turned to pity.

"I gotta go get my momma," Jewel finally said, quietly.

"No!" Blair said, not much more than a whisper.

Jewel turned her head to look at her.

"We can't just leave it here!" she said.

"We're not going to," Blair said, grabbing the box and heading back to my tree house.

She handed the box to me while she climbed and then reached down from the platform to take the box from me as I straddled the third wooden rung. When we were all inside the four wooden walls, Blair lifted the baby out of the peach box. It was naked and obviously a boy. That's when the baby began to really cry. Blair handed him over to me and I handed him over to Jewel. At the mention of calling the police, Blair had again protested.

"Not yet!" Blair replied, with an unmistakable I-want-to-be-a-mother-for-a-day look in her eye.

I didn't want to call the police yet either but I said nothing.

Now beside me, Monica is deftly putting her baby to her breast under the receiving blanket. I watch, remembering.

"This baby needs to eat," Jewel had said next.

"Well then, let's feed him something," Blair replied, as if all problems everywhere have a simple solution.

"You can't just feed a baby *something*," Jewel said. "It needs mother's milk or formula." She was rocking the baby back and forth in her arms. Then she stuck the tip of her pinkie in his mouth. He stopped wailing.

"Well, don't you have some of that stuff?" Blair said.

I can still see Jewel's face as she looked up from the name-less infant in her arms. She was incredulous.

"You want me to go to my momma and see if she don't mind breastfeedin' this here baby that we just found on the church steps?" Jewel said.

Blair narrowed her eyes. "I'm talking about the formula," she said.

"We don't have to buy none of that. My momma feeds her baby on her own," Jewel answered.

"Well, what *do* you have?" Blair said in exasperation.

Jewel sighed. I could tell she wanted no part of this. She was the same age as Blair and me but she was older than us just the same. She was already living in the real world of cooking, housekeeping, and minding her younger brothers and sisters. She was a follower of rules because for her, like so many people with genuine responsibilities, there are so many. She wanted to do the adult thing. She wanted to call the police.

"I can get you an empty bottle," she said instead. "But one of y'all's gonna have to go to Kroger's and buy some Similac. And it's expensive."

Blair stood up as high as she could under the pitched roof of my tree house.

"I have money," she said. She began to climb down. "I'm taking your bike, Tess," she continued as she jumped to the ground from the third step.

Blair walked over to my three-speed bike lying in the grass in my backyard. When she picked it up, a cloud of napping mosquitoes arose from the grass.

"He needs a diaper too," Jewel called down to her.

"Don't you have those either?" Blair asked as she gripped the handlebars.

"My momma uses cloth," Jewel replied, nearly proud of it.

"Do you at least have those wipe things?"

"We got those."

"I'll be right back," Blair said, and then she flashed me a look that said, *Don't let Jewel call the police.*

I remember that I had nodded.

A loud burst of laughter brings me back to the present.

"It's more wonderful than I thought it would be, Tess," Monica is saying as I pull myself back from that hot Arkansas morning fifteen years ago.

"I know it's none of my business but I hope one day you and Simon get married and that you will have a child together, Tess," Monica adds, looking at her baby, not me.

She says nothing else because we've had this conversation before. She knows I am at a loss to explain why I often don't accept good things offered me. What she doesn't know is there is a reason. I just can't explain it in words.

I don't stay long after that. I eat a few stuffed mushrooms, a few cream puffs. Then I look at my watch. A quarter to ten. I wonder if Simon is home. If he is okay. I decide it's time to go.

I say goodbye to Monica and thank Yvette for inviting me. On the drive home, I try to empty my mind of everything—Monica's baby, the abandoned infant from my past, and the way Simon made me feel earlier in the evening—so that I can concentrate on him alone.

But he is not at home.

As I slowly get ready for bed, I try not to worry. I lock the front door only after making sure Simon's apartment keys are nowhere to be found, which must mean he has them with him. I try to read in bed for a while, wanting to stay awake, but when the book starts to fall repeatedly in my face, I get out of bed and head to the bathroom. I tape a note to the mirror above the sink:

> Wake me when you get home.

I sign my name and draw a little heart, which I hope communicates that I fell asleep concerned for him.

As I crawl back into bed, I am aware of the scent of Monica's baby all over me—on my arms, in my hair, and in my lungs.

CHAPTER 4

Notes on the Mirror

The soundtrack from the London performance of *Les Miserables* rouses me from sleep as my CD alarm clock clicks on.

My first waking thought is of Simon: *He did not wake me up last night.* I turn abruptly in my bed, first relieved that his sleeping form is beside me and then miffed that he said nothing to me when he came in.

I wait for several minutes while the song plays through to see if the music will awaken Simon, but he does not stir.

Sighing, I switch off the music and get out of bed. I make my way to the bathroom, where I see that my note to Simon has been replaced with one of his own:

> Tess,
>
> It was late when I got in last night and I didn't want to wake you. Let's talk tonight when you get home. There's something I need to tell you.
> Simon
> p.s. I'm sorry about what I said.

I reach out to touch his note, his words. Something has changed for him; I can sense it. Something broke through his wall of despair last night. It should fill me with relief but it fills me instead with fear. I am afraid he has decided to move on. To leave me. To leave the woman he lives with but who will not marry him. A man can only handle so much disappointment in his life. The accident is already too much for him to bear. With me out of the picture he would have one less thing to cause him unhappiness.

I am tempted to run back into the bedroom, wake Simon, and beg him not to leave me, but I don't do this. I instead spend several minutes trying to convince myself that it is unwise to jump to conclusions. Maybe all that Simon wants to tell me is that he has finally decided to go back to work.

I go about my morning routine as if I have nothing to worry about. I shower, dress, dry my hair, and put on my makeup, thinking only of what lies ahead for me at the boutique. When I get to the kitchen I notice with a start that the three cereal bowls from yesterday have been washed and left to dry in the drainer. So Simon, who got in so late last night that he didn't have the heart to wake me, felt compelled instead to wash a few dishes? By hand? In the middle of the night?

My careful attempts to stay focused on just the ordinary details of the day begin to quaver. I walk back to the bedroom and stand in the doorway, watching Simon sleep. He has not moved since I got up. I walk back into the bathroom, grabbing a pen from his dresser by the door on my way. I reread his note to me, and then in small letters I write my response:

I'm sorry about what I said too. See you tonight.

I love you.

If he's thinking of leaving me, those last three words will sound like a desperate cry for him to reconsider.

And that's what they are.

I get to *Linee Belle* at nine—an hour before we open—but there's new inventory to bring out, and the sitting areas we have set up around the boutique to make people think they are in their own home, not in a mall, need tidying. Antonia likes to keep the coffeemaker busy all day, brewing strong European coffee she buys at considerable expense. She also likes to have her grandmother's silver tray filled with Italian cookies, which anyone rich enough or brave enough to ask to try something on will be offered. I get these things ready.

At ten, I raise the cage that opens out onto the second floor of Water Tower Place and then set the store's CD player to random play. A few minutes after ten, Antonia breezes in, stopping to look at my island scene in the front window.

"*Eez* very good, *Tezz*," she says. She left Italy for America twenty-five years ago, but her accent is as strong and alluring as ever. "Where *deed* you get the beach umbrellas?"

"From Bahama Llamas, on the first floor," I answer. "Rent free. All we have to do is tell people where to get them if they ask."

"Smart girl," she says and heads to the back of the boutique, where she pours herself the first of what will be many cups of coffee for the day.

The rest of the morning passes by slowly, and business doesn't start to pick up until the noon hour. By one-thirty, things haven't slowed down and I am starving.

"*Juz* go," Antonia says to me. "You need to eat. Elena will be here in fifteen *meenits* anyway."

The phone rings then and Antonia picks it up after the first ring. She shoos at me and mouths the word *go* before saying, "*Linee Belle. Theez eez* Antonia," into the mouthpiece.

I grab my wallet from my bag under the cash register and start to walk away.

"*Juz* a moment," I hear her say and then she calls me. "*Tezz. Eez* for you."

I turn back and take the phone from her. She walks away to help two women looking at silk scarves.

"This is Tess," I say into the phone.

There is a slight pause.

"Tess?" says a woman's voice at the other end. The owner of the voice sounds unsure of herself.

"Yes," I say. "This is Tess. Can I help you?"

"Tess, it's Blair."

I am utterly amazed to hear her voice. She has never called me at work before, not even during a time of crisis, which is usually when she calls. Blair and I talk to each other by phone every other month or so, but always at home and always on the weekend. She lives in St. Louis, a day's drive away, with her husband, Brad, and twin girls. Sometimes Brad's business will bring him to Chicago, and she will call me if she comes with him so that we can get together for lunch. But I am struggling to remember when was the last time we did that. Has it been a year? I can remember the last phone call, however. It was two months ago, in February. She was lamenting her depressing lack of true friends. She was tired of cocktail parties and Mah Jongg lunches and country club weekends. I didn't know what to say to her. What do you say to someone who has just realized money, even a lot of it, can't buy good friends? Then she began to tell me she feels like she and Brad are drifting apart, that it seems like her marriage has lost its momentum. I have always known Brad's money can't buy a happy marriage either, but of course I did not say this. I just told her maybe they should see a counselor. As if I know anything at all about marriage.

In any case, her calling me at work in the middle of the day is not like her. It occurs to me maybe she and Brad are in Chicago and she wants to get together.

"Blair! What's up?" I say.

"I called your apartment," she is saying. "Simon gave... Simon gave me this number. He said you wouldn't mind..."

But Blair's voice fades away before she finishes her sentence.

"Blair?" I say, wondering if we have been cut off.

I hear a choked-back sob on the other end. Blair is crying.

"Blair," I try again. "Are you okay?"

"Tess, Brad collapsed while jogging this morning," she says. "They're thinking he had a heart attack. He's...he's in a coma."

Blair's voice sounds weaker and weaker with every word. I can't help but think of Simon, lying wounded in our bed, but not in a coma.

"Blair, I am so sorry," I manage to say. I can hardly believe what she is telling me. Blair's husband is only in his early thirties. It doesn't seem possible that he could have had a heart attack this young.

"Tess, the doctors say it was a bad one," Blair says, her voice thick with distress. "They...they aren't sure he's going to pull through. They..."

Another sob cuts her short.

I hardly know what to say. Antonia is looking at me. So are the two women she is helping.

"Blair, do you want me to come?" I say.

That's it. That's all I can think of to say. I am astounded that that is all she wants to hear.

"Could you?" she says, her voice not much more than a squeak. "Could you really?"

"Well...of course," I answer, wondering what in the world makes me think my presence will make things easier for her.

"I...I can't leave the hospital, but I'm sure I can find someone to pick you up at the airport. I'll pay for the ticket," Blair says through her tears.

"You don't have to worry about that," I begin, but she interrupts me.

"No, you must let me. I want to," she says, and I can tell it's important to her that she is in control of at least one little thing this day.

"Okay, okay," I say, and then I suddenly remember her twin daughters. "Blair, where are the girls?"

There is a momentary pause. Blair seems not to have heard me.

"Blair?" I try again.

"They're with Brad's sister," Blair finally says. "Can you come today, Tess? I don't care how much the plane ticket costs. I will pay for it. Can you come today?"

"Yes, I will," I answer, but I feel anything but confident. "I need to hang up now, Blair, so I can make some arrangements, okay? I'll try and get there this evening sometime."

"Okay," Blair whispers. "You still have my cell phone number?"

"I've got it at home," I assure her.

"Okay. Call me when you land and I'll find someone to come get you."

"Blair, I'll just get a rental car at the airport. I'll call you from the rental agency, okay? You can tell me how to get to the hospital."

"All right," Blair says. "Thank you, Tess. I…I didn't know who else to call."

For a moment I am deeply touched that Blair thought of me first, but then I realize that well-to-do Blair with her million-dollar home, beautiful children, and silver Mercedes has really never been subjected to weakness and powerlessness, not even when we were kids. She probably believes that most of her affluent St. Louis friends are just like her, unaccustomed to misfortune and therefore unable—unqualified—to help her. She knows I am familiar with grief. Of course she would call me.

"Blair, I'm going to go now and call the airlines. You hang in there. I'll see you soon," I tell her.

"Okay," she says. "Tess, come as quick as you can."

"I will. I'll see you tonight."

It doesn't take long to explain to Antonia that I am going to need a few days off as she practically heard the whole conversation. She tells me to ring up the scarves while she calls her travel agent. By the time I close the cash register drawer,

Antonia has secured a seat for me on a flight that leaves O'Hare for St. Louis at 5:10 PM.

Elena arrives as I am hugging Antonia goodbye.

"Thanks, Antonia," I say. "I'll make it up to you."

"*Yez*, you will!" she says with a wink and then adds as she raises her hand in farewell, "*Ciao*."

"*Ciao*," I say back as I make my way out of the boutique.

I am halfway home before I realize that Simon and I sort of have a date tonight. A date to talk. I inwardly groan as I realize how bad the timing is. Blair's emergency couldn't have come at a worse time. I spend the rest of the drive home wondering how to explain things to Simon.

But again, Simon is not home when I arrive. There is no note to let me know where he is. He must be planning on getting back before the time I usually get home from work, which is six o'clock. I'll be in the air by then. His cell phone is sitting uncharged on his night table, so I cannot call him.

I yank out a suitcase and begin tossing things in it, pausing at the slightest sound to see if Simon is coming through the front door. By three o'clock I am anxious to get going. I have to get through afternoon traffic, drop my car off at the park and ride, and make it through security at the airport. I can't wait any longer.

I grab a piece of paper and a pen to write a hurried note.

Simon,
I wanted to wait until you got home to tell you this in person, but I ran out of time. Blair called me this afternoon after she talked to you. Brad

is in a coma, docs think he's had a heart attack and they don't expect him to live. I'm taking a flight that leaves for St. Louis at 5:10. I expect I may be gone a few days, maybe a week. It depends on what happens next. I know we were supposed to talk tonight and I am honestly sorry about this. But Blair needs me, Simon. She asked me to come. I'll call you tonight from Blair's house. I'll leave my car at the park and ride. Missing you already.

Tess

I read the note twice to make sure he will understand I want him here when I get back. Then I tape the note to the bathroom mirror, right over the note that reminds him that I love him.

I grab the suitcase and my canvas bag, noticing for the first time since I got home that the light on the answering machine is blinking. I rush to it thinking it might be Simon letting me know where he is. I press the button. Instead of hearing Simon's voice, I hear my dad's.

Hey Tess, it's Dad. You're probably at work, but I just wanted to let you and Simon know that Zane and I are throwing a surprise fortieth birthday party for Shelley on the twenty-ninth, and we're hoping you guys won't mind the drive and can come. Or maybe you will want to fly in. Just let me know. You can call me back

tonight; just don't say anything to Shelley about
the party if she happens to answer the phone.
Well, talk to you later. Bye.

I don't have the time or the energy to consider how I feel
about my stepmother's upcoming fortieth birthday, nor my dad
and my half-brother's covert attempts to make her feel wonderful about it. The drive to Dayton, Ohio, where Dad and
Shelley live isn't that bad, but I can't picture Simon making that
kind of trip right now. And I don't feel an urge to spend several hundred dollars on plane tickets. I wouldn't mind seeing
Zane, though. He's not too bad for a kid brother. But going to
Shelley's party? Where I know no one? Does my dad really think
I will come? Does he really want me to come? Is he just asking
for the sake of asking?

I can't think about this right now. I have to go. I can't miss
my plane.

On impulse, I go back to the bathroom to take one more
look at the note on the mirror. I read it, and then I pick up
the pen that I had left on the counter by the sink. I add a few
X's and *O*'s after my name.

CHAPTER 5

Answers to Prayer

The gate is crowded with other travelers as I wait for my flight to be called. I am anxious to be airborne. The longer I sit in the terminal at O'Hare, the more I feel like Simon has arrived home and has seen my note. I want to be far away when he reads it. I don't know why.

A woman is sitting next to me as we wait in plastic chairs. She is holding a baby. Two other children are sitting at her feet as all the other chairs are taken. I've seen many tall, slender black women in Chicago in the five years I have lived here, but this is the first one who looks so much like Corinthia Mayhew. I catch myself looking at her purse as her little girl, whom I guess to be three or four, rifles through it, pulling out keys, a comb, and a tiny package of tissues.

"Abigail, put that stuff back," the woman says to the little girl. "When they call our seats, we need to be ready."

The little girl looks up from the purse.

"I want gum," she says.

The mother, jiggling the baby in her arms to keep it distracted or contented, I can't tell which, says, "Well, I don't have any. Put it all back."

The little boy at her feet looks up at his mother. He looks like he's about five.

"I gotta go potty," he says.

"Lordamercy, Simon, I told you to go before we left Nana's," the mother says.

I am startled to hear Simon's name.

"But I didn't have to go then. Now I do," the little boy named Simon says.

"King Jesus, You better help me out," I hear the mother whisper under her breath. She looks at her watch, at the gate where the airline employees are getting ready to announce our flight, at the restrooms across from our chairs, at the baby in her arms, and then back to her little boy.

"Simon, you're just gonna have to wait and go on the plane," she finally says.

"But I can't wait. I gotta go now!"

I feel funny sitting there, watching the little drama, fully able to help this woman who looks so much like Corinthia, but doing nothing.

"Can I help you?" I suddenly say, surprising myself.

The woman turns to me.

"Beg your pardon?" she says.

"I can go tell the people at the desk not to leave without you," I said. "And I can come into the bathroom with you and hold the baby while your little boy uses the toilet."

"Lord, that was quick," she says, but not to me.

"What?" I say.

She turns to me and her eyes lock onto mine.

"That's very kind of you, Miss. Very kind." This she says to me.

I smile. "I'll be right back," I say as I get up and make my way to the desk. I tell a Northwest Airlines employee not to leave without me and the family behind me, that we need to make a quick trip to the restroom.

The employee grins. "Okay," he says. "But make it quick. We're starting to board the first-class passengers."

I thank him, and then I walk back to the woman and her children.

"Okay, Simon, Abigail, let's go," the woman says, grabbing a diaper bag, her purse, and a sack full of books and toys, all the while holding the baby.

We get to the ladies' restroom, and the little boy named Simon begins to complain.

"This one's for girls!" he says.

"Simon Nathaniel, you know I can't go in the men's room, and you know I will not let you go in there by yourself. So it's either the ladies' room or you wait and go in the restroom on the plane."

Simon looks downcast, but he trudges into the ladies' room and the rest of us follow. Thankfully, the restroom is not crowded. The woman picks the handicap accessible stall to give her plenty of room.

"I have to go too," the little girl named Abigail says.

"Of course you do," the woman says, looking at me in mock exasperation. She drops her bags inside the stall, ushers her son and daughter into it, and then turns to me. She hesitates a moment before handing the baby to me.

"I promise I won't move a muscle," I say to her, trying to assure her that she can trust me.

She pauses another moment and then her face relaxes. She places the baby in my arms.

"I know you won't," she says to me. "You're the answer to my prayer."

She turns, walks into the stall, and closes the door. She doesn't see my shocked expression. Within five minutes the children are at the sinks and their mother is helping them wash and dry their hands.

"Okay," she says to me, trying to adjust her bags and purse so that she can take the baby, who has been studying my face the whole time.

"Would you like me to just follow you onto the plane and give your baby to you after you get the little ones seated?" I say.

She grins. "You're one of the best ones He's ever sent," she says quickly and then turns to her children. "Let's go, let's go."

We file out of the bathroom and I follow them to the gate as our seats have already been called. Once inside the plane, the woman settles Simon and Abigail into their seats and then reaches for her baby.

"May God bless you for your kindness to me," she says to me, and I can scarcely take my eyes off her. She is like Corinthia's twin, come to soothe my soul with words from heaven itself.

I hand her the baby and mumble, "You're welcome."

I find my own seat several rows away and slide into it. The experience of helping the woman, short as it was, has left me feeling emotionally drained. It cannot be possible that I was the answer to her prayer. Cannot be possible. God feels as far away to me as He has ever been.

I try to let my thoughts wander as the plane prepares to taxi
down the runway. I look at the airline's magazine in the seat
pocket. I stare out the window. I close my eyes and try to
imagine my island. But my thoughts keep turning back to
Corinthia.

My father and I did make it to the Mayhews' for supper the
day the movers came to our Arkansas house. Dad was a little
hesitant to accept the invitation, not wanting to impose, he said.
But I think he was also a little afraid he was going to get
preached at. I had told him about meeting Corinthia in the
backyard and that she had five kids, that one was my age, and
that her husband was the pastor of the church on the corner
of our street. When I told him that, I could see his eyes widen
a bit. He didn't want anyone pressuring him to go to church—
the church on the corner or any church. It wasn't that my dad
thought church was a bad thing; he just didn't want it for himself. "Church is for people who need God like a farmer needs
rain," he told me once. He didn't need God like a farmer needs
rain. He didn't *need* God at all. It wasn't that he minded the
people who were like farmers when it came to God; he was
just a man of science. There are limitations to everything. Even
God. And church people—people who need God like farmers
need rain—think God has none.

In the end, though, he agreed. He and I were both tired of
fast food and SpaghettiO's at the TLF. And the kitchen wasn't
fully unpacked by six o'clock anyway. So we walked across our
front lawn to the Mayhews' house. Over their front door was

a little wooden plaque that said "The Mayhews—Peace to all who enter here."

A young boy answered the door and then opened it wide for us to enter. He didn't say anything, so it was kind of awkward for my dad and me. But then Corinthia came around the corner and welcomed us warmly.

"Come in, come in," she said. "Welcome, welcome. Samuel, the neighbors are here!"

A tall black man—tall as any man I had ever seen—stepped around the corner, smiling widely. He stuck out his hand to my father.

"Pleased to meet you," he said. His voice was very low. I liked it. "I'm Samuel Mayhew."

"Mark Longren," my dad said, returning the handshake.

"You must be Tess," Samuel Mayhew said, looking down at me from what seemed like three stories. I just nodded.

"Let's get you inside and get your jackets," Corinthia said, helping me off with my coat and taking my dad's as he handed it to her. "We can sit in the living room for just a few minutes while you meet the rest of the Mayhews."

The house was warm and clean, but the carpet was worn in places, and the furnishings were simple and sparse. Dad and I sat on a sofa that was soft and lumpy. Over its back was a beautiful hand-stitched quilt. Corinthia called for her other children.

The oldest I recognized right away as being Jewel even before Corinthia said her name, not just because Corinthia had told me she had a twelve-year-old daughter with that name but also because I had seen the girl at school. Jewel smiled at me. She was holding an infant in her arms. Corinthia moved on to the other children.

"Now this is Noble; he's next after Jewel and he's ten. This here's Shepherd, who opened the door for you and he's eight. Here's Renaissance—we call her Rena—and she's four. And Jewel's holding Marigold who is four weeks old today!"

I think my dad was on the verge of laughing. Neither one of us had heard such interesting names before. I think he thought they were kind of silly. But I thought they were wonderful. Each one meant something, made you think of something. I didn't know if Tess meant anything at all. My dad had told me it was just my mother's favorite name.

We were invited into the dining room, which was long and narrow; the table in its center filled it from one end to another. Jewel placed the infant in a cradle next to her chair like she already knew it would be her job to tend to her littlest sister if she made a fuss during the meal.

"Tess, you can sit by Jewel so y'all can get to know each other. Dr. Longren, you can sit by Samuel," Corinthia said.

"Oh, you can just call me Mark," my dad said nonchalantly as he took a chair on the end by Jewel's dad.

"No, no," Corinthia said. "You worked hard to get that title. I'm surely going to use it! Now, Rena, you help me bring in the serving dishes."

I recognized the meat as being ham, but there were some other things I hadn't seen before. Okra was new to me then, as were the yams. But everything smelled wonderful. I was not used to being in a home where there was a mother who cooked.

When all the dishes were in place, Corinthia took her place at the other end of the table.

She held her hands out to Noble and Rena on either side of her.

"If it wouldn't be too much trouble, may we hold hands while we ask the Lord to bless this meal?" Jewel's father said to my dad.

My father looked a bit taken aback but he lifted his hands from his lap and extended them. "Sure," he said. I lifted mine too. Jewel's hand was soft and slender.

Pastor Mayhew then began to pray.

"We thank You, Almighty God, for Your abundant goodness toward us, for Your tender mercies, for Your everlasting kindness. Bless this meal to our bodies. May it make us strong to live our lives in ways that please You. Bless our new friends Dr. Longren and Tess. May they always have Your kind favor upon them. In the blessed name of Jesus, amen."

I felt funny opening my eyes after that. I think my dad did too. We both looked at each other for a split-second. Then Jewel squeezed my hand and the prayer was over.

Jewel kept eyeing me during the meal like she wanted to talk to me but didn't know where to begin. And I did the same thing. The adults found things to talk about; most of the dinner conversation centered on the places my dad had been stationed in his nearly twenty years in the Air Force.

When the meal was over, Corinthia invited me to help in the kitchen, which surprised me but touched me too, as I think she knew it would. I had been asked to take part in a mother-child mini-event—the washing up of the dishes. Renaissance and Jewel started bringing dishes into the kitchen. Pastor Mayhew took the baby into the living room, where he and my dad continued their conversation on the political problems in the Middle East. I scraped the dishes while Corinthia rinsed them and then placed them in a dishpan of hot, soapy water. Dad and I did the dishes all the time like this, but it was different somehow doing it with Corinthia.

"I sure like your name, Tess," she said to me as she plopped a plate into the water.

"You do?" I said. I was a bit stunned. Unlike the names of her children, my name didn't conjure up an image of anything.

"It sounds soft like a lullaby," she said. "I wonder what it means. Do you know?"

I shook my head.

"My dad just told me it was my mother's favorite name," I said. "I don't think it means anything."

"Oh, all names mean something," she said to me. "Maybe someday we should find out."

I shrugged my shoulders. "Okay," I said.

"I like the names you have for your kids," I added after a moment of silence.

"They are a bit different," Corinthia said, "But each one means something precious to me. Would you like to hear how Samuel and I chose them?"

I nodded. Jewel and Rena just kept bringing in dishes, not saying a word.

"Well," she began. "Jewel was our firstborn of course, and I had no idea how precious a child could be until we had her. She was beautiful and wonderful and I just wanted the world to know that her worth, like that of all children, is beyond reckoning. So, she's my Jewel. Now noble is a good thing to be when you are a man. The world could use more noble men, don't you think? So, Samuel and me, we named our first son Noble to remind him that he is to be an honorable man who seeks after God."

Corinthia took another dish from me and went on.

"We gave Shepherd his name because the Bible tells us Jesus is the Good Shepherd, that He looks after us the same way a shepherd cares for his sheep, not just in any way but in the *good* way. Now Renaissance is a long, fancy name that most folks can hardly get used to using, but I love what it means. You ever heard of the Renaissance, Tess?"

I wasn't sure.

"Does it have to do with art museums in France?" I asked.

Corinthia smiled.

"Well, yes, in a way it does," she said. "Renaissance means 'rebirth.' An' there was a time when art had itself a kind of rebirth back in history. But all of us needs to have a rebirth, Tess. All of us needs to be re-created new. And do you know why? 'Cause we get born the first time in a broken world that doesn't know God or love God. We get born the first time needin' someone to rescue us. You know Who that someone is, Tess?"

I just blinked at her.

"Why, it's Jesus," she said simply, like she was saying, "Why, it's seven o'clock."

I was pondering the whole notion of a rebirth, thinking how wonderful it could be if I could just go back and do it over and this time my mother would live, when Corinthia moved on.

"Now, my Marigold, well, her name just makes me think of sunshine and flowers, like the most beautiful place you ever saw. Like heaven."

Corinthia laughed and continued.

"People don't mind Marigold's name as much. I think they're just glad I didn't name her something like 'Beautiful Day' or 'Third Pretty Girl.'"

I laughed too.

By this time, Jewel and Renaissance had joined us in the kitchen as all the dishes had been brought in.

"Jewel, why don't you take Tess up to see your room? Rena and I can finish up here," Corinthia said.

Jewel smiled shyly at me.

"You wanna come?" she said.

"Okay," I answered.

I followed her to a staircase by the front door that led up to the second story. Jewel's room was the first one at the top of the stairs. It was painted yellow, and there were books everywhere.

"I guess you can tell I like to read," she said softly, smiling like she was embarrassed.

"I like to read too," I said.

Then I noticed that on her desk was an open sketchpad. A half-finished drawing of a giraffe was visible.

"That's really good," I said. And it was.

She just shrugged.

"The neck isn't long enough," she said.

She showed me the rest of her drawings and some of her favorite books. She was quiet and very unlike Blair, but I liked

Jewel. She didn't seem like the kind of person who would ever astonish me. I felt like she was transparent, honest. It was hard for me to imagine her ever being silly or disrespectful. Or unkind.

My dad called up the stairs a few minutes after that and said it was time to go. We still had to make up the beds and such. He seemed relaxed and at ease as we got ready to leave, and so I was pretty sure Samuel Mayhew had not preached to him. I was glad my father seemed happy because I liked this house and I wanted us to come back. I liked how it smelled. I liked the sound of other children playing. I liked Jewel. And I liked Corinthia.

Over the next few weeks and months I spent a lot of time at the Mayhews' house and with Jewel especially. A couple times I convinced Blair to come with me, but Blair liked being able to call the shots. For some reason, she didn't feel comfortable doing that at Jewel's house. She didn't mind doing it at mine, though. When the three of us were at my house, we usually did what Blair wanted to do.

One day in February, Corinthia sat me down at her kitchen table, where she had a library book lying open.

"Remember how I said all names mean something?" she said to me, and her eyes were twinkling. "Well, I found out what *Tess* means."

She pointed to a place on the right-hand page of the open book. I read what was written there:

> Tess: From the Spanish and Portuguese name
> *Teresa*. Believed to be derived from the Greek
> word *therizein*: "to harvest."

She smiled broadly, like she had just discovered gold. It *was* like gold. *From the Portuguese*. I was speechless.

"So now you know why this was your Momma's favorite name," she said. "Harvest is a time of blessing, Tess; a time when the fruit of all your hard labor is finally realized. It's a time for gathering in all the good things you have worked hard for. Isn't that amazing?"

I nodded and read the entry again. It felt weird to realize I had a name that actually meant something. I couldn't help but wonder when I would be gathering in all the good things. It surely couldn't have happened yet.

In fact, a few months later, everything shifted for me. A strong gust pulled at my sail, and I found myself on a new course on unfamiliar seas. One unforgettable day in May—the day I found my mother's medical records—I pretty much ceased to contemplate what good things awaited me. I began instead a different kind of meditation, one I still can't seem to wring free from my thoughts.

I was looking for summer clothes. I knew they had to be in a box that my dad and I hadn't had to open yet since moving in. There were several boxes marked MISC sitting in the garage, filled with unrelated things that the movers had thrown together when they had just odds and ends from various rooms left to pack. Dad was at the base. It was a Thursday afternoon, about four o'clock.

The first box I tried was stuffed with appliance manuals, a bag of fishing tackle, a set of Tupperware bowls, a broken soap dish, and two empty photo albums. The second had a set of ugly brown curtains on top and then, thankfully, my shorts and summer shirts. I started pulling them out and was almost finished when I came across a couple file folders bound together with a thick rubber band. On the tab of each was my mother's name: Madeline Longren. Stamped across the front of both were the words Medical Records.

I had been on my knees, but the moment I realized what I was holding, I sat back on my bottom, nearly stunned. I fingered the tabs for several minutes before taking the rubber band off, as I knew I would.

It didn't take long to find what I was looking for. Every entry was in chronological order. I just headed to the entry that bore my birthday. There was a lot written there. Several pages. I didn't understand most of it, but I was really just looking for one word. *Embolism.* I figured when I found it, I would find out how in the world my mother got one. Eventually I saw the word, though I almost missed it because there were two other words in front of it. It was on a document labeled Post-mortem. I read the three words, saying them out loud.

"Amniotic Fluid Embolism..."

A tremor ran through me. I knew what amniotic fluid was. I had been swimming in it when I was living inside her. My heart began to pound as I read more:

Amniotic fluid embolism suspected by attending when seizures started. Shortness of breath began

during last stage of labor. Pt. became slightly
cyanotic during episiotomy repair, alterations in
mental status preceded coma. Traces of lanugo
and vernix found in lungs on histological
examination indicative of AFE.

Something was being revealed to me, I could sense it. But
I didn't know what it was.

I took the files into the house and into my dad's study. I
looked at the books on his shelves, hoping that the one I wanted
wasn't at his office on base. I figured it wouldn't be. It was a
college textbook on medical terms. He hardly used it anymore.
I saw its blue binding and stood on his desk chair to reach it.
I turned to the A's. Within moments I found it. Amniotic fluid
embolism. I read in silence, understanding at last what had happened. Amniotic fluid had entered my mother's bloodstream
and had flowed into her lungs where it wasn't supposed to be.
Whose fault was that? I wondered. I didn't know what lanugo
and vernix were, but her records said they were indicative of
AFE, of amniotic fluid embolism. I turned to the L's and read
in horror. I turned to the V's and my shock turned to despair.

Lanugo was the soft downy hair that had covered my tiny
body inside her.

Vernix was the white, creamy protective layer that had covered my skin.

My hair, my skin.

Bits and pieces of my little body had floated off into her
bloodstream and suffocated her.

I sat there in my dad's office, choking back sobs that I would have been wise to just let flow. I wanted so much to ask my dad if it was true, did this really happen, because like all people who are suddenly given bad news, I wanted it to be a mistake.

But I didn't do it. I went back out to the garage and put the records at the bottom of the first box, underneath the appliance manuals and fishing tackle. I replaced the tape and then shoved the box back where I found it. When my father came home that night, I pretended to be sick with menstrual cramps. I had only been menstruating for four months, but Blair had recently told me cramps were a good excuse for hiding other kinds of aches. He gave me Tylenol, and I spent the evening in my room, on my bed, wishing with all my heart that Corinthia was right, that there was a way to be reborn. To go back and do it over and this time get it right.

I shake this image of me lying miserably on my bed in Arkansas out of my head. The plane is now starting its wild, rushing jaunt across the tarmac in preparation for its lift skyward. I want to convince myself that Simon is right, that I did not kill my mother. I didn't mean to. But he didn't mean to kill that woman and her daughter either, and look at him. He is languishing in his regret.

Regret.

That single word brings Corinthia back to the forefront of my troubled mind.

A few days after I learned the truth, when I was still walking around in a fog of remorse, Corinthia had asked me what was bothering me. We were in her backyard and I was helping her hang laundry on her clothesline. I wanted to tell her everything but I was afraid. I just told her I had done something I wish I hadn't.

"Well, you know what the remedy for regret is, don't you?" she said.

I shook my head.

"Find a way to make it right," she replied.

Her answer left me feeling hopeless and I started to cry in front of her.

"What if there is no way I can make it right?" I said.

She must have wondered what it was I had done, but she didn't ask.

"Well, can you live with it?" she said instead.

I wasn't sure. I didn't think I could.

"No," I whispered.

She leaned down so that her eyes met my eyes and rested her hands on my shoulders.

"Then find someone who *can* make it right," she said, looking deep into my soul.

I think even then I knew whom she meant. But that was also a hopeless suggestion. Even God has limitations.

Give it a rest, Tess. You didn't kill your mother.

Simon's angry words are repeating themselves in my head as the plane surges forward. I want to believe he is right but that's not how it feels. Now everything else is suddenly swirling in my head: Simon's grief and his unrevealed news, the remembered scent of Monica's baby, memories of the abandoned infant in the peach box, my father's phone call earlier today, the sound of Corinthia's voice, and lastly the face of the woman in the airport who told me I was the answer to her prayers.

I feel weighed down. I want to be above it all. I want my own world to be far behind me as I rush to Blair's side.

The plane pushes upward against the gravitational pull of the fallen earth, willing itself heavenward, but I can feel the resistance all around me, that force that wants to send me back to the broken world where I belong.

CHAPTER 6

Alone

St. Louis, Missouri

As I get off the plane at the St. Louis airport, I am only vaguely aware that this place is unfamiliar to me. I have never flown into the St. Louis airport before. The few times I have been to this city, I have come by car. Like all major airports I have been in, this one is bustling with activity and I am alone in it. No one is here to greet me, and though this does not surprise me, it doesn't bother me either. Dad and I traveled so much when I was a child, by plane and by car, that I grew up accustomed to living out of a suitcase for weeks at a time and being in a strange place where I knew no one.

I make my way to baggage claim, watching all the travelers around me, who I can tell have just come home to St. Louis. I can see it in their walk and in their faces. They look relaxed and nearly bored. The thrill of travel is over for them. They are from here. They are home.

I find it interesting and unsettling that one of the first things people want to know about me when I meet them is where *I* am from, where's *my* home. It shouldn't be that difficult a question to answer, and for most people, it probably isn't. But like a lot of children of military parents, I struggle with the answer. In the past I have been tempted to say that I am from everywhere and nowhere. But even in jest, that sounds far too poetic.

Or arrogant. Like I believe myself to be above space and time. Like God.

But the truth is, I don't feel like I'm *from* anywhere. I am not from the Azores, though I was born there. I am half British, but I have never been to England. I have lived in Virginia, Maine, Nebraska, Arkansas, Ohio, and lately Illinois, but I don't feel like any one of these places is where I am *from*. If I were to die today, I suppose my father would bury me next to distant, deceased Longren relatives who lie under the grass in a small cemetery in central Wisconsin near where his parents live. But I have never called Wisconsin home. Chicago is beginning to feel like home to me. And since it has always been Simon's home, I feel a growing attachment. But I doubt I will someday be buried there. I doubt I will ever say it's where I am from.

The luggage carousel for my flight is empty and unmoving when I reach it. I lean against a wall, waiting with dozens of others who were on my plane for our suitcases to find their way to us. I think about the other times I have been to St. Louis as I wait.

The first time can hardly be counted. Dad and I drove through St. Louis two weeks after Blair, Jewel, and I found the baby and reluctantly gave it up. We were on our way to Wisconsin to see his parents, my grandparents. We looked at the famous arch from the air-conditioned confines of our car as we crossed the Mississippi River into Illinois. I don't remember much about that particular trip. Too much had happened in the preceding few weeks. I do remember Dad asking me, more than once, what I thought of Shelley. But there was nothing to think of Shelley at that point. I had only known her for about a month, about as long as he had.

The second time was about a year later, for my fourteenth birthday. Dad took Blair, Jewel, and me to downtown St. Louis, where he got us our own hotel room—right next to his, of course. This time we went up inside the amazing arch. I began to hyperventilate when I saw the arch's shadow swaying in the muddy river below us. Blair thought it was hilarious. Jewel began praying under her breath that I would not faint. I was glad to come back down and touch solid ground. Two days after we came home from that trip, Dad gave Shelley an engagement ring.

The third time was when Blair, who had moved to St. Louis after college, got married and I was her maid of honor. I decided to drive out from Ohio for the wedding. My address at the time was the spare bedroom at Dad and Shelley's, where I was contemplating going back to college. I was in sort of a mental in-between place. I was twenty-three, not dating anyone, and very unsure of what I wanted to do with my life. I still needed eighteen credits to complete the business degree I thought I wanted, but I had no motivation to do anything about it. I had no job then either. At Dad's urging, I had returned to the house we had moved into—him, me, and Shelley, his now pregnant wife—after we left Arkansas. That move took place in the middle of June, three weeks after I turned fifteen. It was the house where I spent the last three years of high school, where Zane was born, and where Dad hung up his Air Force uniforms after deciding Zane needed a normal, stationary life. His orders to Wright-Patterson Air Force Base in Dayton were to be his last. My father retired from the Air Force the same month I graduated from high school, and he began his new career as a lecturer at a medical school. Shelley, who was just a new second lieutenant when she met my dad in Blytheville, gave up her commission as soon as her four-year commitment was over so she could be a full-time mother to Zane.

So there I was, five years out of high school and still looking for my place in the world. I had changed my major three times, had worked part-time at an animal shelter, a French restaurant, an antique store, and a private school for gifted children. I had moved away from Dayton and come back twice.

My father was actually very patient with me during this chaotic time in my life. Too patient, really. I wanted him to sit me down and talk some sense into me. But he didn't. He just kept writing out checks to Wright State University for the phantom degree I pretended to pursue. To her credit, Shelley tried to find ways to help me, but she really had no idea what it was like to stare at a big world with no idea of where to go in it. So nothing she said really mattered to me. That she is only twelve years older than me probably had something to do with my indifference to her counsel as well. Not because she wasn't old enough or smart enough to know anything, because I am sure she was. It's just that I couldn't—and still can't—think of her as a mother figure capable of dispensing advice.

So when Blair called me after tracking me down at my dad's and asked me to be the maid of honor at her wedding, I decided a road trip was in order. She offered to fly me out then too, as she had already gotten quite adept at spending Brad's millions,

even before the wedding. But I was glad for the opportunity
to be alone in my car for the long stretch of hours between
Dayton and St. Louis. It was actually one of the best decisions
I had made in a long time because on the way back from the
wedding, I took a side trip to Chicago to visit a friend from
my sophomore year of college, which incidentally I spent at
the University of Ohio. It was this same friend, Emily Trowdell,
who now lives in Atlanta, who convinced me to stay in Chicago,
helped me get the job in the Customs Office at O'Hare where
she also worked, and who later introduced me to Simon—a
friend of a friend of a friend.

I met Antonia at O'Hare too. She made several trips to Italy
that first year, and I came to know her on a first-name basis
because she always seemed to come through customs when I
was on duty. She intrigued me and I apparently intrigued her.
She told me on our second meeting she would give her left foot
to have hair the color of mine, but not her left or right arm
because she would need them both to style it. Antonia said my
auburn hair was the exact color of the sky over the Mediterr-
anean at sunset. She also told me, on our third meeting, that
I was very wise to stay away from beige. I had laughed. Veronica
Devere, Blair's mother, had told me the same thing when I was
fourteen. It was one of the few things I remember her ever saying
to me. I went to work for Antonia at *Linee Belle* my second year
in Chicago when she offered me two dollars an hour more than
what the customs office paid, plus a regular work schedule and
an impressive title—assistant manager.

So in a sense, St. Louis, with its celebrated Gateway to
the West, became a gateway for me personally. I used it as a

passageway to move out on my own—for the last time—away from Dad and Shelley, away from the place where my childhood was supposed to have ended and my adult life was supposed to have begun.

My suitcase is one of the first to be deposited on the carousel, and once I have it, I follow the Ground Transport signs to the rental car agencies section. I pick the one with the shortest line, but I soon discover the lone woman ahead of me wants a white Cadillac Seville, not a blue one, and that she is prepared to be adamant about it. While the flustered rental car agency explains there isn't a white one available, I take out my cell phone and press the speed dial button for Blair's number. I hope she will be mentally able to give me good directions to the hospital. I have no idea where anything is in relation to this airport.

Blair's cell phone number rings six times before her voice mail picks it up. In a sunny tone that doesn't fit the day, Blair's recorded voice asks me to leave a message. I quickly leave one, telling her I am at the airport, in line to get a rental car, and waiting to hear back from her before I leave.

Fifteen minutes later I am sitting in a red Camry in the rental car parking lot and my phone call has not been returned. I decide to try again and I get the same message after six rings. I hang up without leaving a second message and whisper, "This is not good," to the steering wheel. I have Blair's home address but not a clue as to how to get to her house. I have no idea to which hospital Brad was taken. I lean my head against the driver's side window and try to consider my options. I can probably get directions to Blair's house from the rental car agency, but I doubt anyone will be at home. I can call a couple of local hospitals and ask to speak with the family of a patient named Brad Holbrook and see what happens. I can look for a hotel room near the airport and at least have a place to sleep tonight while I keep trying to reach Blair.

I decide on choice number three, but I dial Blair's number one more time before starting the car. Blair's number rings five times and I am almost ready to hang up when I hear a man's voice say hello.

It can't possibly be Brad. I do not know the voice.

"Hello?" I say. "I'm looking for Blair. Do I have the right number?"

There is a pause.

"Can I ask who this is, please?" says the voice.

If I had the wrong number, he would not have asked this, so I must have gotten through to Blair's phone. But I am hesitant to give this stranger my full name.

"This is Tess. Can I speak to Blair, please?" I say, trying to inject a little authority in my voice.

Another pause.

"She can't come to the phone right now. You'll have to call back some other time," the man says.

"Wait!" I yell into my phone, fearing he is going to hang up on me. "Blair called me earlier today. She told me Brad had a heart attack and she *asked me* to come to her. I just flew in from Chicago and I am sitting in a rental car at *your* airport, okay? Now can you please let me talk to her?"

A third pause.

"Just a minute," he says and I can tell he has placed his thumb over the mouthpiece of Blair's phone. Several long minutes pass.

"Look," he says and his voice sounds softer, but strained. "This is just a really bad time. Brad...Brad died half an hour ago and everything is a little crazy."

As he says the word "died" I feel my breath catch in my throat.

"Brad is dead?" I say, because no one can believe the announcement of death the first time they hear it.

"He...he never regained consciousness after he collapsed," the man said, emotion lacing his words. "They don't think he suffered."

"And Blair?" I say, emotion now thick in my own voice.

"She's taken it pretty hard," the man continues. "A doctor here at the hospital has given her a sedative. We are getting ready to take her home."

I have no idea who he means by "we."

"Can...can I ask who you are?" I venture.

"My name is Peter Agnew. Brad was a partner in my investment firm. He worked for me."

"I am so sorry," I mumble because nothing else seems adequate. I am aware that my cheeks are wet and that the lump in my throat has expanded into something larger and heavier and has moved down into my chest. I am aching for Blair.

"My wife and I are going to stay with her tonight," Peter Agnew is saying.

"Does she know I'm here?" I say, feeling alone in a strange place. It's a new feeling.

"She's not very lucid right now," Peter says. "It might be best if you got a hotel room for the night. There's a Holiday Inn just across the freeway from the airport. I can call ahead and tell them you're coming. I can put it on the company credit card. What's your last name?"

"You don't have to do that," I start to say.

"I'm sure it's what Blair would want," Peter assures me. "I will come and get you in the morning and bring you to her, okay? Now, what's your last name?"

"It's Longren," I answer, and then I have a sudden thought. "Mr. Agnew, if she wakes in the night and asks for me, please tell her where I am. If she wants me to come to her, I will. I don't care what time of the night."

"That's very kind of you, Miss Longren," Peter Agnew says. "I promise I will tell her. I will try and come for you around nine tomorrow."

"Okay," I say.

We say our goodbyes and I click off.

It takes a tremendous amount of effort to maneuver the unfamiliar car out of the lot and to look for a way to get across the freeway where a cluster of hotels is located. I finally locate a street that takes traffic under the busy freeway to the other side. It does not take long to find the Holiday Inn and true to his word, Peter Agnew has called ahead. My room key is waiting for me. It's after eight and I'm as hungry as I am weary. The hotel clerk must sense this because when I ask where to get a quick bite to eat he suggests I call a nearby pizza place that delivers free to the hotel. He gives me the phone number and I head to the elevator and my room on the fourth floor.

Once inside the room, I fling my suitcase onto one of the two double beds. I make the call to the pizza place as I sit on the other bed and kick off my shoes.

I am exhausted, but I should call Simon.

In a few minutes, I think to myself. I stretch out on the bed to rest my eyes for just a moment but my body willingly gives in to the pull of sleep.

Chapter 7

Open Wounds

I am barefoot on a deserted street on Terceira. In one hand I hold my canvas bag, in the other, the smaller hand of my half-brother, Zane. I am young. Too young to have the canvas bag that I carry as an adult and too young to have a little brother named Zane. I realize both of these things at the same moment that I drop the bag and pull Zane close to me.

"Watch out!" I yell as the pounding of hooves fills my dream.

I pull Zane away from the bulls as they race past us down the empty street, angry and afraid. The sound of my voice yelling out a warning to Zane wakes me. The pounding of hooves is replaced by a pounding at my hotel room door.

"Pizza delivery!" I hear someone yell from the other side, probably for the third or fourth time.

I am dazed and disoriented as I grab my wallet out of my bag on the bed beside me. I make my way to the door and open it.

"Sorry," I mutter to the young man standing there holding a flat box with a spinach, black olive, and feta cheese pizza inside it. I hand him fifteen dollars for the nine-dollar small pizza, telling him to keep the change and hoping my generous tip will make up for my slow response. He pretends not to be surprised by it.

"Have a good evening," he says as he stuffs the bills in his pocket and hands me a receipt.

"You do the same," I say, closing the door as he walks away.

The bottle of water I had brought with me on the plane is warm and half-empty, but I don't feel like leaving the room to get ice or a fresh drink. I fill the bottle the rest of the way with tap water from the bathroom.

I eat the pizza slowly, trying to clear my head. As I chew, I dismiss the dream and concentrate my thoughts on making the call to Simon. When the small pizza is half gone and I feel somewhat satisfied, I close the lid on the pizza box and push it away from me. I hold my cell phone for several minutes before pressing the button that will speed dial my phone at home in Chicago.

I can't seem to shake the dread I feel. I am afraid that Simon won't be there and equally afraid that he will be. I am painfully aware that the last spoken words between us were unkind words. Words meant to wound.

Don't let him leave me, I whisper to no one as I press the button.

I nearly collapse in relief as Simon answers the phone by saying my name as if he's been waiting to say it all day. I know caller ID has allowed him to see that I am calling, that he answers by saying my name because he knew it was me, not because he hoped that it would be. But it sounds like there is hope in his voice, and I have not heard such a thing in quite a while.

"Oh, it's good to hear your voice," I say to him, because it is.

"Is everything all right? Are you with Blair?" he asks.

"No and no," I answer, relaxing back on the headboard of the bed. "I'm actually at a Holiday Inn by the airport. Simon, Brad died half an hour before I got here. His employer got this room for me. I won't be seeing Blair until tomorrow. She's sedated right now."

"Oh, Tess," he says, but nothing else. We are both weary of bad news.

"I feel so bad for Blair," I continue without thinking. "She's so young to be a widow."

But of course Simon doesn't want to contemplate Blair's future without her husband. It must surely remind him of the man whose wife and daughter died when Simon's phone-fumbling and ill-timed pass sent them to their deaths. I am wishing I could take back what I just said. I am about to apologize when Simon asks me how long I think I will be gone. I'm only too happy to change the subject.

"I'm not sure yet, Simon. If Blair wants me to stay through the funeral, well, I think I should."

"Yeah, I suppose that would be the right thing to do," he says, and I can tell he wants me to come home, but I can't tell why. I decide I cannot bear another moment not knowing.

"Simon, is it good news or bad news?" I ask.

"What?"

"Whatever it is that you want to talk with me about," I answer. "Does it have to do with us?"

He pauses for a moment. I hold my breath.

"Well, yes," he replies.

I close my eyes as if that will keep me from hearing whatever it is he will say next.

"Tell me," I am able to say.

I can sense that he is thinking of how to say what is on his mind. I hold on to the bedspread under me like it is the handle of a roller coaster car.

"Tess," he begins. "I think I know what's wrong with us."

I grip it tighter.

"Wrong with us?" I say, pretending I don't have the foggiest notion where he's headed.

"Yeah," he continues. "I think I know why you don't want to get married yet. Why I pretend it doesn't matter. Why you still grieve for your mother. Why I can't seem to forgive myself for what I did to that family."

Every word from his lips pokes at me. I feel afraid, like the roller coaster ride has started but I can't see the tracks ahead. I don't know where we are headed.

"What are you saying?" I manage to say.

"I am saying I think we need help, Tess. Both of us."

I am not sure what he means, but I'm beginning to think that he is not planning to leave me. At least not yet.

"Help?" I echo.

"We're going nowhere, Tess. We're just spinning in circles. I didn't realize how bad off we were until my accident and I finally understood how debilitating it is to live without peace."

"Peace?"

I cannot seem to stop myself from sounding like a parrot, repeating everything he says. I would laugh if I weren't so stunned.

"Tess, last night when...when I left the apartment, I walked around for a long time. I had maybe walked two or three miles when I suddenly knew that if I didn't do something, the guilt I was feeling was going to kill me. I had to do *something* to try and make it right."

The face of Corinthia rises up before me, behind my closed eyes, as he says this. I can see her bending over a basket of wet laundry, picking up a limp dish towel and saying, "Well, you know what the remedy for regret is, don't you?"

I want to say now like I wanted to say then that there are limits. You cannot put a broken egg or a broken mirror or a broken window back together again. You can't. Some hardships cannot be made right, no matter how much you desire it.

"Tess, I went to Brian Guthrie's house last night," Simon says when I do not immediately respond.

At this I am truly speechless. Brian Guthrie is the man whose wife and child died in the accident. Simon's accident. I can't even say *You what?!* but I am thinking it.

"Tess, are you there?"

"Y...yes," I say. "You went to his house? How did you...how did you know where he lives?"

"He's in the phone book. It wasn't that hard. I hailed a taxi and just went over there."

"But, Simon," I say. "Was that really wise? I mean, he might have hurt you."

"Well, I wanted him to," Simon replies easily. "When I rang the doorbell, I wanted him to see that it was me. I wanted him to open the door with a shotgun in his hand. I wanted him to blast me to hell where I thought I belonged."

I taste bile in my throat. The roller coaster car is tumbling down a cold, cavernous valley, gathering speed as it rushes forward in the darkness. I cannot comprehend what I am hearing.

"Simon," I begin, and my voice doesn't sound like my own. I can't keep back the image of Simon lying on a Chicago porch with a chest full of lead. I can't finish.

"Tess, it's what I *thought* I wanted to happen, but that's not what happened."

I wait for the image to fade before asking him what *did* happen.

"Well, he was surprised to see me, and his first reaction was revulsion."

I wait.

"But he didn't hurt me like I wanted him to, Tess. And when he didn't hurt me physically, I wanted him to curse me to my face. I wanted him to damn me to the Devil. But he didn't."

The ride seems to be slowing. I use the moment to catch my breath. "What did he do?" I say.

"The longer I stood there mumbling about how sorry I was, the more his face softened," Simon replies. "The disgust faded away and what I saw instead was sadness. When I finally realized he wasn't going to give me what I deserved, I began to weep right there on his doorstep. Right in front of him."

Simon's voice is beginning to falter. To weaken. I too am feeling very weak. The ride has slowed to a steady creep.

"What happened next?" I ask.

"He invited me in, Tess. I refused at first, but he kept insisting, so I went in. He sat me down on his couch, got me a drink of water, and then called his pastor."

"His pastor?" I said, immediately thinking of tall Samuel Mayhew.

"Brian told me there was no way he could help me, but he knew someone who could," Simon continues. "Brian said only God could heal a wound as big and deep as the one I carry—as big and deep as the wound he also carries."

Simon is not leaving me but I feel like he's pulling away nonetheless. He is moving in a direction that is unfamiliar to me. I feel him edging away from me and toward a God I have never understood.

"I think he's right, Tess," Simon is saying. "What Brian said is true. I can't fix this on my own. It's too big and deep, just like what you carry is too big and deep for you."

He gives me a moment to digest this but it is nowhere near enough time.

"Tess, Brian's pastor took me over to his house. I talked with him and his wife until two o'clock. His name is Jim. His wife's name is Emily. We talked about everything—the accident, you and me, my whole life..."

"You talked about me?" I interrupt, feeling a twinge of anger.

"Yes, Tess, I did. I love you. I want to marry you. You can't keep living with your open wound just like I can't keep living with mine."

In my mind I hear Corinthia's voice. She is standing above me, placing a clothespin on a dishtowel and hanging it on a clothesline.

"Find a way to make it right," she is saying.

I am sitting on the grass next to her laundry basket.

"What if there is no way I can make it right?" I am saying back to her.

"Well, can you live with it?" she is asking, bending down to look at me.

"No," I am saying, because I don't want to believe that I can.

"Then find someone who *can* make it right," she says, with her strong arms on my trembling shoulders.

I let the voice fade away. It's just not that simple.

"Tess?" Simon is saying.

"There is no way either one of us can make *these* things right," I tell him, and I cannot mask the anger in my voice.

"That's exactly right, Tess," Simon says boldly. "You and I can't. But Jim told me God can put things to right, no matter how big they are. He can carry what we can't carry."

"Even God has limitations," I say softly, quoting my father though I don't want to.

"I used to think so too," Simon says in reply. "I think we've been wrong about that, Tess."

I am starting to get a headache.

"I don't see what this has to do with us," I say.

"Because, Tess, you are just like me, only worse off. I have been struggling with this open wound for just two weeks. You've been suffering with yours for years."

I wince at this, not because it's news to me but because it hurts to hear the truth sometimes.

"And it's not even the wound you think it is, Tess."

Now he has thrown me for a loop.

"What?" I say.

"Maybe we should continue this when you get home," he says after a momentary pause.

"What do you mean it's not even the wound I think it is?" I say, unwilling to just let it go.

"Never mind, Tess. I shouldn't have brought it up right now."

"Brought *what* up?"

"I spoke in haste, Tess," Simon says quickly. "It's...it's just your dad and I had an argument on the phone tonight, before you called. I got a little angry. I'd really rather talk about this when you get home."

"You talked to my dad?" I asked, thoroughly perplexed.

"He wanted to make sure we got the message about Shelley's surprise party because you hadn't called him back."

"What did you argue about?" I ask, having a hard time picturing my dad and Simon having a conversation lasting more than ten minutes. They've seen each other maybe three times in three years. But Simon doesn't answer my question.

"Are you going to call him back tonight?" he says instead.

"I don't know," I answer in a huff. "I haven't had a minute to think about Shelley's birthday, and you and I haven't even talked about it."

"If you call him tonight, see if he mentions talking with me, Tess," Simon says, and it's obvious he's confident my dad *won't* mention it. I don't know what to make of this. Something is going on and I don't know what it is.

"Didn't you tell him where I was?" I say.

"I did," Simon assures me. "He's not expecting you to call back tonight."

"Then I'll call him tomorrow."

"Okay. But when you do, don't mention that you know he and I talked. See if he brings it up first. Will you do that?"

What on earth did you argue about? is all I can think of to say, but I know Simon will not tell me until I try his little experiment.

"All right, I will," I say wearily.

"Tess?"

"Yes."

"I'm going back to work tomorrow."

For the first time since we began this conversation tonight, I am starting to feel a little of the hope that his voice sounds saturated with.

"You are?" I say.

"Yes. Just half days at first. We'll see how it goes."

"Simon, that's...that's wonderful."

"Yeah. The more I think about it, the more I'm feeling ready. Call me tomorrow night after you talk to your dad. But don't call until after ten. I am going over to Jim and Emily's for dinner."

"Oh, okay." I wonder if he can sense my unease.

"Give my condolences to Blair, would you?"

"Sure," I say.

"Goodnight, Tess. I love you."

"I love you too," I reply. And I do. But I feel very alone.

I lay my phone on the bedside table and rub my throbbing temples. I had dreaded making that call for no reason, but I feel scared and vulnerable nonetheless. I decide a hot bath will ease some of the tension I am feeling.

It does, but only while I am in it.

Fifty minutes later when I am lying alone in bed, a gallery of images begins to parade around in my head—racing bulls, Brad lying dead on a hospital bed, Simon weeping on the porch of a stranger, Corinthia hanging up her laundry to dry. They vie for my attention, and sleep eludes me until after midnight.

CHAPTER 8

How to Mourn

I am seated in the lobby of the Holiday Inn by ten minutes to nine the next morning. I awoke early, as I knew I would, after a restless night of sleep. I am hesitant to see Blair and yet impatient for Peter Agnew to come for me. I wonder how she spent the night. Did she wake up this morning, as I did, forgetting for just a fraction of a moment that Brad is dead? I wonder if she will want me to stay for the memorial service. It occurs to me that I haven't brought anything appropriate to wear to the funeral of a rich man. Antonia will chide me someday about this. She has told me repeatedly to never go on any trip of any kind without a little black dress.

A few minutes after nine, a bronze Jaguar pulls into the carport of the hotel's parking lot. A man with graying hair and wearing an expensive suit of the same color steps out of it. His face looks careworn. This must be Peter Agnew.

He steps in through the front doors and I rise, offering a tiny smile that lets him know I am the woman he is expecting.

"Miss Longren?" he says to me.

"Please call me Tess," I say, offering my hand.

"And you must call me Peter," he says, shaking my hand and then looking down at my feet, like he is searching for something. "If you don't mind, Blair would like you to stay with her for the rest of your time here. Is that all right? Do you mind getting your things and bringing them?"

"No, of course not," I say. "I'll be right back."

It doesn't take long to get my suitcase and return to the lobby. Peter tells me he has paid one of the hotel desk clerks to take my rental car back to the airport on her lunch hour. There are plenty of vehicles at Blair's house if I need to use one, he says. I hand over the car key and my room key and he takes my suitcase.

"Ready?" he says.

I nod and we make our way outside to his car. In less than a minute we're on our way. Peter tells me the drive to Blair's home in the bedroom community of Ladue will take about twenty-five minutes.

Peter Agnew looks tired and preoccupied, but he makes an attempt to get to know me. He asks me what I do for a living and where I am *from*, of course, and I answer as best I can. Then he tells me that Blair asked about me right away when he came downstairs to breakfast this morning. She had apparently awakened first. Peter does not know when she came downstairs but she was already sitting in the breakfast room with a cup of coffee when he joined her.

"So, how is she?" I ask.

"I don't know," he says thoughtfully. "She was hysterical yesterday, and this morning she just seems shell-shocked."

"Are her parents coming?" I ask. "Will they be able to help her with...with the details?"

"They're flying in this afternoon from Dallas, but they won't have to do much on that end," Peter answers. "Brad's lawyers will take care of Blair's interests when it comes to his estate. He has left her a wealthy woman. She won't have to worry about keeping her home or putting the twins through college. Or anything financially, really."

"That's something to be grateful for," I say. "And Brad's parents and his brother? They live here in St. Louis too, right? And his sister, Annette?"

"Yes. They were all at the house for a while last night too. Except for Annette and the girls. Annette kept the girls at home with her. She was reluctant for them to see Blair in the state she was in."

I think of Chloe and Leah, just three years old, most likely unaware of how much their lives have changed in just one day.

"They won't remember him," I say rather absently.

We ride the rest of the way in silence.

Blair had sent me pictures of the house she and Brad had built two years ago. I knew it was spacious and elegant, and I knew that it cost more than three million dollars to build and furnish. But I have never been in a home that boasts more than seven thousand square feet, and I certainly never have had a housekeeper take my things "up to a guest suite" upon entering a tiled entryway crafted of Italian marble. It's even more impressive than I expected.

Peter ushers me into a room off the main entry that is nearly wall-to-wall windows with no drapes or blinds of any kind. A set of wrought iron benches and chairs, adorned with black-and-white striped cushions, are placed around a glass table whose center is nearly covered with a huge arrangement of pale pink daylilies. An ebony baby grand piano fills one sunny corner; its black shiny top is up and is glistening in the morning sun. To the left of the piano is another seating area. Two fat white chairs sit on a small Persian rug and another glass-topped table separates them. On this one is a Lladró sculpture and three lead crystal candlesticks. The room looks empty of people. I almost miss seeing Blair sitting on the piano bench. The open piano top nearly hides her.

"I'll leave you two alone," Peter says softly.

He walks quietly out of the room and I take two steps toward Blair and then stop. I am afraid to be alone with her. She doesn't know how to play the piano. I don't know why she is sitting there.

"I don't know what to do, Tess," she says, breaking the silence, inviting me to approach her.

I walk to the piano and sink down beside her on the bench, wrapping an arm around her. She feels weightless.

"I don't either," I say.

She leans into me and rests her head in the crook of my neck and shoulder. I'm afraid she will start to weep and I don't know what to say to her if she does, but she doesn't.

We sit there like that for maybe five minutes, not saying anything.

"I don't know what to do," she says again.

I am nervous about what to say in response. I came here to help her. She asked me here for support and encouragement. I can think of nothing wise and wonderful to say. Instead, I think of something wild and wholly inappropriate and before I can stop myself, it's out of my mouth.

"Let's go paint our toenails."

She starts to shake and it is on the tip of my tongue to begin a lengthy apology, but then I realize she is laughing. I start to laugh too. Pretty soon we are laughing so hard, the tears we had wanted to shed all along are streaming down our faces.

I am so glad Peter shut the door behind him.

The morning passes quietly. Blair and I do not stay long in the sunroom after gaining back our composure. When we emerge, looking puffy-eyed and red-faced, Peter assumes we had been deep in grief for Brad. It was so much more than that, but I cannot explain it to him or anyone else.

A little before noon, we decide to sip some tea on the patio in Blair's expansive backyard. Peter's wife, Shar, joins us for a little while, but then she leaves to go make lunch arrangements. After Shar goes back into the house, Blair tells me the doctors told her Brad had four blocked arteries—probably a hereditary condition. No one knew. Not even Brad. The cholesterol levels in his blood were sky-high. He would have been a good candidate for quadruple bypass if his condition had been caught earlier, but Brad wasn't in the habit of seeing a doctor regularly. He was fit and trim and hardly ever got sick so he never saw the need. He attributed recent dizzy spells to a busy schedule and lack of sleep. In the five years they were married, Blair never once took him to a doctor and he never went on his own.

"He always ate and did whatever he wanted," Blair tells me.

She takes a breath after saying this, like she is going to say something else, but then she stops. She has changed her mind. She looks off in the distance, her thoughts far away.

"Blair, what can I do for you?" I ask. "Are there any arrangements I can make? Do you want me to go get the girls?"

She blinks long and hard.

"Brad's parents are taking care of all the arrangements. He is their son. Their heir."

Blair sounds almost aloof as she says this. I am not sure what she is thinking.

"Well, do you want to pick out some flowers for yourself?" I ask.

"Flowers?" she says, turning to me like I am suggesting something foreign.

"Well, maybe you'd like to have a flower arrangement for the funeral that is special to just you and Brad," I reply. "You know, like maybe the same flowers you had at your wedding."

"Is that what you would do?"

Blair is looking at me with those big, liquid eyes of hers that all the boys loved when we were in middle school. They look too big today, wide-open and searching.

"Who knows?" I say to her, dropping my eyes. "I'm not even married."

"Yet," she says, like she still has hope for me.

After a few minutes of silence I ask her again if she would like me to get the girls for her.

"No," she says and again she sounds aloof. This is a side of grief I have never seen.

After lunch, Peter heads over to the airport to get Blair's parents, and Shar returns to their home. When he leaves, I convince Blair to rest awhile. I head to my guest suite, as the housekeeper called it, and unpack my things. The closest thing

I have to a black dress is a purple bolero jacket and gray skirt
that Antonia says I look captivating in. I wonder if I will have
a free moment to find something more appropriate to wear.

When I'm finished, I make my way back to the main part
of the house and tiptoe up the stairs to the family bedrooms.
I pass an oak-paneled study, another guest suite, and a sitting
room. At the top of the stairs I find the twins' rooms—two large
bedrooms that are joined by a common play area. The rooms
are splashed with yellow and pale lavender. I feel a stab of envy
as I think about how wonderful it would be to have two curly-
headed daughters like Chloe and Leah. I walk past these rooms
and up a few steps to the master suite. Blair is lying on the king-
size bed; its massive four posts seem to guard her like knights.

I stand there for a few minutes. Her back is to me.

"I'm awake," she says. "You can come in."

I walk in and she turns her head toward me.

"Maybe you could just sit here with me. You don't have to
say anything, Tess."

"Sure," I say and I slip into a soft armchair by a window
that I think no one has sat in very much. We stay this way, in
silence, for quite a while.

I have dozed off when I hear footsteps on tile and voices.
I snap my eyes open. Blair is sitting up on the bed and running a hand through her hair.

"They're here," she says to me without emotion.

I follow her downstairs. In the entry, surrounded by brown
leather suitcases, are Veronica and Jack Devere. He looks pretty
much the same as he did at Blair's wedding five years ago, a
little less hair, a few more inches around his middle. Veronica,

not surprisingly, looks younger. She is wearing a taupe-colored rayon suit and a silk scarf around her neck that resembles the tawny hide of a cheetah. Gold glitters on her fingers, wrists, neck, and ears. She holds out her arms to Blair and waits for her daughter to come to her.

"There, there," she says, enclosing Blair in her arms. Jack takes a few steps closer to his daughter and rubs Blair's back. Neither one says anything else. They have absolutely no idea how to comfort their daughter.

I step away toward the sunroom to let the display of sympathy run its course. I stand in the doorway between one room and the next, leaning on the frame of the door. I can't help but think—I'm ashamed to admit it—that Veronica is hoping the embrace won't rumple her suit. I try to tell myself it's not as bad as that, but I'm remembering all those afternoons and evenings Blair was left home alone when her dad was flying sorties and Veronica was out shopping, sightseeing, dining, and doing who knows what else an hour away in Memphis. I'm remembering all the times we went into Veronica's closet and tried on all her clothes while she was out. We didn't even have to be sneaky. We knew she wouldn't be home for hours.

I'm remembering the pity I used to feel for Blair when we were young. I'm remembering that Veronica had a dozen different purses, and none of them ever interested me.

Veronica pulls away from Blair and flicks a stray hair from her daughter's forehead.

"We'll get through this, you'll see," Veronica says. "Won't we, Jack?"

Jack Devere finds his voice and chimes in.

"It'll be okay, babe," he says to Blair, still stroking her back.

Veronica suddenly notices me standing at the far end of the room.

"Oh, Tess. How good of you to come!" she says, and Jack turns and smiles halfheartedly at me.

"Hello, Veronica, Jack," I say as politely as I can.

"Now, let's get settled in so we can see where you need help," Veronica says as she turns back to Blair and Jack. "Grab those hangers off the back of that smaller suitcase, Jack, and I'll hang those up so they don't get wrinkled."

I watch as Veronica takes Blair's hand and they begin to ascend the staircase. Jack follows holding two matching, navy blue sailor dresses, size three.

Later in the afternoon, Brad's parents, brother, and sister arrive with the twins. I offer to watch the girls so that the family can plan Brad's funeral. Annette hands the twins over to me with what appears to be a mixture of relief and pain. The task of watching her nieces probably distracted her from the nasty business of mentally dealing with her brother's death. The girls are wearing matching pink outfits. They are chattering to Blair about what Aunt Annette's cats did last night, but it's obvious Blair is numb and only half-listening. She looks like she has far more on her mind than Brad's death. Perhaps she is wondering how in the world will she be able to tell her daughters that their daddy is dead. It doesn't appear yet that anyone has told them.

"Chloe is the shorter one," Annette says to me after we have been reintroduced. I have not seen her since Blair's wedding five years ago.

I leave the grieving family members to their grim task and ask the girls to show me their rooms, which they happily do, scampering up the stairs as if it's just another ordinary day in April. I follow them.

In their rooms, Chloe and Leah bring out every toy imaginable and provide a running commentary on each item in their unperfected, three-year-old English. I have a bit of difficulty distinguishing one from the other and am glad of Annette's tip. After the full toy inventory, they announce they're hungry and I take them downstairs to the kitchen. The housekeeper, who is named Vera, fixes us a snack and I suggest we take it outside.

When they are finished with their cookies and apple slices, they run to a massive wooden play gym and begin to climb it. I walk over to a patio table nearby to watch them, taking my cell phone out of my pocket. It's 4:30 PM. Dad should be finished with his last class and is most likely back at the clinic where he works part-time as a general practitioner. I contemplate making the call I owe him, wondering what I should expect. Simon is quite sure my father will not mention they had an argument. He is also quite sure this fact is significant. I am sure of nothing. I decide before I press the button that the purpose of the call is to tell my dad that, regrettably, Simon and I won't be able to make it to Shelley's surprise party at the end of the month. I will have just spent time away from work for Brad's funeral, and Simon will have just returned to work after his long absence.

I punch in my dad's cell phone number and he picks it up on the third ring. I can tell from the background noise that he is in his car.

"Hey, Dad, it's me," I say.

"Tess!" he says. "So sorry to hear about Blair's husband. That's very sad news."

"Yeah. It is. He was only thirty-two, Dad. The doctors here are saying it was a hereditary thing and not age-related."

"Yes, unfortunately sudden cardiac arrest can happen to a man as young as Brad if cardiac disease runs in the family. Guess his dad and his siblings will take note. Too bad it's too late for Brad, though."

"Yes. Um…Dad, I don't know how long I am going to stay here, but it might be a week or so. And Simon's going back to work, so I'm afraid the timing is a little bad for Shelley's party. I don't think either one of us will be able to get the time off to come."

"Not even a couple days, huh?" he says, but I don't get the impression he's really expecting us to try. Nor is he especially disappointed.

"I don't think so, but it sounds like a lot of fun and I hope you can pull it off," I say. "You'll have to tell Zane to call me and tell me all about it."

"Well, I guess it can't be helped," Dad replies.

"Sorry, Dad. But we'll try and get out there this summer sometime."

Try is a very useful word. It promises very little.

"Sure, I understand," Dad says.

There is a slight pause in our conversation and I decide to make use of it.

"So, is everything going okay?" I ask.

"Yep…well, things are busy of course. Zane's playing C-squad baseball this year, so we've been going to a lot of games. And I think I already told you Shelley has a new nursing job with a hospice provider. Excellent pay and she can pick her own hours."

Okay, strike one.

"And how about you?" I say. "How are you doing?"

"Oh, you know. The usual. Finals are coming up next month. There'll be lots of essays to read."

"Sounds like fun," I say. *Strike two.*

I wait for him to ask how I am. How Simon is.

"Yeah, well, I should probably let you go," he says, ending our conversation himself. *Strike three.*

Simon was right.

"Okay, Dad. Tell Zane I'm really sorry about not being able to make it to the party. I'll make it up to him."

"Will do. And please pass on my sympathy to Blair and her family, would you?"

"Sure, Dad."

"Take care, Tess. Call me when you get home, okay?"

"Okay. Goodbye."

I click the phone off. So that's that.

Chloe and Leah are beginning to squabble over who gets to be in a swing and who has to push it. I place the phone on the patio table and make my way to them. I tell them they can both be in a swing and I will push them both.

The rest of the day is a mixture of trying to meet Blair's needs, helping with the girls, staying out of Veronica's way, and being impatient to talk with Simon. By nine-thirty I have the girls in bed, Blair has been given a sleeping pill, and Veronica and Jack have closed themselves off in their own suite.

I'm glad to get to my room, where nothing has to be done for anyone. I just have to wait until after ten to call Simon. I get ready for bed. I pull a novel I read six years ago off one of the shelves in the room and read until a few minutes after ten. Then I can wait no longer. I press the speed dial for home. Simon answers.

"So how's it going?" he says.

"It's going," I say. "Blair has a lot of family here and Brad has left everything to her in his will, so she will never have to worry about money. But it's hard, Simon. I don't know what to say. And she seems so detached. I don't know what to do."

"Give her a few days," Simon replies. "She's probably in shock. Or denial. Brian Guthrie told me he went through both."

I'm kind of surprised to hear him mention Brian Guthrie's name again.

"So are you guys, like, friends now?" I say, and he can tell I'm not quite serious.

"No," Simon says. "But at least I'm not his enemy."

I decide to change the subject. "So how was work today?"

"It went really well, Tess. Everyone was glad to have me back. And they were patient with me while I re-familiarized myself with what we do all day long."

"Direct air traffic?" I question him, like it would be impossible for Simon to forget how to do that in two weeks.

"Getting planes full of people safely onto the ground," he replies.

"Oh. Sorry, Simon. I should have figured that out on my own."

"It's all right, Tess. It wasn't your problem."

Which I know leads us to what is *my* problem. Or at least what he thinks is my problem. I know he is going to ask me if I called my dad. He does. I tell him I did.

"And?" Simon asks.

"He didn't mention the argument."

For a moment neither one of us says anything. I wish I could see Simon's face as he realizes he was right. Is he satisfied? Disappointed? Relieved? Sad?

"So are you going to tell me what that means?" I ask. "I did what you said."

"Not over the phone," he replies, and I have at least one answer. His voice is full of sadness.

"You told me you would tell me," I counter. I feel like I'm being treated like a child. Or like he is acting like a child.

"I will tell you, Tess. I promise. But I am not going to do it over the phone."

"Why not?"

"Because I'm just not. You'll be home in a week or so. One more week can't matter."

"Simon…" I begin, but he cuts me off.

"Tess, you're going to have to trust me on this. Right now you need to concentrate on being a good friend to Blair."

"You think I won't be able to handle whatever it is you have to tell me?" I say, and I try to keep the irritation I am feeling out of my voice.

"I don't know. Maybe not."

"How can it be that bad, Simon, when I already know I am *wounded,* as you say?"

"Because you think you know where the wound came from, Tess. But you don't."

I'm getting angry and I don't want to be angry with Simon. He is assuming too much. He has only known me for four years, and lived with me for just two. He doesn't know everything. And he can't possibly know something about me that I don't know.

"Fine. We'll talk about it when I get home, then," I say curtly.

"Tess."

"What?"

"We'll get through this," he says.

Funny, that's the same thing Veronica said to Blair earlier today. But it sounds different somehow falling off of Simon's lips. Perhaps that's because, deep down, I trust Simon. And despite the annoyance I have for him at the moment, I know that he is motivated by his surprising love for me. So when he says it, I can almost believe it.

CHAPTER 9

Beautiful Lines

I have been to a handful of funerals in my life, but I must say Brad Holbrook's was the most masterfully arranged. It was held at the spectacular Cathedral Basilica of St. Louis near downtown—a beautiful piece of architecture. There were flowers everywhere and the music that poured forth from the pipes of the great Kilgen organ was magnificent. In the end though, the tears that flowed from the heavy-hearted congregation were just like those that flow from the poorest of parishes in any city you please. Funerals may differ but death is the same everywhere you go.

I sat a few rows behind Brad's family, where I could see the back of Blair's head. Chloe and Leah sat on either side of her in the matching sailor dresses. Brad's brother, Dane, gave a eulogy, as did Peter Agnew. I didn't know Brad very well, but my impression of him at his wedding five years ago, as well as the few times I saw him and Blair in Chicago, led me to believe he had been a man who always went after what he wanted. Driven, intelligent, and charismatic, he likely would have made his own millions if his parents had not already been wealthy. This was more or less the same picture painted of him at his funeral: Brad was a determined man who lived life fully and was taken far too soon.

The interment followed, which was probably the hardest part of the day for Blair. This time I was standing where I could see a portion of Blair's face, but her eyes were concealed behind a pair of sunglasses. It was difficult to see how the interment was affecting her. She stood motionless by her mother.

I couldn't help but notice how stunning they both look in black.

Now we are back at Blair's house. A caterer has brought an elegant spread of food, and most of the family and Brad's closest friends are huddled in intimate groups, sitting on rented folding chairs with white porcelain plates on their dark laps. I am not hungry but I take a plate anyway and look for a quiet place to eat where I won't have to mingle with people I don't know. I see a gazebo on the far side of the backyard lawn with a bench inside and I head for it.

I am nearly finished when I see Blair walking toward me, alone. The girls are scampering off in another direction behind her and Annette is following them. I can see that there is purpose in Blair's steps. She is walking toward me to speak with me. Perhaps she is going to ask me how long I can stay.

"You ate something. Good," she says, like I am the one who needs to be watched for signs of refusing to eat.

"Did you?" I ask.

She shakes her head. "I will later. I promise."

She sits down by me and I can see that she is drained of energy. She turns to me and sighs.

"That's a pretty color on you," she says suddenly, speaking of my purple bolero jacket. In four days I did not find a free moment to go dress shopping. I guess it doesn't matter.

"Antonia dresses me these days," I say.

She manages a weak smile, remembering, I think, all those times she told me what to wear, and more importantly, what *not* to wear.

"So tell me, what does *Linee Belle* mean?" she asks.

"It means 'beautiful lines,'" I answer, smiling back at her. "Antonia says fashion and style are all about lines. Make your lines beautiful and you will *be* beautiful. That's her motto."

"Make your lines beautiful," Blair echoes, looking away toward her daughters, who are far away on the other side of the yard.

We are both silent. I let her choose what to say next and when.

"Tess," she says a few minutes later, but she is not looking at me.

"Yes?"

"He was cheating on me."

I am at a complete loss for words. I feel tricked. This can't be true.

"Blair! Are you sure?" is all I can say.

"He was going to divorce me. I found the papers in his study the morning you came. He was getting everything ready. He had already contacted a lawyer. I found everything. I even found out…what her name is."

Blair looks down at her lap and I see the first tears of the day slip down her cheeks.

I close the distance between us and put a protective arm around her. This is too much. Too much for one person! Why does it always seem like it's too much?

"Blair, I am so, so sorry," I say as I start to tear up as well.

"No one knows," she manages to say through her tears. "I don't want anyone to know."

"I won't say a word," I assure her. "Are you sure he didn't file anything already?"

"I don't think he did," she says, shaking her head. "Everything was all in one place. I think he was just getting everything ready to...ready to tell me."

She covers her face with her hand. Blair's body shakes with grief and with what must be a horrible sense of rejection, which no one will probably ever know about, so no one will be able to help her through it.

We are lost in our own thoughts and tears for several long moments. I remember how dazed Blair looked when I came into the sunroom four days ago and found her sitting at the piano. I remember how Peter Agnew had said Blair had been hysterical the day Brad died, but appeared numb the morning after when he came into the kitchen and found her already sitting there. She had just come across the sad evidence of Brad's unfaithfulness. And no one knew it. I wonder why she kept it a secret from me these past four days when she had been so candid about everything else.

"Blair, I wish you would have told me sooner," I say, patting her shoulder. "I feel bad that you've had to bear this alone on top of everything else."

I don't know what I would have said to her had I known, but it is true that I am aching for her in a fresh way.

"It wouldn't have mattered," she says miserably. "You wouldn't have been able to stop it."

"Stop...stop what?" Surely she can't mean I wouldn't have been able to put an end to Brad's affair. His own death had already taken care of that.

"I think I know why all of this is happening to me," she says, ignoring my question and looking off toward her girls, two dark blue dots at the far end of the expansive backyard. "I think I know why."

Then Blair wipes her eyes and looks at me.

"Tess, I think I'm being punished."

"Punished?" I say, and I'm sure surprise is written all over my face. "By whom? For what?"

She looks down at the moist tissue in her hands.

"It must be God. I think God is mad at me."

"Blair, I don't think…" I start to say.

"Why else would this be happening?" she interrupts, looking again at her little girls off in the distance.

"Blair, you are not to blame for Brad's unfaithfulness! He's the one who blew it! And you certainly cannot hold yourself responsible for his heart attack. He had a heart condition no one knew about."

But I can see by the look on Blair's face that she has already given the matter hours and hours of desperate thought. She has mulled it over for four days. She doesn't see how incredibly irrational she is being. All she sees is a horrible situation that must have a divine cause.

"Blair, listen to me. You haven't done anything to deserve…" I begin, but she cuts me off.

"I think maybe I have," she says, fixing her eyes on her lap again.

"What? What is it that you have done, Blair?"

She dabs at her eyes but keeps them trained on her lap. "I have something that doesn't belong to me. I have had it for a long time."

I can think of nothing that Blair has that she couldn't pay for herself. I have no clue what to say to this. The idea of Blair stealing anything is ridiculous.

"I had it hidden away and I kind of forgot about it, but I found it awhile ago. And when I found it, I thought maybe it was because it was time to return it. Like maybe I was *supposed* to return it. But I did nothing."

She pauses and I nervously raise my head, looking past her to see if the minister who performed the funeral is still here. He should be here listening to this, not me. I am searching the torsos of the men on the patio, looking for someone in all black except for a square of white at his Adam's apple. I need help. Blair needs help.

"Blair, I am sure whatever it is you have done…" I start to say.

But as I am saying this, Blair reaches into the pocket of her black linen jacket and pulls out a tiny, worn piece of paper and a silver locket on a chain. She hands them to me.

"Read that note," she says.

I stop mid-sentence and look at the piece of paper she has handed me. It fits in the palm of my hand. I carefully open the yellowed note, which is folded in quarters, and read what is written on it:

> I am sorry.
> I am only sixteen.
> I am going home.
> I will always love you.

I have no idea what the note means or who wrote it. I am beginning to wonder if Blair might be losing it mentally.

"The locket and the note were with the baby, Tess," Blair says softly, not daring to look at me. "They were underneath the baby. When you went to get the blanket and Jewel went to get a baby bottle, I found them in the peach box. There were left there by the mother. She wanted the baby to have them…"

Blair is weeping again. I am in shock at this revelation, but I put my other arm around her to hold her as she cries.

"I didn't mean to hurt anybody. I just wanted to keep something that belonged to that baby. The note was so beautiful, Tess, and her locket…I was just so taken by her affection for him. I just wanted to imagine what it must be like to be loved like that. I know I should have given them back but when the police came and took the baby I didn't want to yet. And then when I wanted to, it had been more than a year! I was afraid. I was afraid, Tess!"

She clings to me, sobbing like a child, and I hold her, remembering that day, seeing it all in my mind…

Blair had come back from Kroger's with a couple cans of Similac and a package of newborn-size Pampers. She climbed up the tree in my backyard with a white plastic bag hanging from her arm. The baby had fallen asleep in Jewel's lap.

"Jewel, did you get the bottle and the wipes?" Blair said as she reached the top step and crawled into the tree house.

"Well, no, I've been sitting here holding this baby!"

"Well, go get them!" Blair commanded as she pulled out a can of formula from the bag and started to shake it.

Jewel sighed, placed the baby gently back in the peach box, and climbed down the stairs.

"That sweatshirt he has been lying on is wet and it stinks," I remember saying.

"I should have told Jewel to bring us a baby blanket," Blair said, peering out the tree at Jewel's retreating form.

"I know where my baby blankets are!" I said. "I'll go get one."

I had remembered that my grandmother had convinced my dad to save some of my baby things for me, and I knew just where they were—in a box in the closet of the spare bedroom.

I had left then. I was not there for what happened next but I can picture it now.

Jewel was in her house sneaking a baby bottle out of the kitchen. I was in the spare bedroom of my house, opening a box of my old baby things. Blair was alone in the tree house with the infant. The baby began to cry. She lifted him out of the peach box and the wet sweatshirt started to come with him. She started to pull it away and she noticed something was in the corner of the peach box under the sweatshirt. It was a locket. And a note. As she read the note and fingered the locket, a place that was already hurting in her heart began to throb. When Jewel and I started to make our way back to the tree house, Blair made a split-second decision. She shoved the note and the locket into her pocket. And never mentioned it to anyone.

When Jewel and I were back in the tree house and the baby was properly diapered, wrapped in a blanket, and starting to suck formula out of a bottle, Jewel said that we simply had to let her mama call the police.

"Why the police?" Blair had said.

"*Because* it's against the law to abandon your child," Jewel replied plainly.

"Well, maybe the mother had no choice," Blair said pointedly.

And I remember now that Jewel and I were both struck by Blair's sudden compassion for the anonymous mother. She knew what we didn't. She knew the mother hadn't abandoned the child because she wanted to. She left him because she was not much more than a child herself.

"Blair," I say, coming back to the present. "Listen to me! God is not punishing you. You meant no harm. And keeping the note really didn't change anything for the baby, Blair. This note doesn't have a signature or an address. The police wouldn't have been able to use it to find the mother."

Blair pulls away from me.

"How can you say keeping the note really didn't change anything for the baby?" she says to me. "It changed everything! He has grown up thinking his birth mother didn't want him, didn't love him. But I know that she did. And I am the *only* one who knows!"

Blair's big eyes are wild in a way that frightens me.

"Don't you see, Tess? I have to make this right! I have to."

I can scarcely believe she is saying these words. These same words. Corinthia's words. They are like a spell I cannot seem to come out from under.

"I have to find him, Tess," Blair says. "I have to find him and give him the note and the locket. They are his. She meant for him to have them. I have to find him or I will never again have a moment's peace!"

My mind is spinning. Blair is blowing this completely out of proportion. I don't know much about God but I am fairly sure Blair is wrong about this. She is young and attractive, she has two beautiful little girls, and she is financially set for the rest of her life. It's terribly unfortunate that Brad had been cheating on her. But I don't think this is the end of Blair's charmed life. She still has so much to be thankful for. So much that I confess I envy. But she apparently sees the rest of her blessings as handy, additional assets that God can strip from her if she doesn't rid herself of this skeleton in her closet.

I don't know how to combat this "the gods must be angry" state of mind. Blair is in a place of grief I have only ever read about: She wants to bargain her way out of sorrow.

Besides, what Blair is proposing is probably impossible. The baby was adopted eight months after we found him. We never knew the family's name. We were way out of the picture by then. I don't know much about family law, but I'm fairly certain adoption records are closed to the general public.

"Blair, I don't think it's that easy," I say.

"I don't care. I don't care how long it takes or how much it costs."

"I don't think it's a matter of time and money, Blair; I think it's a matter of the law. I don't think..."

"It's not like we're strangers!" Blair says. "We rescued this baby. And I even remember the names of the people who adopted him. That social worker I kept calling told me a couple by the name of John and Patricia were going to adopt him."

This surprises me. I didn't know Blair had kept tabs on the baby by calling the county social worker assigned to him. But I suppose hiding the locket and the note had kept her somewhat on edge.

"She told you their names?" I say. "And you remembered them?"

Blair nods. "I know it must seem weird to you, Tess, but I loved that little baby. I really did. I thought John and Patricia—whoever they were—were the luckiest people in the world. I used to pretend I *was* Patricia, that I was the mother of a sweet little baby who needed me."

She stops for a moment and sighs and I see again how mightily Veronica Devere failed her daughter. And how Blair tried to make up for it.

"John and Patricia who?" I ask.

Blair blinks at me.

"I don't know their last name. She never told me."

"I'm afraid no one is going to tell you their last name, Blair," I say gently. "I don't think anyone can."

"I don't see why this has to be such a big deal. I already *know* the first names!" Blair says defensively. "And *we* rescued that baby! It's not like we're not a part of this."

Blair's use of the words *we* and *we're* silence me. She is including me somehow in something she is planning, I am sure of it.

"I have to find that boy, Tess. I have to. I have to make this right before something else happens to me."

I can think of nothing to say in reply.

"I am going back to Blytheville," she says. "I am going to start there. And...and I want you to come with me."

"I couldn't possibly!" I stammer. "Blair, I have a job back in Chicago. And Simon needs me at home."

"I'll pay you what you would make at the boutique. I'll pay you double. If Antonia fires you, I'll buy you your own boutique. I don't care what it costs, Tess. And Simon is a man, not a little boy. He can live without you for a few months."

"A few months! Blair, this could take years!"

"Maybe, maybe not. Tess, please come with me. I won't make you stay more than a couple months, I promise."

"Blair, I can't just take off for two months."

"Yes, you can. I'll pay for everything."

"But what about Chloe and Leah?" I say, trying another approach.

"I would bring them with me if I could, but I can't. You know I can't," Blair says. "I know Brad's mother will keep them for me. And I have to do this, Tess. I have to or it won't stop. If we can't find him, I'll come back. But only for a little while. I won't rest until I find him."

She sounds like she is making a holy oath, and perhaps in her anguished mind she is. I am about to come up with another protest when it suddenly occurs to me I have just been afforded a wonderful opportunity. Truly splendid. Suppose I join Blair on her campaign for inner peace. Suppose I undertake with her this quest to "make it right." It is highly probable we will not be able to find a fifteen-year-old boy who was left as a baby on a church doorstep. And of course we are assuming he is still alive. But yet it is possible. It is possible we can find him. And if we do, we can show him his mother loved him. We can tell him it didn't matter about the leg. We can make it right. And I will have been a part of it.

I cannot give my mother back her life, but perhaps I can give a son back his mother, in a figurative sense. If I can make that happen, then perhaps it will not matter what Simon thinks he knows. Maybe then it won't matter what he and my father argued about. I will have bargained for my own peace, participated in my own act of restitution. I will have found and drunk my own remedy for regret.

"All right," I say to Blair. "I will come with you."

CHAPTER 10

The Road Home

Telling Blair's parents and in-laws that she and I have decided to take a little road trip is easy. No one raises an eyebrow, not even when Blair says she doesn't know how long we will be gone. They are all supposing that a trip to a childhood home full of happy memories will act like a tonic on the young widow. Blair does not mention the real reason for the trip.

"The girls can stay with us," Brad's mother says as soon as Blair stops talking, as if she is afraid Veronica will ask to keep the twins first. I can't imagine Veronica volunteering to take those little girls for who knows how long.

Blair nods and says thanks.

Brad's father wants to know where we will be staying and if Blair needs any cash. He also wants to know which car she is taking so that he can make sure it's ready for the trip. Blytheville is only three and a half hours away—not exactly a taxing drive for a top-of-the-line car—but I say nothing. This is Mr. Holbrook's way of showing concern for Blair. She is lucky to have him for a father-in-law. I wonder if this man has any idea what his son had been planning.

"Brad had plenty of cash here at the house," Blair answers. "And I guess we'll take the Lexus. We'll get a hotel room in Blytheville. I'm sure the Holiday Inn is still there."

"I think this is a very good idea," Veronica chimes in. "You need to get your mind off these troubles, Blair. Go and have a good time. Forget about all this."

I have a hard time not snickering. Those last two sentences of Veronica's are like her dual-sided mantra. Have a good time. Forget what waits for you at home.

"Tess and I will leave in the morning," Blair says, and the mission seems to be set in motion even though we have not left yet.

In a few hours, Veronica and Jack are gone. Dane takes them to the airport to catch their flight back to Texas, back to whatever life they have managed to carve out for themselves.

After they leave, Blair and I take the twins upstairs to pack their clothes and get them ready for the extended visit with their paternal grandparents. As we head up the stairs, Brad's father goes into the garage to check on the Lexus, and Brad's mother heads into the kitchen to find leftovers for a light supper. The housekeeper has gone home for the day.

The twins' immature chatter as we pack is soothing, though each one asks at different times if their daddy can change his mind and come back home. I was not in the room when Blair told the girls their father had died. I'm not even sure she told them he died. Does the word *died* have any meaning to a three-year-old? I don't know. Chloe and Leah seem to know that their father is gone and that he is far away, and I suppose that is sufficient for the time being.

There is a palpable heaviness in the entryway as Blair hugs her girls and her in-laws goodbye after we eat. Dwindling afternoon sunlight is filtering through tall windows above and on the sides of the front door, bathing the little group in hushed light. Perhaps Blair's eyes are empty of tears and need replenishing, but I am still a little surprised at her dullness in saying goodbye to Chloe and Leah. When they are gone and the door is closed behind them, I say what is on my mind.

"You are so lucky to have those little girls," I tell Blair.

Blair, looking out one of the panes on the side of the front door, nods and says nothing.

"Blair, I know it's none of my business, but..."

"You don't have to say it, Tess," she says, interrupting me. "I'm not going to do to them what my mother did to me."

Then she turns to me and looks at me like it's very important that I understand something.

"I'm doing this for *them*," she says. "I'm doing this so God will leave me alone. So He will leave us alone."

There is nothing I can think of to say in response to this. If I thought it would interest Blair, I would say that it's amazing that she attributes the grief in her life to God's intrusions, while the grief in mine I attribute to His absence.

"You probably have calls to make," she says as she turns and walks toward the stairs. "You can use Brad's study."

Simon. My father. Antonia. None of them will be thrilled with my change of plans. Actually, my dad will think it's a little odd, but he won't lose sleep over it. He may even think it's a quaint thing to do. A proverbial sentimental journey. Antonia will be annoyed. She can get along without me but she doesn't like to. Elena and the other girls can take up my slack. Elena in particular will be thrilled. She has been asking Antonia for more hours for weeks. And Antonia is not planning to go back to Europe until September. I will be back way before then.

I'm not sure what Simon will think. He's not the tortured man I last saw sitting in our hand-me-down chair. Through our phone conversations I can tell that he is slowly returning to the confident, shrewd man I fell in love with three years ago. He will think this is a fool's mission, that we won't find the boy. He may even be disappointed I'm not going to be home in a few days to hear his startling revelation about me.

I will call him last.

I look at my watch, noting that it's five-thirty. I can call Dad at the clinic where I know I will get his answering machine. That will make for a quick, uncomplicated call. Then I can catch Antonia just before she leaves for the day, which will be better than catching her at the beginning of one, as she would then have the whole day to stew over what I'm going to tell her.

I pick up the black handset on Brad's phone and try not to think about the plans he had been making at the desk it sits on. I dial my dad's direct line at the clinic and leave a cheery message saying that Blair and I are going down to Blytheville for a little R and R. I say that I will tell him all about it when I get back. Just before I say goodbye I tell him to be sure and wish Shelley a happy birthday and to let her know I will pick something up for her in Arkansas.

One down.

The boutique sounds busy when I call. I can't decide if that is good or bad. Like I had imagined, Antonia isn't pleased when I tell her I'm accompanying my grieving friend to a childhood home in another state for a visit.

"I can't *beleef* you are doing *theez* to me at the beginning of the season," she says, like spring arrives at *Linee Belle* and nowhere else.

"Just give Elena more hours, and maybe hire that girl from the school of design who came sniffing for a job last week," I say. "Maybe she won't mind taking something temporary. I took her resume to be polite, Antonia. It's in the desk. Third drawer."

"I hate training new people!" she says.

"Let Elena do it," I reply. "Antonia, it will be all right. And I simply must do this for my friend. She just lost her husband."

"*Sheez* most likely better off without *heem*," Antonia says gruffly, ever the believer in the carefree, single life.

"Antonia, I promise I will come back as soon as I can."

"I won't be able to *juz* do whatever I want when you are gone. I will have to be in charge!" she says in a resigned tone that lets me know this is her final volley.

"Then you will appreciate me that much more when I come back," I say, hoping my return volley will come across light and casual.

"So what is in Arkansas?" she finally says after a pause. "There is nothing in Arkansas. Why *doan* you take her to New Orleans or Miami or New York? Why you take her to Arkansas?"

"It's where we met, Antonia," I say. "There are a lot of good memories there."

And some troubling ones too, but I don't mention this.

"You call me the *meenit* you get back, yes?"

"I promise," I reply.

"Okay, okay. *Ciao*."

"*Ciao*, Antonia."

Two down.

I dial our number at the apartment and there is no answer. Simon must be putting in a full day at work. That's a good sign. I dial his cell phone, hoping he has started charging it again and using it. After four rings, he answers. I hear the sound of a moving car beneath the sound of his voice.

"Simon, it's me. Are you driving somewhere?"

"Hey, hi. Yeah. Just leaving O'Hare. I picked up your car today at the park and ride."

"Oh. That's great."

It's actually astounding. Simon is not only driving a car but he is also using a cell phone at the same time. I am amazed.

"So, you're just getting off then?" I continue.

"Yeah. I worked a full shift today."

"I'm really glad, Simon."

"Me too. But I don't want to talk too long, okay? Traffic is bad. It would be better for me if we didn't."

"Of course," I say quickly.

"So the funeral went okay today? Do you know when you're coming home?"

Well, here goes.

"Yes, the funeral was very nice. But...um, Simon, Blair told me something afterward that kind of changed my plans for coming home right away."

"What do you mean?"

"Well, she found out the day after Brad died that he was having an affair and was getting ready to file for divorce."

"Oh man, that's...that's terrible."

"No one else knows, Simon, so we can't tell anyone."

"Sure, sure."

"But Simon, Blair has it in her head that God is punishing her," I say, wondering what Simon will think of this.

"Punishing her? For what? What did she do?"

"Well, it might sound a little outrageous, but do you remember me telling you that when I was thirteen, Blair, Jewel, and I found a baby on Jewel's church's doorstep?"

"Yes."

"Well, the thing is, Blair had found a note and a locket in the box we found the baby in. They were from the baby's mother. See, the note explains why the mother left him. She was just too young to be a mother. And the note says that she will always love him. But Blair never told anyone. She still has the note and the locket. She showed them to me."

"And Blair thinks God is mad at her for keeping them and not telling anyone? She thinks that's why Brad was having an affair and why he died? Because God is mad at her?" Simon asks.

"Well, yeah. Pretty much."

"Tess, that can't possibly be true!"

I'm about to ask Simon what do he and I really know of God when I realize he may have discovered all kinds of things about God in the past few days that I don't know about. Simon has been with his new friend Jim daily since I left. But I have to admit it doesn't seem likely that God is punishing Blair.

"I know, but that's what she thinks," I say.

"Well, did you tell her that's not true?"

"Simon, she wouldn't listen to me. She has it in her mind that she needs to find this child and give him the note and the locket because she thinks he has grown up his whole life thinking his birth mother rejected him. She says she has to let him know his mother loved him."

"So that God will stop bullying her."

Simon makes it seem like Blair is naive. It makes me feel like I am naive.

"Simon, she has been through a lot. Maybe she isn't seeing this clearly, but I have to say, I can see how finding this child could have an enormous healing effect on her."

"Well, you're probably right there," he says.

There is a slight pause. I am trying to think of a way to tell him that I am going with Blair but he beats me to it.

"And I suppose she has asked you to help her find him."

There. It is out.

"Yes, she has."

"So you're going."

"Simon, I feel I owe it to her."

I say nothing of how this quest fits my own agenda.

There is a measurable pause before he speaks.

"How long will you be gone?"

"I'm not sure at this point. I have my doubts we will be able to find him. But we have to try," I reply.

"And what about your job?"

"I already called Antonia. She was a bit miffed but in the end I think she understood."

"So you called her before you called me?" he says, sounding a little hurt.

"Simon, calling her was easy. Calling my dad was easy. I knew calling you would be hard. I really don't care if Antonia or my dad think this is crazy. But I do care if you do. Please don't tell me you think we're crazy."

Simon sighs and I hear the rush of passing cars.

"I don't think you're crazy. But I think you are going to be disappointed. What's going to happen to Blair when she can't find him? How is she going to feel then?"

I want to say that Blair will become skilled at living with her regrets, because when you have no choice, you simply learn to breathe with your troubles pulling at you. It can be done. But this is not what I say.

"She will know she tried her best to make it right," I say instead. "Surely that counts for something."

"I miss you," Simon says in softer voice.

My throat feels thick as I tell him I miss him too.

"Call me often," he says. "Every day."

"I will. I love you, Simon."

"I love you too."

I hang up the phone and sit sort of dazed in Brad's expensive leather chair. Simon is probably right. God is not punishing Blair. But Blair is right too. The child we found needs to see the message his birth mother left him. It could change his life. Maybe it will change Blair's. Maybe it will change mine.

I rise from the desk and leave the study and its emptiness. Blair told me earlier that we would go through her closets and pick out some clothes for me to bring to Arkansas since I came with just a few things in my suitcase. It will be just like old times. Me, sitting on the bed, watching her pick out hanger after hanger and saying things like, "This will look good on you," and "This is definitely not your color," and "This one has always been one of my favorites."

Just like old times.

It occurs to me as I climb the stairs to Blair's room that I will be able to see Corinthia for the first time since I left Blytheville thirteen years ago. I hope I will see Jewel too. I have the strangest feeling as I consider this. It's the feeling I would expect to have if I was planning a trip to my hometown, to the place where I am from.

CHAPTER 11

Square One

Blytheville, Arkansas

Our drive to Blytheville would seem uneventful to an unknowing observer. There are no maps to continually turn to since Blytheville is a straight shot south from St. Louis on Interstate 55. There is no excited conversation about where Blair and I are headed, no hotel reservations to confirm or carefully laid plans to discuss for the days that lay ahead. We have brought no camera with us, no film. There is nothing to indicate that we are on a pilgrimage of sorts except for the suitcases in the trunk.

Despite my offer to drive, Blair insists on being at the wheel. She assures me she slept fine last night and that driving will keep her focused on what lies ahead and not what lies behind. I slept fairly well myself last night. The enormous house was like a tomb without the girls and Blair's family sharing it with us.

For the first hour there is little conversation. We sip coffee that we bought at a Starbucks on our way out of St. Louis and Blair asks me little questions here and there about my life. I'm afraid to ask too many questions about hers. I don't know what hurts too much to talk about.

"You know, I'm surprised you didn't become a map-maker

or whatever they are called," she says, getting an update on Antonia. "You were always so crazy about maps."

"A cartographer," I say, almost sheepishly. "I *was* crazy about them, wasn't I? I thought about it as a career for a while. I even changed my major to geography my sophomore year. Went to this island off the coast of Argentina to map its topography with a bunch of other students ..."

"So what happened?"

"I don't know," I answer honestly. "I just got cold feet. Or lost interest. I'm not sure."

"So you like what you are doing now?" Blair asks.

"Well...yes, I do," I answer. "I kind of have you to thank for it."

"Me?"

"I never thought about fashion and style until I met you."

Blair says nothing as she contemplates this. I meant it as a compliment but I'm not sure she's taking it as one. The expression on her face is difficult to read.

"It just seems to me you're too intelligent to be dressing mannequins," she finally says. "You were always the smart one. Smarter than Jewel. A million times smarter than me. You should be doing something brilliant."

"Well, like what?" I say, laughing nervously. Once again, I'm completely surprised by something Blair has said.

"Like making maps or solving mysteries or finding a cure for cancer. You're too smart to sell clothes. I could do that. My mother could do that."

I sit in wordless wonder. In the back of my mind I'm aware that this is the conversation I had wanted my dad to have with me when I was twenty-three, living at home and unable to motivate myself to go back to college and finish my degree.

"None of my St. Louis friends care what my degree is in, Tess," Blair continues. "You know why? 'Cause it doesn't matter. I went to Boston University to find a rich man to marry. And I did. I found Brad. Who cares what my degree is in? It doesn't matter. It doesn't prove I'm good at anything or smart in anything. It just shows I went to a good East Coast school where I was lucky enough to meet a rich Midwest man."

"Blair," I begin, but she does not want to continue this conversation.

"Sorry I brought it up, Tess," she says. "Get me a bagel, will you? I don't want to talk about this."

I reach into a bag between our seats and pull a bagel out for her. As I hand it to her I see lines on her face and around her eyes that seem to have emerged overnight, as if her woes have aged her. Then it occurs to me. Blair had only one day to grieve for the man she loved. Not even that. It was less than an hour. In those hours between the time she called me in Chicago and I arrived in St. Louis, she was still clinging to the hope that Brad would live. She was not yet grieving then. But then Brad died and her immediate sorrow was too much for her. Half an hour later, Blair had been sedated; medicated so heavily that she could not take my phone call. In the morning, before anyone else was awake, she had gone into Brad's study, probably to recapture the feeling of being close to him. Perhaps she had been in there for ten minutes, maybe fifteen, when she opened a drawer or looked in his briefcase and found papers that Brad surely had thought were in a safe place until he needed them. Thirty minutes of grief the night before, fifteen minutes of grief the morning after. Then everything changed for her.

She had forty-five minutes to mourn the death of the husband she loved. Less than an hour. And now it seems like she faces a lifetime of loathing the husband who was unfaithful to her, a lifetime of bitterness and resentment. I'm thinking, as I look at her, that plain, uncomplicated grief would be less devastating.

We are quiet for the next ten minutes or so. Then Blair motions to an envelope by the bagel bag.

"Take a look in that envelope," she says.

My interest piqued, I pick up the envelope, place it on my lap, and reach inside. I draw out a folded newspaper clipping. When I unfold it, I gasp. I haven't seen this in years. It's the article from the local Blytheville paper about the baby we found.

"Oh, my gosh! You kept it!" I say.

"Didn't you?" Blair replies.

"I think it's at Dad and Shelley's. I'm not sure. I haven't seen it in so long. I kind of forgot about it."

"I read it again last night. It had been a while," Blair says.

The photo of the three of us standing outside Jewel's church is grainy with age. The baby isn't in the picture. By the time the local press had heard what had happened it was close to four in the afternoon. An ambulance had come for the baby shortly after Jewel's mother called the police—without its sirens blaring, thank goodness. That had been at noon, three hours after we found the baby. We told everyone we found him around eleven-thirty. Actually it was Blair who did the outright lying.

No one asked Jewel or me to verify the time. But I know had someone asked Jewel, she would have told the truth. I still feel a pang of guilt just thinking about what we did.

I look at the photo next to the story. We are sitting on the steps where we found the baby. We have nothing to show to the camera. The baby was long gone and the police had taken the peach box and the soiled sweatshirt. Jewel and I didn't know that there was, in fact, tangible evidence of what our amazing morning had been like. We didn't know that in Blair's front shorts pocket was a folded note and a locket on a chain.

I sit back in my seat in Blair's car and read:

Infant Found on Church Doorstep

Blytheville, Ark.—Local authorities are looking for the mother of a day-old infant who was found on the steps of the Church of the Beautiful Gate sometime Wednesday morning. Three Blytheville teenagers, Blair Devere, Tess Longren, and Jewel Mayhew, all thirteen, found the baby boy late Wednesday morning while walking through Mayhew's backyard. Mayhew's father is Samuel Mayhew, pastor of the Church of the Beautiful Gate. The church adjoins the Mayhews' home.

According to the police report, the girls were walking from Mayhew's house to the Longren home next door when they heard a faint cry. Following the sound, the girls came upon a wooden produce box sitting on the church's west entrance steps with the infant inside. Jewel Mayhew informed her mother, Corinthia Mayhew, who then called the police. The baby was taken to Chickasawba Hospital, where he will be under observation for several days. Mississippi County authorities told the *Courier News* that the infant will be placed in foster care while the search for the infant's parents or other family members continues.

"He is such a sweet little baby with such beautiful blue eyes," Blair Devere told the *Courier News* a few hours after the baby was taken to the hospital. "We are so glad we found him before anything bad happened to him."

The girls told the *Courier News* that they bought diapers and formula for the baby and that they wrapped the infant in one of the girl's old baby blankets. The police report states the girls waited half an hour after finding the baby before telling Corinthia Mayhew.

"He was so hungry and he needed a diaper," Tess Longren told the *Courier News*.

Police have the wooden produce box the baby was found lying in and a plain, gray sweatshirt that was also found in the box but no other clues. The infant is believed to have been less than twenty-four hours old at the time of the discovery. He is Caucasian, blue-eyed, and has a clubfoot on his right leg. Anyone with

information about this incident is asked to contact the Blytheville Police Department or the
Mississippi County Sheriffs Department.

"This was the first and only time I have ever been in a newspaper," I say to Blair, looking at the article.

"It was my first too. My second was when I got engaged."

I put the article back in the envelope and help myself to a
bagel. We listen without talking to a Norah Jones CD until we
cross the state line.

The transition from one state to the other is seamless. We
cross into Arkansas and are promptly welcomed to the City of
Blytheville. I cannot tell if things look the same or if they look
incredibly different. I didn't pay attention to those details when
I lived here. We take the first exit, one of only two, and see
the first familiar sight, the Holiday Inn sign. Blair and I came
here often for Sunday brunch with her parents. Blair managed
to sneak a taste of champagne once when the buffet had been
particularly busy. She had urged me to try it but I had been
too scared.

We pull into the familiar parking lot and Blair and I get out
of the car and stretch. She takes care of getting the room. I'm
glad that she wants to share a room with me. She can afford
to get separate rooms, but I find it touching that she doesn't.
I wonder what it's like for Blair to get a room in an ordinary
Holiday Inn. She has led a life of luxury for five years, but she
says nothing about the commonness of the room when we step
into it. We open our suitcases and wordlessly hang up the few

things we brought on hangers. I'm pretty sure Blair will waste no time in getting started on what we came here to do.

"We'll eat something and then we'll go to the county offices," Blair says. "Maybe we'll get lucky."

"Don't you want to drive by our old houses?" I ask. I'm anxious in a childish kind of way to see Corinthia. It feels strange that she is just a few miles away from me.

"There will be plenty of time for that," Blair says, "You can have those two drawers and I'll take these."

She points to the dresser drawers and I'm reminded as Blair deftly changes the subject that for her, this is not a pleasure trip.

We get back in the car and head toward the main business district, driving slow and causing other drivers to impatiently ride our back end. It's a little difficult to remember where everything is. It doesn't appear that the town of 30,000 has changed that much, but we didn't drive anywhere by ourselves when we lived here before. We were just kids. By luck we find the Sonic drive-through that had been our favorite place for hamburgers and shakes. My old street is only a few blocks away from this fast-food place, but Blair doesn't seem to care about this as we eat. I'm itching to at least drive by my old house, but Blair has only one thing on her mind. She wants the last name and the address of the family that adopted an abandoned baby fifteen years ago.

When we are finished, Blair asks our server where the county offices are, and we are directed to a four-story gray building a few blocks away. Within minutes, Blair is parking her Lexus across the street. We stare at the building in silence for a few minutes.

"I suppose we could start with the county recorder," she says.

"That sounds good," I say, but neither one of us move. We both know the real search starts here. It could also end here.

"C'mon," Blair finally says. "Let's do it."

It's a little after one in the afternoon. We hope that whoever works in the recorder's office will be back from lunch. The air inside the building is cool and the hallways are dimly lit. A wide, graceful staircase leads to the other floors. The recorder's office is on the first floor. Our steps echo on the linoleum as we walk to the office and step inside.

A woman looks up from one of several desks as we approach a customer counter. Two other employees are in the room, and a woman is sitting in a chair in a waiting area just inside the door we came in.

"May I help you?" says the woman behind the counter with a Southern accent I haven't heard in a long time.

"Yes," Blair says, trying to sound confident. "Births and adoptions are recorded in this office, right?"

"Yes."

"Well, my friend and I used to live here, and fifteen years ago we found an abandoned infant on the doorstep of a church here in town."

The woman's eyes get a little wide. *There's something you don't hear every day,* they wordlessly say.

"The baby was adopted eight months later in this county. My friend and I are traveling through Blytheville and we would like to see how he is doing. We're hoping you can tell us where we can find him. I know the first names of the couple who adopted him but not their last name. I need to get in touch with these people because I have…there's something I need to give that boy."

It would sound like a reasonable request if we lived in a world without pedophiles or sociopaths or stalkers. But you can't just give information like that to a stranger off the street. I can see it in her eyes before she says anything.

"Well, I'm sorry, but that information is protected by law. I wish I could I help you, but I am afraid I can't" she says, her accent making every one-syllable word a two-syllable word.

"I can assure you I mean this child no harm," Blair says, reaching into her purse and pulling out the envelope that had been between the seats in the car. "Look. Here is the newspaper article about it. See? That's me. And that's my friend Tess here. And this is Jewel Mayhew. She lives in Tennessee now. But her father and mother still live here. In the background is the Church of the Beautiful Gate."

The woman is looking and nodding but I can see she will not budge. How can she?

"Well, the law doesn't allow me to give out that kind of information, no matter what the circumstance. I'm really very sorry. But I can assure you that the county most certainly did a thorough background check on the family that adopted him. I'm sure he is doing just fine."

"No, you don't understand," Blair says, all confidence lost in her voice. "I already *know* the couple's first names! John and Patricia! I just can't remember the last name. And I have to find this child. I…I have something that belongs to him."

I watch as Blair reaches into her pocket and brings out the locket. But not the note. I am certain she will show no one the note.

"This locket belongs to him! It was in the box when we found him. It somehow got misplaced that day. But I'm sure his birth mother wanted him to have it. So you see, I need to give it to him. Maybe… you could call the family and tell them I'm looking for him."

"Oh, I don't think..."

"Please," Blair is pleading.

I want to leave before she totally loses it. The other two women in the office have raised their eyes from their desks and are watching the whole thing. I can see the woman in the waiting area is watching too with a look of dismay on her face. I wonder whom she is feeling sorry for—Blair, the adopted boy, or the harried employee.

"Maybe you can come back tomorrow when someone from court administration will be here. Maybe you can see if there is a way to petition to the court for the information you want."

"Will…that work?" Blair asks. Her hands are shaking.

"Well, I'm not sure, Miss. But I think it's a better place to start than here, okay?"

She says "okay" like "oak high." She is being very patient with Blair.

"No one is there today?" Blair says.

"No, but they will be there tomorrow."

"All right," Blair says, defeated. She puts the locket back in her pocket.

"Thank you," I tell the woman as Blair turns to leave.

"Yes, thank you," Blair says.

We walk out of the office and I can feel every pair of eyes on us: the woman at the counter, her two coworkers, and the woman in the waiting area.

Blair says nothing as we get back into the car.

"So what do you want to do until tomorrow?" she says quietly, starting the engine.

"I think you know," I say, trying to lighten the mood.

She offers me a half-smile.

"Okay, but we'll look at my old house first. It won't take as long. You'll probably want to see Corinthia when we get to yours."

Oh, yes. I probably will.

CHAPTER 12

Where Time Stands Still

The person who coined the phrase, "You can't go home again," probably did so after visiting a childhood home after many years away and finding that time did not stand still for him while he was gone. Blair and I are halfway prepared to visit her home at the air base, but only halfway. We know everything about her old neighborhood will be very different, for mostly physical reasons.

The air base in Blytheville was deactivated a few years after both our families moved away from it. Maybe the mission of the command changed or maybe the money ran out or maybe it was some other reason altogether, but one day the squadrons of B-52s and KC-135s flew away from the base and did not come back. I didn't think much about it at the time because we had already moved away, but now as we drive onto Memorial Drive, past the base's once-guarded entrance, I can see that going home for Blair will be different than for me. Her house on base is no doubt still there, but everything else about the base is very different.

The wide streets are quiet and the flight line and the sky above it is eerily empty. Some of the old buildings have found new uses in the private sector, but many more sit quiet and vacant. The housing area has been taken over by a property management company that specializes in active retirement communities. We are glad to see the geraniums, spurting sprinklers, and gazing balls on the front lawns that declare that people still live here. But none of the cars in the driveways bear Department of Defense stickers; none of the people living inside wear Air Force uniforms. No children are here.

It takes a little while to find Blair's duplex because the street names and house numbers have all been changed. But we finally find it, tucked away on a quiet cul-de-sac that used to be officer housing. The yellow brick looks the same, the white carport too. Missing from the driveway is Jack Devere's roadster, but everything else about the house looks like it did thirteen years ago when Blair and her family moved to their new base in Idaho and I moved to mine in Ohio.

"Do you want to ring the doorbell and see if anyone is home? They might let us in to see the inside," I ask.

"No," Blair says. "It was just a place to live. I never felt like this was home for me."

We head out of the housing area through the unmanned front gate and make our way back to town. Again, we have a little trouble finding our way, but soon the Sonic drive-through is in sight and I know where we are.

"Turn here," I say, pointing to a street just past the Sonic.

"I know," Blair says. "I know where we are."

We see the white steeple of the Church of the Beautiful Gate first and my breath catches in my throat. Then we see Jewel's old house, the one Corinthia and Samuel Mayhew still live in. I can't help smiling. Then there is my house, the two-story, ageless brick one. Blair pulls up to the curb on the opposite side and stops the car.

"Nothing has changed here," she says, looking at the two houses and the white church.

I just nod.

The driveway of my old house is empty and the garage door is closed. No one appears to be home. The same is true of Corinthia's house.

"Let's see if Corinthia is home first," I say, and I get out of the car.

We walk across the street and up the cement path to Corinthia's front door. The metal screen door is new. I wonder when they got rid of their old wooden one. I liked the way it squeaked. I ring the bell and we wait. I ring it again.

"She's not here," Blair says.

I am disappointed to say the least.

"Let's see if anyone is home at my old house," I say, and we walk across the grass separating the two houses. I ring that bell twice too. No one answers but I do not want to go.

"We can come back," Blair says. "I want to go to the library, where I can use the Internet. I want to know what the adoption laws are in this state."

She starts to walk away.

"Blair, I think I'll stay and see if anyone comes home," I say. "You can go on to the library. I don't mind waiting. And Corinthia might return while you're gone."

Blair hesitates for a moment and then shrugs. "Suit yourself," she says. "I might be an hour or more."

"It's okay. I'll be fine."

"I'll be back," she says, and she starts across the street.

I watch her drive away and then turn my attention back to the two houses, wondering if I would attract attention if I just sat at the patio table in Corinthia's backyard. The yard is open to the street and the table is in plain view. Then it occurs to me that maybe Corinthia is at the church. I wonder why I didn't think of this sooner.

I walk over to the Church of the Beautiful Gate and stop for a moment at the sign that bears its name. I can remember seeing the sign for the first time two days after we moved in. I remember being puzzled by it since there is no gate on the church grounds. I had asked Corinthia about it the third time she invited my dad and me over for dinner. It was another conversation that had taken place while we did the dishes.

"Well, in the book of Acts in the Bible, Tess, there is a story of a man who had been crippled from birth," she had said, plunging a dish into soapy water and scrubbing it. "Every day people would bring him to the city gate to beg for money. The gate had a name. It was called 'Beautiful.' Well, one day—now, this is all after Jesus rose into heaven—the apostles Peter and John were walking through the Beautiful Gate and the crippled man asked them for money. Peter said to the crippled man, 'Silver and gold have I none. But such as I have give I thee. In the name of Jesus Christ of Nazareth, rise up and walk!' And do you know what happened, Tess?"

I had given her another scraped plate and shaken my head.

"The man who had been crippled from birth got up and he walked! The Bible says he was so overjoyed that he started walking and jumping and praising God!" Corinthia replied, her eyes bright and animated.

"That's why our church has that name, child," she continued. "All of us need to come to the gate called Beautiful. All of us are crippled from birth. I don't mean in the physical sense, Tess. I mean in *here*."

And then she had touched my chest with her wet finger. It left a little watermark.

I have not thought about that moment in her kitchen in a long time. I don't even know how long. There weren't many dinners at her house after that. In the following weeks my father began to politely decline every dinner invitation Corinthia extended to us. I'm fairly certain that that same night, Samuel Mayhew, in his own way, had approached my father about his own need to come to a gate called Beautiful. And my father had quickly decided, "Well, that's enough of that." I ate with the Mayhews whenever I spent the night with Jewel and whenever my dad had to go out of town. But he and I never went over to the Mayhews' again as a family to share a meal with them after that night.

Standing here now and looking at the sign, I'm struck by something that I have never thought of before. The baby we had found—the same baby Blair and I have come back to Blytheville to find—was also crippled from birth. Just like the man in the story. Just like me. No wonder that like Blair, I had wanted to keep the baby as long as we could that day. I identified with him. In a way, I felt crippled from birth too. The difference is that no one has ever been able to see my deformity.

No one really knows what my birth did to my mother and what it subsequently did to me. Except perhaps for Simon.

I leave the sign and these heavy thoughts and walk up the front steps to the church. The wooden double doors are both unlocked. I step inside the darkened church sanctuary, where rows of dark wooden pews sit empty. All the inside lights are off and I can see that the altar and the pulpit are dark and empty as well. I know how different this big room can be on Sundays. I had gone to church with Jewel several times when we lived here. I remember feeling awkward being the only white girl in the little congregation, but it didn't seem to bother anyone else. The services, unlike the few I had gone to with other friends at other bases, were anything but boring. There was a lot of singing, clapping, and shouting. The women and girls dressed as if they were going to a fancy wedding with lots of beautiful hats, shiny high-heeled shoes, and white gloves. The men, and even the littlest boys, wore starched white shirts and ties. These memories stand in stark contrast to the quiet room I am now standing in.

I walk to the front of the church to the side door by the organ that leads to the Sunday school rooms, Samuel Mayhew's office, and the door whose outside steps once bore a peach box with a baby inside it. The Sunday school rooms are all empty. Samuel's office door is closed and there is no answer when I knock on it.

I walk back to the sanctuary, disappointed. Sighing, I slide into a pew near the front and stare for I don't know how long at the plain wooden cross that hangs in front of me against a backdrop of stained glass.

Many minutes later or perhaps just a few minutes later—I don't know which—I feel a hand on my shoulder and I hear a familiar voice.

"Can I help you, friend?" Corinthia says.

I turn around to face her. Despite the darkness of the unlit room and the passage of time, when she sees my face Corinthia knows who I am. I stand and she enfolds me into a tight embrace as I knew she would. As if I were her child.

By the time Blair returns it is nearly four o'clock. Corinthia and I are sitting in her backyard sipping sweet tea, talking as if no time had escaped between us. I have told her about the death of Blair's husband, the note, and the locket. I have also told her about Simon, calling him my fiancé and causing her to immediately ask if we have set a date. I told her about Simon's accident, his dark days, and his new friend Pastor Jim, but I couldn't bring myself to tell her we are living together. I know this would make her sad. I told her about my little brother Zane, my hopscotch college days, and my job at *Linee Belle*.

Though I am nothing like the teenager she last saw, Corinthia looks the same except for strands of gray at her temples. All of her children except for Marigold are grown and have left home to build their own lives. She has five grandchildren, counting Jewel's three boys. Corinthia has also told me that no one is presently renting my old house, that the owner has had some trouble keeping it rented since the air base closed and the steady flow of newcomers to town abated.

Corinthia is telling me she will try to contact the owner if I would like to see the house, which I would, when Blair arrives.

She gets out of her car and begins walking toward us. Corinthia stands, embraces Blair warmly, and invites her to sit down.

Blair accepts a glass of iced tea and sneaks a look my way that says, *How much did you tell her?*

I have no idea how to communicate to Blair that I told Corinthia nearly everything.

"My dear, I am so sorry about the loss of your husband," Corinthia says, patting Blair's hand. "I truly am."

"Thank you," Blair says and again looks my way to see how much Corinthia knows. I shake my head just once and I trust it is barely perceptible. I did not tell Corinthia that Brad had been unfaithful.

"I will be praying that God will heal your heart, Blair."

"Oh. Um...thanks."

"Do you have pictures of your little girls?" Corinthia asks.

"Oh. Yes," Blair says, reaching into her purse and pulling out her wallet. She opens it and flips to two pictures side-by-side. Chloe and Leah.

"How beautiful they are! Oh, my, how precious!" Corinthia says.

"That one is Chloe," Blair says, relaxing a little. "And the other one is Leah."

"Truly enchanting. I will have to show you pictures of my grandchildren when we go inside," Corinthia says, handing the wallet back. "Y'all can stay for supper, can't you?"

"Sure, we'd love to," I say before Blair can say anything.

"Samuel will be so happy to see you. Marigold won't remember you, of course, but she knows your names. We've never forgotten you girls."

When she says this I can picture the Mayhew family gathered around their beds, offering up nightly prayers year after year for Blair and me. It makes me wish I had written Corinthia or called her from time to time.

"Did you find what you needed at the library, Blair?" Corinthia asks, refilling our glasses.

Again Blair looks to me for a cue. Corinthia sees it this time.

"It's all right, Blair. You can speak freely. Tess has told me why you've come. I'd like to help you if I can."

"Well," Blair says, looking from Corinthia to me to Corinthia again. "It looks like I will have to convince a court to open the files. Adoption records are sealed by state law and cannot be opened unless a judge rules otherwise."

"I see," Corinthia says. "That's not what you were hoping to hear."

"No," Blair says, and it seems like her load is lightened a tiny bit now that one more person is in the loop.

"May I see the note, Blair?" Corinthia says.

Blair pauses a moment and then reaches into her pocket where the note has been all day, close to her body. She hands it to Corinthia.

Corinthia unfolds it carefully and reads it. When she is done she refolds it and gives it back.

"Here is the locket," Blair says, extending her hand and giving the necklace to Corinthia.

Corinthia is pondering something as she fingers the necklace, but she says nothing for a few seconds.

"What's the worst that can happen?" she says to Blair.

"Well, I guess the worst would be that I petition the court and I'm turned down," Blair says.

"Would you tell the court about the note and the necklace?"

"Yes," Blair says, swallowing hard.

"Do you suppose you could get into some kind of trouble for having kept these?" Corinthia asks.

"I don't know. I hope not," Blair answers honestly.

"But you'll try anyway."

"Yes."

Corinthia stretches out her hand and gives the necklace back. "I think it's a very admirable thing that you want to do for this boy, Blair," she says.

I'm wondering if I should have told Corinthia Blair's motives are little more selfish than that.

"I'm thinking you are going to need a little help," Corinthia continues.

Blair's face brightens in a way I haven't seen all week.

"You know someone who can help me?"

"Oh, indeed I do," says Corinthia.

And I know exactly whom she means.

"You do?" Blair asks, leaning forward.

"I know someone who *knows* where this boy is," Corinthia says plainly, leaning back.

"Who? Who is it?" Blair says excitedly.

"I know someone who knows if this boy needs to see this note and this locket."

Blair sits back. The words, *Who could know a thing like that?* are written all over her face.

"Who?" Blair says, with slightly less intensity.

"God knows, Blair. He knows where this boy is. He knows if it would help him to see this note and this locket. You don't need a courtroom to ask Him for help. You don't need to file any papers to ask Him to help you find the boy."

"Yeah, but why would God do that for me?" Blair says, looking downhearted, as I knew she would when she figured out where Corinthia was going.

"Why, indeed?" Corinthia said, grinning. "We won't ask Him to do it for you. We'll ask Him to do it for this boy. Isn't that why you're here?"

I have watched the dialogue take place like a spectator at a tennis match, saying nothing. If I didn't know better, I would say Corinthia knows more than I have told her.

Corinthia holds out a hand to both Blair and me.

"Let's ask Him. Right here. Right now. Go on, join hands."

We take Corinthia's hands and join our own. Corinthia bows her head and we follow suit.

"O Father God, You know all things. You know the dilemma we face. You know whether or not there is a young man hurting out there who needs to know he had a momma who loved him just as he is. We don't know what is best, but You do. It doesn't look like there's a way to find out where this boy is on our own. We don't know what a judge might say, but Father God, it doesn't look good. So if there is a way You can show us where this boy is, then we just pray You'd show us. We ask forgiveness for the many times we have failed to do the right thing and ask that You would help us do the right thing now. In the mighty name of Jesus we ask, amen."

We lift our heads and open our eyes and Corinthia is beaming at us.

"I am so glad y'all are here," she says, as if the last few minutes weren't fraught with philosophical questions about the goodness of God.

Blair looks stricken and pale, but hopeful too. I don't know what expression I wear on my face—a mixture of shock and awe, probably. A breeze overhead causes me to look up and I notice for the first time that we are sitting underneath a giant magnolia tree, and the blooms are as big as dinner plates.

CHAPTER 13

The Power of a Name

I awaken in our hotel room to see that Blair, lying in the bed next to mine, is awake also. She is watching me, expressionless.

"What time is it?" I ask, yawning.

"Eight-thirty," she says softly. Her voice doesn't sound sleepy. I wonder how long she has been lying there, awake and unmoving.

"Did you sleep okay?" I ask, facing her with my head on my pillow, the mirror image of Blair.

"Sort of," she says. "I woke up early and couldn't get back to sleep."

"Too much on your mind?" I ask.

She neither nods nor shakes her head. Blair says nothing for a moment.

"I should have guessed," she finally says. "He was spending so much time at the office and he kept taking all these *business* trips. I bet they weren't all business. I bet she was meeting him at those places."

"Blair," I start to say, but she just continues.

"But I was too busy being the socialite, too busy showing off my girls. What an idiot I have been."

"Blair, you're not the one who messed things up," I say, raising my head and resting its weight on my elbow.

"He had all those papers in his desk. In our house. He had a note from her in his *pants* pocket, Tess. He must have thought I was truly brainless."

"Blair, he was the brainless one. Only a foolish man would leave things like that lying around his own house."

"Or a desperate one."

"What?"

"I wonder if he was leaving clues for me so that I would find out on my own. I would've gotten mad and confronted him. I would have yelled at him and told him to get out of my sight. It would have been so much easier to walk away from an angry wife than a wounded one."

"Blair, don't do this," I say, sitting up in my bed and throwing my legs over the side. "Don't torture yourself like this. You didn't do anything you should be sorry for."

"I'm just saying I should have figured it out," she says, rather emotionless.

I'm about to say something else, something about not letting her bitterness ruin the rest of her life, when the phone rings in our room.

I reach over to the bedside table between us and pick up the receiver.

"Hello?" I say.

"Good morning, Tess. This is Corinthia. I hope I haven't called y'all too early."

"No, no, Corinthia. We're up."

Sort of.

"Well, I waited as long as I could. I have a visitor here at the house. A lady. She would very much like to meet you and Blair."

"Corinthia, what's this about?" I say.

"Let's just say I think you will very much like to meet her too. Can you come over?"

"Um…yeah, sure. We haven't eaten yet, so it might take a little…"

"Oh, just come on over. I'll make y'all some waffles."

"Well, all right. We'll get there as soon as we can. Bye."

I hang up. Blair is sitting up, looking a little peeved.

"What is so important that we have to go over there right now?" she says.

"She said there is a lady at the house who wants to meet us," I answer. "She said we would want to meet her too."

"Is this about the baby?" Blair says, interest entering the picture.

"She didn't say."

"Well, if it doesn't, we're not staying. I want to go to see the court people first thing."

By nine o'clock we are on our way, this time finding my old street without any wrong turns. As we pull up to Corinthia's house, I can see that Samuel is walking toward the Church of the Beautiful Gate. He waves to us but keeps walking. It had been a very pleasant evening the night before, sharing a meal with Corinthia, Samuel, and Marigold, although it had seemed a very quiet affair compared to the old days when the house was full of children. I was sort of disappointed that Corinthia insisted Blair and I relax in the living room after supper while she put the dishes in the sink to soak.

As we get out of Blair's Lexus I notice a blue sedan parked in front of Corinthia's house. We walk up the cement steps and knock on the screen door. Corinthia is there in seconds.

"Come on in," she says warmly. "Come on into the kitchen."

We follow her into the kitchen and right away I notice a woman whose face is vaguely familiar. She's sitting at the kitchen table where Jewel and I used to do homework, where Corinthia showed me what my name means.

The woman stands up.

"Tess, Blair, this is Penny Mollet. She lives here in Blytheville too, but she and I have not had the pleasure of meeting until today," Corinthia says.

"Nice to meet you," I say, but I'm struggling to remember where I have seen her face before. Is she an old teacher of mine whose name I have forgotten?

"Please have a seat," Corinthia says. "I'll pour y'all some coffee and get the waffle iron goin'."

Blair mumbles a greeting as she shakes Penny Mollet's hand and sits down. She's anxious to get back to the county building.

Corinthia places hot mugs of coffee in front of Blair and me and I see that her eyes are twinkling fiercely.

"Penny, why don't you tell these girls what you told me?" she says, turning to the waffle iron and pouring batter into it.

"Well, it's like this," Penny Mollet begins. "I had a real hard time sleepin' last night and I awoke at first light with this heavy on my mind."

Blair and I just sit and stare at her when she pauses.

"See," she continues. "I remember you girls."

Then she reaches down by her legs, picks up a brown photo album, and lays it on the table. She flips through some pages and then stops. She turns the album around so that Blair and I can see it. Under a cheap, plastic-covered sheet is the fifteen-year-old article from the *Courier News,* the same article I read in Blair's car yesterday.

I glance at Blair and see that she is now very interested in Penny Mollet.

"I remember when you girls found that baby," Penny continues. "I remember how y'all cared for him until the police arrived. How you fed him and wrapped him in one of your own baby blankets. I thought what you had done was very kind and y'all were just young girls. That's why I saved this article."

As she says this I suddenly remember where I have seen this woman before. She was waiting in the chair behind us at the county recorder's office yesterday. She had heard Blair's desperate plea for information. She had heard every word.

"I didn't mean to eavesdrop, but I couldn't help hearing what y'all were saying at the county recorder's yesterday," Penny continues. "I was sitting behind you. I heard what you asked for and I heard what the answer was."

Blair's face is unreadable. I look over at Corinthia who is practically glowing as she lifts a golden waffle out of the black iron.

"Ms. Mollet," I say, "Can you help us find this boy?"

"Yes, I think I can," she says.

"Do you know where he is?" Blair says, suddenly finding her voice.

"Well, no, but I know the last name of the family who adopted him and I know where they lived when they got him."

"That's great!" Blair says and her eyes are misty. "What is it? What's their last name?"

"Well, perhaps I'm not supposed to say, and I wouldn't if I thought you weren't going to do right by this boy, but I think he should have that locket."

"Yes, yes," Blair says, impatient to hear the name.

"See, I had overheard a conversation between my daughter—she was a court clerk back then—and another court employee while I was waiting to take my daughter to lunch on her birthday. She and this other person were talking about that baby that had been abandoned, that it was being adopted by a family that lived in Paragould."

"Paragould," Blair echoes. This is her first big clue.

"Just like this time, I didn't mean to eavesdrop. I just couldn't help hearin'. And I wouldn't have remembered the last name except that it's the same as my first name. Penny. Only they spell it with an *e* before the *y*. I know because I heard my daughter spell it."

"John Penney," Blair says, and she sits slowly back in her chair.

Corinthia turns to us with a plate full of hot waffles in her hands.

"Who wants waffles?" she asks gleefully.

Over bites of waffles, Blair pores over a fairly recent phone book, looking for a John Penney in Paragould. There isn't one.

"There's a John Penney in Jonesboro," she says. "Think that could be him?"

"It's worth a try," Corinthia says.

"Can I use your phone?" Blair asks Corinthia.

"Well, I suppose."

"You're going to call right now?" I say, my own mouth full of a bite of waffle.

"Why not?"

"Well, what are you going to say?"

"That we want to see him. How could his parents refuse? We rescued him."

"Well, what if they say no, Blair?"

Blair stands up and walks over to the phone on the wall.

"Then I'll find another way to see him."

The three of us anxiously wait as Blair dials the number. Within seconds she closes her eyes in frustration. She hangs up the phone.

"That number is no longer in service," she says, coming back to her chair. "And there's no new number."

There's a collective sigh around the table.

"They must have moved recently," Blair says. Then she stands up. "I've got to get to a computer. I've got to get on the Internet to see how many John Penneys are out there."

"You go on over to Samuel's office," Corinthia says to her. "He's got Internet over there."

"Great. Thanks," Blair says as she starts to head to the front door. "Oh, thanks, Ms. Mollet."

"My pleasure," Penny Mollet calls out to her.

When Blair is gone, Penny Mollet stands, puts her brown photo album under her arm, and announces she should be getting home.

"Well, I am so pleased we have met," Corinthia says, wrapping an arm around Penny as she walks her to the door. "I hope I will see you again sometime."

"Yes, that would be nice," Penny Mollet says as she steps out into the mid-morning sunshine. "Let me know how things turn out, will you?"

"Of course," I say as I wave goodbye.

When the door is closed for the second time, Corinthia and I head back into the kitchen. I start to stack plates from our breakfast when Corinthia asks if I want to join Blair over at the church.

"Why don't we do these dishes real quick first?" I say.

Corinthia smiles at me.

"Just like old times," she says.

And I smile back.

We work in silence for a few minutes and then I ask what has been on my mind since meeting Penny Mollet.

"So, was Penny the answer to your prayer?"

"Well, what do you think?" Corinthia says. She has always been good at answering a question with a question.

"I think maybe she was," I say, surprising myself a little.

Corinthia just smiles and takes a dish from me.

"How did you know?" I say.

"How did I know what?"

"How did you know God would answer it?"

"Well, Tess, God always answers our prayers. I knew He would answer it because that's the way He is. I didn't know *how* He was going to answer it. I asked Him to help us if this boy needs to see the note and the locket. This boy must need to see the note and the locket."

I hand her another dish and formulate a question in my head that I hope will not hurt her feelings.

"But Corinthia, isn't it possible that Penny Mollet could have come to your house this morning *anyway*, even if you had not prayed?"

But Corinthia's feelings are not hurt. She finds my question amusing, I think.

"Well, one day when I get to heaven—and if I think of it, of course—I will ask God if she would have come anyway."

Then she turns to me and winks.

When Corinthia and I join Blair in Samuel's study, she is sitting in front of his computer with a look of exasperation on her face.

"There are nearly a hundred John Penneys in the United States," she says. "He could be anywhere."

"Any in Arkansas?" I ask.

"Just one, and I already called that number," Blair says. "He's a Catholic priest in Little Rock."

"So I guess that's not him," I say, sitting down in a chair next to her.

"It's quite possible the family stayed in the South, though," Samuel says, leaning against a bookcase with his arms comfortably crossed on his chest. "It's pretty costly to move."

"Well, there are six in Tennessee, another half dozen in Alabama, a couple in Kentucky, some more in Missouri and Texas," Blair says. "I should just go get my cell phone and start calling them."

"I wonder if maybe someone in Paragould—a neighbor, maybe—would remember John Penney and his family," Corinthia says. "If that John Penney is the same one who until recently also lived in Jonesboro, then a neighbor in Jonesboro would surely remember him too. You would have more to go on. And you wouldn't have to make calls to people who don't know you. Some folks don't take to calls from strangers, Blair."

Blair is nodding. She can see the wisdom in this, I think.

"How will we find out where he lived in Paragould?" I ask.

Corinthia smiles and nods her head. She opens up a bottom drawer in a file cabinet and starts pulling out old phone books.

"You just never know when you're going to need an old phone book," she says.

She pulls out half a dozen, the oldest dating back to the year after Blair and I moved away.

Blair picks this one up, turns to the P's, and then her face breaks into a smile.

"Bingo," she says.

I have a pretty good idea where we will spend the rest of the morning.

CHAPTER 14

The Boy with the Limp

I don't remember coming to Paragould when Dad and I lived in Arkansas, but I remember local classmates talking about going there on weekends to visit grandparents or aunts and uncles. It is less than an hour's drive from Blytheville.

Corinthia has been here several times, thankfully, so with her help and her old phone book, we easily find the street where the Penney family used to live. The creamy-white house is smallish and in need of a fresh coat of paint. The flowerbeds underneath the front windows are a tangle of newly sprouted primroses and hearty weeds. There is a rolled up newspaper, yellowed from several days in the sun, sitting on the cement path to the front door. We observe all of this from the windows of Blair's car as we pull up to the curb in front of the house and get out. I am about to walk up the cement pathway to ring the doorbell when a young woman with a stroller steps out of the house next door. Buckled in the stroller is a chubby baby with barely any hair. She looks at me.

"If y'all are lookin' for the Pattersons they're gone 'til next Tuesday," she says across the yards, pronouncing Tuesday like "twos dye."

"Actually," Blair says coming up to stand by me. "We're

looking for someone, anyone, who knew the Penney family who lived in this house some years ago."

The woman casts a long look at the three of us, wondering, I suppose, if we are federal agents looking for a fugitive. But she notices the Lexus and dismisses this, I'm sure.

"I need to find the Penneys," Blair continues. "I have something that belongs to their son."

"Well," the woman says, relaxing a little. "When we moved into this house three years ago, the Pattersons were already here. I don't know any family named Penney."

"Is there a neighbor here on the street who has lived here a long time?" I ask.

The baby in the stroller starts to fuss and the woman pulls a pacifier out of her shorts pocket and sticks it in his mouth.

"Mr. and Miz Taylor across the street in the blue house have been here thirty some years, I think," the woman says, looking up from her baby.

"Thanks," Blair says quickly and starts to walk briskly toward the road.

"Thank you so very much," Corinthia says. "What a cute little one you have there!"

Blair is already across the street when Corinthia and I begin to cross. Blair is looking at us with obvious impatience as if she were holding an hourglass and the sand is nearly gone. When we reach her, she quickly walks up the curving stone path to the Taylors' front door. On either side of the path are neat rows of marigolds, which I see Corinthia is understandably happy to see.

Blair rings the doorbell and a few seconds later the front

door is opened by a petite woman with silvery-gray hair. Her surprise at three strangers on her doorstep is evident.

"Yes?" she says warily.

"Mrs. Taylor?" Blair asks.

"Yes."

"My name is Blair Holbrook and this is Tess Longren and Corinthia Mayhew. We're hoping you can tell us where we might find the Penney family who used to live across the street from you. Your neighbor with the baby thought you might be able to help us. It's very important that we find them."

"Oh!" Mrs. Taylor says, wide-eyed. Then she opens her screen door to us. "Won't you come in?"

At the same moment Blair is about to say, "No, thank you, we don't want to impose," Corinthia says, "Well, that's very nice of you, Miz Taylor. Thank you very much."

So in we go.

"Please sit down," Mrs. Taylor says, directing us to a living room cluttered with dozens of teacups on display, Victorian dolls, and lacy pillow covers. We sit on a chintz-covered sofa that is abloom with fat cabbage roses.

"Can I get y'all some coffee?" Mrs. Taylor says kindly.

"No, thank you. We just..." Blair says, but Corinthia interrupts her.

"Why, we would love some if it's not too much trouble, Miz Taylor."

"It's no trouble at all. It's already made."

Mrs. Taylor disappears into the kitchen and we sit quietly, waiting for her to return. Corinthia is relaxed and at ease beside me. Blair, sitting on my other side, is anything but.

Mrs. Taylor returns with a tray of clattering cups on saucers.

"Here, dear. Let me move these for you," Corinthia says, pushing a pair of teddy bears dressed like ballerinas from the center of the coffee table.

"Thank you," Mrs. Taylor says, setting the tray down. On the tray are four cups of steaming coffee despite Blair having said she didn't want any. There is also a lead crystal creamer and sugar bowl and a plate of Lorna Doone cookies resting on a paper doily. By the time we all have our cups and cookies, Blair seems about ready to explode.

"So, Mrs. Taylor," she says anxiously. "You remember the Penneys?"

"Oh, yes," Mrs. Taylor replies. "They were a sweet couple. Patricia had a way with tulip bulbs. I don't get the blooms she did. I never have."

Blair leans forward and I almost feel like I should hold her down to keep her from pouncing on our gracious hostess.

"And you remember their little boy?" Blair continues.

"Oh, of course. He was a little charmer. In a quiet kind of way. He never said a whole lot, but he was very polite."

"And his name?" Blair says, licking her lips nervously.

"Why, Timmy, of course," Mrs. Taylor says slowly, as if the three of us surely should have known that already.

"Miz Taylor, these girls found Timmy on my church doorstep when he was just a day old," Corinthia says, coming to our rescue. "The Penneys adopted him when he was just a baby and the girls haven't seem him since."

"Oh, my! Well!" Mrs. Taylor exclaims. "They never said he was adopted."

"They didn't?" Blair says, doubt creeping into her voice.

"No. I mean it's not a question you ask people. I just assumed he was their own."

Blair looks at me like she's thinking perhaps Penny Mollet got her wires crossed. There is fear and uncertainty in her eyes.

"Miz Taylor," Corinthia says. "Was there anything...different about Timmy?"

"Different? Well, like I said, he was quiet, kind of shy. Didn't always answer you straight away."

Blair quietly sighs next to me. Maybe we are looking in the wrong direction after all.

"Oh, and he did have a limp," Mrs. Taylor says, like she suddenly remembered something she had almost forgotten.

"A limp?" Blair says, and the hope in her voice sounds like what I'm now instantly feeling.

"Yes. Something wasn't quite right with one of his legs. He had surgery a time or two. He was in a cast more than once as I recall."

"That's him!" Blair whispers, but loud enough for Mrs. Taylor to hear.

"Yes, that's Tim," she says.

"Mrs. Taylor, when did the Penneys move away?" I ask.

"Well, let me see," Mrs. Taylor says, laying a hand on her cheek. "My grandson Philip was about two when they moved in, and Timmy was just about the same age. They came from a house they were renting in the country, I think. I am thinking Philip was eight or nine when they left, so I reckon it was seven years ago."

"Do you know where they moved to?" I ask, knowing how close we might be.

"Well, I think they moved to Jonesboro. John Penney was a schoolteacher, taught at the high school here. I think he got a better payin' job there. You know, they can pay more for teachers in the bigger towns."

But Blair and I really hear nothing she says beyond the word *Jonesboro*.

"Did you keep in contact with them after they moved? Do you know if they're still there?"

"Oh, I wouldn't know," Mrs. Taylor says. "We didn't see or hear from them again, I'm afraid."

"Thank you very much," Blair says abruptly, standing up. "You've been a big help."

"Oh…well, you're welcome," Mrs. Taylor says, her voice betraying that she is sad our visit is over. She stands too, and Corinthia and I follow.

"That was wonderful coffee, Miz Taylor," Corinthia says. Then Corinthia looks down at the end table she is standing next to and notices a photograph of three children in a satiny, pink frame. "Oh, what lovely children! Are these your grandchildren?"

"Yes," Mrs. Taylor says, her voice brightening. "That's Philip. He's fifteen and he's the oldest. He'll be sixteen in August. Next is Eliza Jo, she's twelve, and the youngest is Daisy. She's nine."

"What beautiful names they have," Corinthia says. "You know, I have a daughter with the name of a flower too. My Marigold is fifteen, just like your Philip."

"Well now, Marigold is a very pretty name for a girl," Mrs. Taylor says. "And I happen to like marigolds very much."

"So I noticed!" Corinthia says, smiling broadly.

"Well, thank you again for your help," Blair says evenly. "I'm very grateful."

"Well, I hope y'all can find him," Mrs. Taylor says. "I'm sure it will be nice to see him again after all these years."

"Yes, yes, indeed," Corinthia says. "Goodbye, Miz Taylor."

We make our way across the street, back to Blair's car. Mrs. Taylor stands on her doorstep watching us get in. Corinthia lowers her window in the backseat and waves as we pull away.

"Was all that really necessary?" Blair grumbles low enough that Corinthia may not have heard it.

"Was *what* really necessary?" Corinthia says. She heard it.

"Going inside. Drinking her coffee. Eating her cookies. She could have told us from her doorstep the Penneys moved to Jonesboro."

"Well," Corinthia says, and I can see that she is watching the houses go by as we drive. "I suppose returning courtesy for courtesy isn't necessary, but it sure makes sense."

I turn my head to face the road ahead of us. I can't see her face but I know Corinthia is grinning.

CHAPTER 15

What a Farmer Needs

We formulate a plan on the way back to Blytheville from Paragould. Blair wants to spend the rest of the day on Samuel's computer looking up John Penneys on the Internet.

Blair is convinced she will find John Penney, high school teacher, on a school website. All high schools have websites and a lot of teachers have their *own* websites, so Blair says. *How many high school teachers named John Penney can there be?* Blair postulated halfway between Paragould and Blytheville.

Corinthia and I have decided to drive to Jonesboro and do what we did in Paragould; go to the street where the Penneys lived and hope we find a neighbor who knows where they are.

When we arrive at Corinthia's, we eat a quick lunch of egg salad sandwiches. Blair offers me the keys to her Lexus when we are done, but Corinthia tells me she wants to drive.

"Wish me luck," Blair says as she heads out the door to Samuel's study.

"See you when we get back," I say.

Corinthia grabs her own keys.

"I'm glad you thought of somethin' to say back so quick," she says to me in a soft voice. "I don't do much wishin'! And I don't believe in luck."

I follow her out to the garage and into her aged but well kept Oldsmobile.

The fifty-minute drive to Jonesboro gives Corinthia and me almost an hour of time just to us. Not more than a few miles outside of town, I decide to tell Corinthia about the woman in the airport with the three little children.

"Well, isn't that something!" she says when I finish. "She looked just like me, did she?"

"Yes, it was the weirdest thing," I say with a nervous laugh. "And she was thoroughly convinced I was the answer to her prayer for help."

"Well, why wouldn't you be?"

"Well, Corinthia, I heard her ask for it."

"But she didn't know you heard her ask for it. And so what if you did? How can that mean God didn't put you in that chair next to her so you *would* hear her?"

"Well, Corinthia, it was the last chair at our gate. I didn't have a choice."

"Imagine that," she says, looking at the road and smiling.

We ride for a few more minutes in a silence that seems easy at first.

Then Corinthia turns her head to me.

"You know, Tess, yesterday when we were waiting for Blair in my backyard, I didn't get the chance to ask you how you are *really* doing. You seem a little bit troubled to me."

"Oh, I'm..." I pause and then say softly, "I don't know what I am." I can't say I'm fine because I'm not. It's hard to be misleading around Corinthia.

"Are you unhappy?"

The question isn't one I can adequately answer.

"Sometimes," I reply after a moment's thought.

"What makes you unhappy, Tess? If you don't mind me asking."

Strangely enough I don't mind it when Corinthia asks. I think this is what I've wanted to do for years, to talk with her about what I feel. But here I am with the opportunity to tell her everything and I can't seem to find the words. Or the courage.

"Well, it's a lot of little things, I guess," I say.

"Like what?"

I give her the answers that I think are the easiest to say, at least to her, and the most vague.

"Well, like I don't know if I'm doing anything worthwhile with my life. Like I don't really deserve Simon. Like I totally missed out on knowing my mother. Like I'm never going to be truly content."

She just nods her head, thinking on what I have said. I'm about to minimize one or more of the things, when she turns her head to me.

"Tell me, Tess. What do you believe about God?"

I have never liked to consider such a question. Most of the time I don't have to because no one ever poses it to me.

"I don't know," I say, which is part truth.

"Well, do you believe He exists?"

The question of the ages hangs between us on the front seat of her Oldsmobile, but even so it's not so hard for me to answer. I know God exists. I have felt His weight for as long as I can remember, before Corinthia, before we moved to Arkansas. I know He is there and it has always bothered me. If He did not exist, it would explain a lot of things. A chancy world would naturally provide a life of chance, a life where you can't truly depend on anything. But I know He is there.

"Yes," I say, but only that.

Corinthia does not seem surprised.

"What else do you believe? What do you believe He is like?" she continues.

Now this question scares me more than the first one did. This is not a simple yes or no question. What scares me is that I actually know what I think about God. But I don't know how to say it. I'm afraid to say it.

Corinthia must sense this.

"Just say what's on your mind, Tess. You know I won't judge you."

This surprisingly gives me the courage I need to lay all my cards out on the table—figuratively, of course. *Here they are*, I almost say audibly to the swirling heavens above me.

"I think He is..." I'm searching for the right word to replace the kindergarten word that is on my tongue but nothing else comes to mind. "Big," I say, wincing at sounding like a five-year-old.

Corinthia just nods her head. "What else?" she says.

Somewhat more confident, I search my mind for the other words that describe how I feel about God. They are there in plain sight to my roving inner eye. They alarm me.

"Tess, what else?"

"He is distant," I say, looking at the road ahead. It sounds like an accusation—the very thing I was afraid of.

But Corinthia just says, "What else?"

"He is indifferent," I continue, feeling a little bolder, a little more like the insolent child who yells, "You're not fair!" at the parent who has just disciplined her.

"Anything else?"

"He is...capricious," I say, and this time the word I have chosen makes me sad, not afraid, not angry.

Corinthia is silent for several seconds.

"I think I'm beginning to understand," she says, maybe to me, maybe not. I think I'm beginning to understand too.

"You mean, now you can understand why God has been avoiding me," I say as I see my ugly metaphorical cards on my lap, uncovered.

But Corinthia looks at me in surprise. Her face breaks into a smile. Her eyes, which have always shined brighter than anyone else's I know, are afire.

"Avoiding you?" she says, and I can tell she is amused. "My dear Tess, you have it completely backward!"

I have no idea what she is talking about.

She reaches across the seat and grabs my hand resting in my lap, glancing at the road and then back at me.

"He has not been avoiding you," she says, smiling widely.

I stare dumbfounded as she leans over just a little, all the while watching the road.

"He has been *pursuing* you," she whispers secretively, just like an old pirate might tell another pirate where to find the buried treasure.

Or like one weary farmer might tell another that the forecast calls for rain.

We ride the rest of the way in silence as Corinthia wisely lets me digest what she has told me. When we arrive in Jonesboro, Corinthia hands me a street map and together we find the street where the Penneys are listed in the most current phone book. This time the house is a little larger and the flowerbeds are filled with tall tulips. I am beginning to wonder if perhaps the Penneys simply got an unlisted phone number and still live here. We get out of the car and I rush up the walk to the covered porch. Corinthia is right behind me. I ring the doorbell and wait. I see a portable basketball hoop in the driveway and ring the bell again.

A woman with dark hair and a slight build opens the door.

"Patricia Penney?" I say, nearly breathless.

"No, I'm afraid the Penneys don't live here anymore," the woman says, and I can't keep the disappointment from flooding me.

"Do you know where the Penneys moved to?" Corinthia says, kindly, as is her way. "We have something that belongs to Tim Penney."

"Oh, well, I think they moved to Tennessee," the woman says effortlessly. "I think that's what the Realtor said. I'm not really sure."

"Can you tell us when that was?" Corinthia says. "When they moved, that is."

The woman shrugs.

"Well, it was nine months ago. Just before the start of the school year," she says.

"Do you have their address? Do you know where we can find them?" I say, knowing I must seem a little crazy.

"Well, no, I'm afraid I don't. My Realtor might, though."

"Would you be so kind as to tell us who is your Realtor?" Corinthia says calmly.

The woman pauses for a moment.

"Why don't you two come in? I'll call him for you."

She ushers us into her home and we follow her into her kitchen.

"Have a seat there," she says, motioning to a table where she was obviously making cookies until a moment ago.

Corinthia and I sit and I flash a look to her that communicates, I hope, my joy. She smiles back at me.

The woman picks up her phone and thumbs through a yellow phone book. She punches in the numbers and puts her free hand on her hip.

"Have a cookie," she says, pointing to a tray of cooling peanut butter cookies.

But I cannot eat.

"Hi, this is Carol Ann Marker. Is Jeffrey there? Thanks."

"He's there," she whispers to us.

"Hi, Jeffrey. This is Carol Ann Marker. I have some ladies here at the house that have something that belongs to Tim Penney—you know, the boy who lived in this house before us? Yes, that's right. I don't know. I think they're from the school or something."

She pauses a moment and then says, "He wants to talk with one of you."

I rise and nervously take the extended phone.

"Hello?" I say, trying not to sound edgy. But I know I do.

"Hello. This is Jeffrey Tauer from Tauer Real Estate. And who am I speaking with?"

He sounds very professional.

"My name is Tess Longren," I reply, with not so much as even half the professionalism in my own voice.

"You're with the school?"

"Well, no, I'm not…" I say, but I struggle to come up with a good description of whom I *am* with.

"You a friend of the Penneys?"

"Well, just a friend of Tim's, I guess you could say. I have something that belongs to him. I knew him when he was a baby, back when we both lived in Blytheville."

"Blytheville, huh? I don't recall the Penneys ever mentioning they lived in Blytheville," he says, but not in a mean way.

"No, they didn't actually, but Tim…Tim was an abandoned infant. Two of my friends and I found him. We have something that was in the box he was found in. We'd like to give it to him."

Jeffrey Tauer is silent for a few minutes.

"Well, I'd like to help you but I'm not at liberty to give out addresses of my former clients," he finally says.

I can't help but sigh into the phone.

"So, you know where Tim is," I say.

"Like I said, I'm not at liberty to give out addresses of my former clients."

Then why are we even talking? I want to yell. But I don't. I look over to Corinthia. Her eyes are closed. I imagine she is praying.

"Mr. Tauer, can you at least tell us if the Penneys are in Tennessee? Please?"

There is a long pause. Jeffrey Tauer is probably wondering if I'm telling him the truth. He's wondering if I'm someone he wants to help, even if only a little. I guess he decides I am.

"I think that would be a very good place to start looking," he says. "But since you already know they might be there, I probably don't even need to say that."

He has covered himself well enough. He told us nothing.

"Thank you," I say anyway.

"Sorry I can't help you," he says kindly.

I place Carol Ann Marker's phone back on its base.

She is looking at me with compassionate eyes. Corinthia has opened her eyes and is looking at me as well.

"He says he can't give me their new address. But he did say Tennessee would be a good place to start looking," I say.

"I wonder how many John Penneys there could be in Tennessee," Carol Ann says.

"There are six," I say as Corinthia rises from her chair. "Thank you so much, Mrs. Marker."

"So...so is all that true, then? About the abandoned baby?" she says.

I nod.

"Can I ask what it is you are trying to give back to him?"

"It's a locket from his birth mother."

"Oh! Honestly?" Carol Ann says, amazed.

"Yes," I answer.

"Well, no wonder. Here," she says, thrusting a blank piece of paper to me. "If you want, I'll ask around and see if anyone here on the street or in town knows where the Penneys are. Maybe I can convince Jeffrey to tell me. Just write down a number where I can reach you."

"Thanks," I say, and I give the piece of paper to Corinthia. She quickly writes down her name, address, and phone number.

We thank Carol Ann several times for her kindness, and she stands on her porch and waves as we get back in the car.

Despite having nothing new to tell Blair when we get back to Blytheville, I still feel as if we're miraculously close to finding Tim Penney. I can already taste the sweetness of finding him on my tongue.

Blair is at Samuel Mayhew's computer when we return. Her cell phone is sitting next to a nearly empty bottle of Diet Coke. Her right hand is resting on a yellow pad of paper filled with a list of names and addresses. The word *Texas* is written at the top of it.

"Well?" she says when Corinthia and I walk in.

I tell Blair what the Realtor told us.

"So he practically *told* you they're in Tennessee!" she says, and she tears off the list of Texas John Penneys she had been busily trying to contact when we came in, revealing the list of six Tennessee John Penneys. She picks up her cell phone.

"Blair, what exactly are you telling these people when you call?" I ask.

"I'm not *telling* them anything," she says. "When they answer I say, 'Hello. May I speak to Tim Penney, please?' He's fifteen. He still lives at home."

"But Blair..."

"Then when they say, 'I'm sorry. There is no Tim Penney at this address,' I say, 'Is this the home of John Penney?' to make sure I didn't dial incorrectly. When they say 'Yes, it is,' I apologize, thank them, hang up, and cross them off my list."

"How...how many have you called already?" I ask, amazed at her determination.

"All of Missouri and Texas. I left two messages and two weren't home. But that doesn't matter now. All that matters is Tennessee."

Corinthia squeezes my shoulder and tells me she is going to put a roast in the oven so we'll have something to eat tonight and that she's going to call Jewel and let her know what's going on. She leaves the little office as Blair starts to punch in the first telephone number. I wonder for the first time where Samuel Mayhew is. I am about to ask Blair what she will say if she says, "Hello. Is Tim Penney there?" and the voice on the other end says, "Speaking."

"Hello. Is Tim Penney there, please?" I hear Blair say.

She pauses for a moment.

"Oh. I must have the wrong number. Is this the John Penney residence? Well, I'm sorry to have troubled you. Goodbye."

She clicks the phone off.

"Blair," I say.

"What?" she answers, but she is already punching in the numbers for the next John Penney on her list.

"I'm wondering if maybe we shouldn't think this through..."

She holds up a finger to silence me for a second.

"This is Blair Holbrook calling for Tim Penney. I have something that I think belongs to him. I can be reached at 801-555-2945. It's...uh...four forty-five in the afternoon on Tuesday. Thanks."

She clicks the phone off again.

"Blair, I think you should have an idea of what you are going to say if he answers!" I finally get in.

She's punching in the next set of numbers. "I'm going to tell him the truth," she says. "I'm going to tell him I have something that belongs to him. Because it's true. I do."

She holds up another finger and I shut my mouth.

But then her big, fluid eyes widen in surprise and she pulls the phone away from her ear. She presses the disconnect button like she's sealing the cage of a monster.

"What?" I say.

"You were right, Tess! I don't know what to say!"

"Was that him!?"

She puts the phone down and her hand is shaking.

"It was an answering machine, Tess. It said I had reached the home of John, Patricia, and Tim Penney and asked if I would like to leave a message."

Then she starts to giggle. But she is still shaking.

"We found him, Tess! He's in Memphis!"

I'm starting to shake too. I can't believe the worst part of the search is over. At least I hope it's the worst part.

"Are you going to call him back?" I say.

"Later. I'll try later when I think I might find someone home. Tess! Can you believe it? *We found him!*"

It's a little after seven when Blair decides to try the Memphis John Penney number again. We have finished eating. Samuel, Corinthia, and Marigold are seated in the living room offering a prayer on our behalf. I'm pacing the floor between the kitchen and dining room. I cannot sit still. Blair is seated at the dining

table in Samuel Mayhew's chair. I think she chose it on purpose. This is the chair of a holy man.

She punches in the number and waits.

I pace.

"Hello? Is this John Penney?"

A second of silence.

"Mr. Penney, my name is Blair Devere Holbrook and I'm
calling because…yes, Blair Devere Holbrook. You…you remember my name?"

More silence. I stop pacing and stand at the entrance to the
dining room. John Penney knows her name. He knows the name
Blair Devere.

"Yes! Yes!" Blair is saying, smiling.

"Well, I…we…were hoping to visit with Tim. Would that
be possible?"

The silences are driving me crazy.

"Well, we were lucky enough to find some folks who
remembered you. I've been calling John Penneys all over the
South looking for you. We just…we just want to see Tim."

More silence. This one is longer, much longer.

"Yes, but…well, okay. Sure. I understand. No, we're in
Blytheville right now. Yes, we can be there by tomorrow afternoon. Of course. No, I won't call the house again. Thank you,
thank you so much, Mr. Penney. Goodbye."

She clicks off the phone and looks at me.

"He wants to meet us first," Blair says. "Tomorrow. At the
school where he teaches. As soon as classes let out."

"How did he sound?" I ask, leaning back against the door-
frame.

Blair shakes her head like she's not sure.

"I think he's too surprised to know how he feels," she says. "But he wants to meet us. We might have to convince him to let us see Tim."

Blair looks down at her little silver phone and the list of John Penneys.

It is not over yet. John Penney may decide his son doesn't need to see the necklace or the note. He may decide *we* don't need to be the ones to give them to him.

I need to talk to Jewel. Now.

I step into the kitchen to call her from Corinthia's phone. I know she will want to come with us tomorrow. *I* want Jewel to be with us tomorrow when we go. She needs to be there with us when we go. For as far as we can go.

CHAPTER 16

The First Confession

Memphis, Tennessee

I can't help feeling, as we drive over the mighty Mississippi into Tennessee, that the bridge that carries us is symbolic of what lies just ahead. I feel that I will soon be crossing over into a new phase of my life, one without so many regrets. If God is indeed pursuing me then He will just have to cross over this bridge with me. I'm through with battling ghosts.

I'm glad Corinthia is with us, though Blair is probably not as keen about it. Jewel wants us to stay with her and her family for however long we are in Memphis, but Blair politely told Corinthia last night that she and I would be staying at the Peabody. I would prefer to stay at Jewel's with Corinthia but I don't think it would be right for me to leave Blair alone. It's only been a little over a week since Brad died. She acts like she is finished mourning him, but I'm beginning to think she hasn't even started. And when she does, I'm pretty sure she will mourn not his death, but the death of her marriage. She didn't see either one coming.

I wish I could have told Simon personally about how far we've come in such a short time, but he was out last night when I called to tell him our unbelievable news. I had to leave a message that Blair and I had a last name and an address and would be driving to Memphis in the morning. I also told him to call me back if he got home before eleven, but I guess he didn't because he didn't call back.

We head into downtown Memphis from the riverbank and follow Corinthia's directions to the Peabody Hotel. It's a beautiful morning in April. The financial district is dotted with men in white shirts and ties talking on cell phones, drinking from Starbucks coffee cups, and walking in and out of the Cotton Exchange building. Blair drives to the valet parking area of the Peabody, where we leave her car and head into the elegant hotel. I have been to the Peabody only once before, and then just to see the lobby and watch the famous Peabody ducks arrive from their rooms upstairs to the beautiful fountain on the main floor. Dad and Shelley had been married less than a month and the three of us had come to Memphis for the day. It was our first big outing as a new family of three. It seems like a long time ago, but the hotel lobby looks the same. The floral bouquets look the same. Even the ducks look the same.

Blair has secured a suite that will allow us both to have our own bedrooms and bathrooms and to share a common sitting area. Corinthia and I are both aghast at the opulence of the suite when we step into it. I don't think Blair is the least bit impressed. She likes it—it's not that. It's just what she has come to expect. Blair had the courtesy to ask Corinthia if she would like to stay at the Peabody too, but Corinthia said she'd just stay with Jewel and the family.

"Though I probably won't get an invitation like this again," she had said, shaking her head, but not regretting her decision, I think.

We unpack a few things, but I am anxious to see Jewel. Soon we are back in Blair's car and driving toward Jewel's home.

Jewel's house is about twenty minutes away from downtown in an older suburb where brick houses line nearly every street. Hers is a two-story saltbox with white trim on the windows. The tiny lawn is well kept and the crocuses underneath the front windows are vibrant. When we stop the car in her driveway, the front door opens and a little boy charges out of it.

"Gamma!" he yells and runs to Corinthia as she steps out from the backseat.

"Elijah, my boy, you have grown in just a month, you have!" Corinthia leans down to the little boy and wraps her arms around him.

Then at the door, a tall, slender woman appears with a plump baby in her arms. She is smiling even though her teeth aren't showing. Jewel.

She steps out into the late morning sunshine.

"Oh my word! Tess and Blair, just look at y'all!" she says.

"Here, let me take Jonah," Corinthia says, taking the baby from Jewel.

Jewel comes to me first, enclosing me in her arms.

"It has been *too* long," she says and when we part, her eyes are glistening. "You look wonderful."

"So do you," I say. My own eyes feel moist.

"Oh, Blair," Jewel says, turning to the other third of our long ago trio. She takes Blair gently into another kind of embrace. "I'm so sorry for the loss of your husband. I truly am. I have been praying for you."

"Yes. Thank you," Blair says breaking away first.

"Please come in," Jewel says. "I hope y'all can stay for lunch. I have chicken gumbo on the back burner. And Joseph, my husband, will be here for lunch today. Y'all won't see Matthias until after school, though. He's in first grade."

We follow Jewel into her house as she says this and I wonder what she will think when we tell her we have plans for her for after school.

Jewel's chicken gumbo is quite good and her husband Joseph is very much like Samuel Mayhew. In fact everything about Jewel reminds me of her mother. Her house, her cooking, her husband, and the gentle way she reached out to Blair.

When lunch is over and Joseph heads back to his church office a few blocks away, Corinthia offers to take Jonah and Elijah into the bedrooms for an afternoon nap so the three of us can talk.

We decide to sit outside on Jewel's front steps, something we did countless times when we were young. When we get settled, Jewel turns to Blair.

"Blair, may I see the note and the locket?"

Blair hesitates for a moment and then reaches down into her purse. She pulls the note and the locket out from the inner pocket and hands them to Jewel. Jewel fingers the locket for a moment, opening it to see the tiny blank frame inside. Then she unfolds the note and reads it, probably several times. She fingers its edges and runs her hand over the writing.

"She wasn't much older than we were," Jewel says thoughtfully.

"I'm sorry I didn't tell you and Tess about these," Blair says, needing, I think, affirmation from Jewel that she didn't need from me. She didn't apologize to me.

"It's all right, Blair," Jewel says refolding the note and giving it and the locket back to Blair. "I know why you did it."

Blair takes them and smiles cynically.

"Were my insecurities that obvious?" she says.

"Well, no," Jewel answers quickly. "I thought you were the most confident person in the world. It used to amaze me because I saw the way your mother neglected you."

Blair looks up and a quirky mixture of apprehension and respect quickly replaces the cynicism.

"Guess I had you fooled," Blair says softly.

"Guess we're all a little smarter now," Jewel replies, and from the open screen door we can faintly hear Corinthia singing a lullaby to a child who refuses to yield to rest.

Blair, Jewel, and I arrive at the high school in Germantown about five minutes before the last bell is supposed to ring. We can't help but feel a little out of place walking into the administration offices. We know no one there. We know John Penney's name but not what he looks like.

Blair approaches the reception desk and a woman in a lavender dress looks up from a computer screen.

"May I help you?" she says.

"We're here to see Mr. John Penney. He may have told you we were coming."

"Oh, yes," she says. "He just rang down here not too long ago. You can just go to his classroom. Here, I'll show you where it is."

She pulls out a laminated map of the campus and points us in the direction of the science building. We thank her and begin walking toward John Penney's classroom, dodging students who begin heading toward the exits as the bell rings. None of us say anything. Each of us is hoping, wishing, or praying that this goes well.

When we get to his door, Blair pauses in front of it for a moment and then opens it, walking purposefully inside, and Jewel and I follow.

A man with a trim build, a slightly receding hairline, and wire rimmed glasses looks up from a dry erase board.

"My goodness," he says and he seems shocked, even though he knew we were coming. He walks toward us.

Blair, standing next to me, speaks up first.

"Mr. Penney," she says. "I'm Blair, this is Tess, and this is Jewel."

We shake hands but his shock at seeing us doesn't fade.

"Well, I never thought we would ever meet. When we adopted Tim, the social worker in Blytheville gave us the article from the paper with your picture in it. I would know you three anywhere I think. How did you find us?"

Blair looks to me and I just tell him we got lucky. Dumb answer. Jewel says nothing beside me.

"Can I ask what made you suddenly decide to try and find Tim?" he asks cautiously.

"Well," Blair says, closing her eyes for just a moment to steady her world, I think. "Mr. Penney…"

"Please call me John."

"John," Blair begins and I can tell she is going to confess. "The reason we have come is…well, it's really the reason I have come—my friends are just here for moral support—I have a couple things that belong to Tim. Things that were in the peach box when we found him. Things his birth mother meant for him to have."

John Penney's face is impossible to read.

"What kinds of things?" he says.

Blair reaches into her purse and pulls out the locket and the note.

"Oh!" John says when he sees the locket. He takes it from Blair and fingers the little heart. "Is...is there..." But he does not finish.

"No, the locket is empty," Blair tells him. "But there is this too." And she hands him the note that I have memorized down to the exact way Tim's birth mother made her *m*'s.

John reads the note and then leans against a lab table. His eyes grow glassy. I can see that he is reading it again. Several times. Like all of us have who have read this note.

"John, it wasn't right, but I kept these things because I wanted something to remember Tim by and because I...I was quite taken by the love this mother had for her baby," Blair says and her voice is quavering. "I'm not proud of what I've done. And I'm very sorry. You don't know how sorry I am. But I want to make it right. I want Tim to have these things. Please. Please let me give them to him!"

John is looking at the note again, absorbing it all—the note, Blair's confession, and the reality that fifteen years of history have jumped forward to the present.

"I'd like some time to think," he says slowly, not looking at us, looking only at the note. "Are you staying somewhere in Memphis?"

Blair seems ready to crumple beside me.

"Blair and I are staying at the Peabody. Jewel lives here in Memphis," I say.

"I'm sorry, but I can't just…I need to think."

Blair sighs and then reaches out her hand. She wants the note and the locket back. And I can't say I blame her. It's *her* peace offering.

John Penney hesitates for a moment and then places the note and necklace in Blair's open hand.

"It would mean a great deal to me if I could give these to Tim myself," she says to him, but her voice starts to break. The muscles in her face begin to contort. She cannot control the tears that want to fly down her face. "Excuse me," she says abruptly as they start to come. Blair begins to hastily walk away. Jewel follows her, reaching out to hold her by her shoulders. As they burst through the door into the now-quiet hallway, I can hear Blair losing herself to sobs.

"She just lost her husband," I say to John Penney, feeling a need to explain Blair's obsession with reuniting this boy with his mother's last treasures. "She wants very much to make this right. She thinks God is punishing her for having kept them."

I feel I have said too much.

"Thank you for seeing us today," I say as I start to follow my friends out the door. "We're registered under Blair's name, Holbrook."

John Penney just nods. I can feel him watching us as Jewel and I usher Blair down the hallway.

CHAPTER 17

The Second Confession

There is nothing any of us can do except wait. Well, that's not entirely true. When we get back to Jewel's house and tell Corinthia what happened with John Penney, she promptly disappears into a back room where the boys are napping and begins praying. Jewel asks us to stay for supper, but Blair just shakes her head. She walks toward the front door, opens it, and steps outside.

"Thanks, anyway, Jewel," I say. "I think I'll take her back to the hotel. I don't think she has been sleeping well. She's probably exhausted."

"You can come back over in the mornin'," Jewel says as she walks me to the front door. "We'll find something to do to get her mind off her woes."

No we won't, I think to myself.

Blair lets me drive back to the Peabody. Traffic is snarly and very Chicago-like, but Blair doesn't seem to notice. We ride in silence.

When we get to the hotel, I convince Blair to give the twins a call. Her mood scares me a little. I'm hoping chatting with Chloe and Leah will raise her spirits some, but she doesn't talk to them for very long.

Later, I talk Blair into walking down Beale Street, famed for being the birthplace of jazz, and we find a restaurant that features live music. But Blair just picks at her food. I don't think she's very adept at waiting, and that's precisely what she must do. We don't stay out long. As soon as we get back to the hotel, Blair rushes to the phone in our room to see if we have a message waiting, but we don't. I make a quick call to Simon to fill him in on where things are at in our quest.

We sleep in the next morning and Blair orders room service for breakfast, something I have never done. We take our time showering and getting ready for the day. We wait for the phone to ring but it does not. I offer to drive us over to Jewel's or to a shopping center or anywhere but Blair declines.

"I am not leaving the room until he calls," Blair announces.

After lunch—room service again—I head to Jewel's, hoping it's safe to leave Blair alone. But once I get there, I realize I too am not able to do anything but wait for John Penney to call. I stay for maybe an hour, but I'm back at the Peabody long before rush hour starts.

Blair and I are contemplating our third meal in our room when the phone rings. Blair waits for it to ring twice before summoning up enough courage to answer it.

"Hello?" she says.

Someone is saying something to her on the other end.

"Yes?"

Then she closes her eyes and sinks into the chair next to the phone.

"Thank you, thank you…" she is saying, and she begins to cry.

John Penney has made up his mind.

We will see Tim.

Blair and John Penney arrange to meet the following day at his school, at the end of the school day. From there the four of us will make our way to the Penney home on the eastern edge of Memphis.

As soon as Blair gets off the phone with John Penney, we call Jewel's house to let her and Corinthia know the good news. For all I know, Corinthia is still on her knees in the back bedroom.

The rest of the evening is almost as difficult to fill as the day that led up to it. More waiting. But at least this second round of waiting is a different kind. We eat out, which is a nice change, and do a little shopping. We are back in the hotel by nine o'clock and in bed by ten. Blair simply cannot wait for this day to be over.

In the morning, we again sleep as late as we want and order breakfast in. By ten-thirty we are back at Jewel's, hoping our visit with her will help the hours fly by.

Our visit is wonderful of course, at least it is for me, but the hours slip by slowly. Finally at two-thirty, the three of us get into Blair's car to drive to Germantown. Corinthia has again graciously agreed to watch her grandsons while their mother is out.

"I'll be praying for y'all," she says as she waves goodbye to us.

John meets us by the flagpole at the entrance to the high school. Most of the students are gone and the front of the school is fairly quiet. He looks a little tense. I'm wondering if he's having second thoughts.

He greets us politely, but he's distracted and on edge. I start to feel tense too as I wait for him to say he has changed his mind.

"We'll be getting there right after Patricia gets home from the hospital. She's a nurse. She usually gets home around four o'clock. She doesn't know about this yet. Tim will be home by three-thirty," he says as he starts to walk with us back to the parking lot.

"Do you want us to talk to Patricia first before we talk to Tim?" Blair asks. I can tell she really doesn't want to. I am amazed she has asked.

John looks quickly in Blair's direction.

"I don't think that would be a good idea," he says. "Patricia has always been a little overprotective of Tim. She might be a little ticked off about why you waited so long."

"Oh," is all Blair can think of to say.

"Will this cause trouble between you and your wife?" Jewel says calmly.

"She will come around in time," he said. "Besides, in the end she will see that this came at just the right time for Tim. She knows I'm expecting some company today after school; she just doesn't know it's you."

John Penney stops as we reach Blair's car and I can see that he's choosing his words carefully.

"Tim is going through a tough time right now," he says, and I can tell it hurts him to say this. "He has always been kind of a quiet kid. You don't always know what he's thinking.

Sometimes kids still tease him about his leg. He has a—what am I saying? You know about his foot.

"Anyway, as he's gotten older, kids remark about it less, but I know the smallest comment still bugs him. The thing is, he's got lots of friends in baseball and in track. Every spring it's like this. He would give anything to be able to..."

But John Penney cannot finish. Overcome with emotion, he looks away from us, seeking strength from some hidden place in his heart. It seems like many long minutes before he is able to continue.

"In the past, Patricia and I have always been able to help him through his sad times. We've been able to get his mind off his limitations and onto what he excels at."

John Penney looks back to us and his moist eyes are suddenly bright with pride. "He has a gift with animals. He has his own boarding kennels in our backyard. You should see him with the dogs people leave with him. Some of them are so starved for affection...Some of them have never been taught to mind...Some of them have been abused."

He stops again and shakes his head, like he himself cannot believe what his son can do. And I suppose also at what people can do to defenseless animals.

"They are different when they leave our place. Most owners can't get over it. And it's amazing to me how much the dogs love Tim. They really do. You know," and John Penney starts to laugh. "The dogs don't see the limp!"

My cheeks are wet and my eyes are stinging. I cannot look at Blair or Jewel. I am aching to see and hold that little boy who cried out to me from the peach box.

"He really is an amazing boy," John says.

And then he looks at his watch.

"I think if we leave now, we'll be in good shape," he says abruptly, like the amazing boy is in danger and in need of rescue.

We follow John Penney from the school parking lot to his home on the edge of Memphis, about fifteen minutes away. The house is set back from the road with a long sloping lawn and is shaded by a dozen hundred-year-old trees. The house is creamy white brick with four stately pillars in front. The shutters are deepest green and tendrils of ivy grace their frames. Below the front windows are rows of pink, red, and yellow tulips. They wave a greeting to us.

"It's a beautiful house," Jewel remarks as we get out of the car.

"It was my grandmother's," John says. "She died last year and left it to me. That's why we moved here."

"I'm sorry," I say. "About your grandmother."

John nods his head and slings the strap of his briefcase over his shoulder. "It was hard. Tim was very fond of her. He has such good memories at this place. So do I."

We approach the front door and just before he opens it, John turns to us.

"If you don't mind, just let me do the talking until you have a chance to sit down with Tim," he cautions us.

We just nod our heads and then follow him in.

"Anybody home?" he calls out cheerfully from a cool, tiled entryway.

"In the kitchen," says a female voice from a couple rooms away.

We follow John through a sitting room into a large kitchen that opens out onto a screened porch in the backyard. I hear a dog barking from beyond the screens.

Patricia, wearing a set of purple scrubs and a hospital name tag, is sorting through the mail. She looks up when we come in. Her eyes betray her surprise.

"Patricia, remember when I said I had some special guests coming home with me today? Well, you'll never believe who these women are!" John says brightly, as if we were princesses from a faraway country.

Patricia attempts a polite smile but is only slightly successful. She wants to think we are just former students of her husband, but something tells her we are not.

"Patricia, these women are the girls that found Tim when he was just an infant. On the church doorstep back in Arkansas!"

John makes it seem like it is all just a happy memory to be embraced like recollections of a wonderful trip to Disney World.

Patricia looks stricken and John closes the distance between them.

"Honey, they've gone to a lot of trouble to find us, to find Tim," he says softly, but loud enough for us to hear. "They have something special they want to give him. I think he could use something special right now."

"John," Patricia says, but nothing else.

"It will be all right," he tells her.

Patricia studies his face for a moment and then I guess she decides she will just have to trust him. She looks past him to us.

"I'm very pleased to meet you," she says with effort. "I am Patricia Penney, Tim's mother."

We step forward and introduce ourselves and shake hands. Patricia Penney's hand is cool and clammy.

"Tim is out with the dogs," she says, trying to sound at ease but I can tell she's not.

"Why don't we go outside onto the patio?" John says. "We can get situated there and I can go get Tim, prepare him a little bit, okay?"

"Of course," Jewel says, the most at ease of all of us.

We follow John and Patricia through the kitchen and the screened porch to an outside door that leads to a wooden deck and a set of patio furniture.

"Here, let me just wipe these chairs," Patricia says, grabbing a little whiskbroom by the door to the porch. She begins to methodically tackle each chair cushion with gusto. But then our collective attention is quickly drawn to the sound of a barking dog and Patricia pauses, the broom in midair. We look past a vegetable garden and a row of rose bushes to structures at the far end of the backyard. We can see a large yellow dog and a smaller black one jumping and skipping around the legs of a tall young man with curly brown hair. In the distance we can see the young man pick up something and throw it and the two dogs bound away from him. The young man takes two steps forward and the hitch in his step is unmistakable.

Tim. Our baby.

"I'll...I'll go fetch Tim," John says.

"Please," Patricia says, and for a moment I think she will finish the sentence with "Go away!" But she doesn't.

"Won't you sit down?"

We each take a chair and watch, riveted to the little drama at the far end of the backyard. John has reached Tim and he is telling him something. He points in our direction and we see Tim turn his head to look at us. Blair and I nearly flinch in our seats. John talks to his son for another moment. Tim leans down to pat one of the dogs that has come running back to him, but he is still looking at his dad. Then he looks down at the dog, like he's thinking. He stays that way for several seconds.

It seems like everything is being weighed in a set of scales while Tim crouches down by the dog. I don't know what Jewel is feeling, but I know for Blair and me, everything hinges on what Tim will do next. I'm itching for my freedom, as she must be itching for hers.

Finally, Tim stands and looks again in our direction. John says something to him. And then they begin walking toward us, John with a measured step that matches the slower pace of his limping son.

Each imperfect step brings Tim's face closer to my own. For some reason I'm drawn to his eyes and yet apprehensive of meeting his gaze. When Tim and his father reach the patio, Blair, Jewel, and I stand up.

He is nearly as tall as John, and his brown hair is flecked with golden highlights. His eyes are blue, the same shade as his infant blue eyes, and his cheeks are speckled with light freckles. He is handsome in an easy, boy-next-door way. His face looks kind and gentle, but also cautious.

I see Tim's sapphire blue eyes and I'm transported back to the day we found him, to the first time I saw those eyes. We had kept him for three wonderful hours, and then we finally took him to Corinthia, who immediately called the police. Blair, Jewel, and I took turns holding him until the police arrived, followed by a county social worker and an ambulance. Blair did most of the talking and all of the lying. The last one of us to hold him was me. He was asleep in my arms, wrapped in my yellow baby blanket, and I leaned down to kiss his forehead, above the row of mosquito bites that looked just like Orion's Belt...

The two dogs jump up onto the patio, fracturing the frozen moment in time.

John Penney is calling their names. "Bandit! Cosmo! Get down!" I am standing closest to Tim and our eyes meet. There is commotion all around us and yet I hardly sense any of it. It's like everything around us is happening in slow motion. I smile at him and the corner of his mouth lifts a fraction.

He was too young to know how to smile the last time I saw him. But those eyes are the same.

"Hi, I'm Tess," I say, thrusting my hand forward.

He takes it and grasps it more firmly than I thought he would.

"Tim," he says, like I don't already know his name. He realizes this and the rest of the smile comes, awkward and sheepish, the way fifteen-year-old boys smile when being introduced to women in their late twenties.

This eases the tension on the patio and we all laugh. John has corralled the dogs and sent them off to play in the yard.

"Hi, Tim. I'm Jewel," Jewel says, extending her right hand. "And I'm Blair."

When Blair offers her hand, Tim pauses for a moment before taking it.

"You look just like your picture," he says to her.

"My picture?" she says, blinking several times.

"The photograph in the newspaper article," John says. "Tim has it in his baby book."

"Oh," Blair says, wondering if that is good or bad.

There is an awkward pause in conversation. Patricia invites us to sit back down and then excuses herself to get us something to drink. We spend the next twenty minutes in tedious small talk, telling Tim and his parents where each of us lives now, where our lives have taken us since the last time we saw Tim.

When Blair shares that her husband died of a massive heart attack less than two weeks ago, Patricia is appalled. I'm sure she is wondering why Blair is looking for Tim when she should be at home grieving with her two little girls. She will never know Blair's true reason for coming, just as she will never know mine.

John stands up then and suggests to Patricia that we might like to visit with Tim alone for a few minutes.

Patricia is not enthusiastic about this idea in the least. But she gets up and flashes a look at Tim that says something like, "I will be just a few feet away." Tim looks a little nervous too, but he says nothing. He watches his parents disappear into the screened porch and then into the kitchen. He looks back at us.

Blair clears her throat.

"Oh, God…" she says, and I think she might actually mean it. "Tim, I…" but she stops. I can imagine that her heart is racing, that her mouth feels dry.

"Okay," she says as she tries again. "Tim, I have to tell you something. When we found you in the peach box, there was something, two things actually, inside the box with you. Jewel and Tess didn't know about them, Tim. Only I did."

Blair reaches into her purse and pulls out the locket and the folded note. Her hand is shaking a bit. Tim's face is expressionless.

"Your…mother left these for you," Blair is crying now, softly, but it is hard for her to talk. My own throat feels tight.

"She meant for you to have them, Tim. I am so sorry I kept them. I am so sorry! I just…I was…I didn't want to give you up. I didn't want the police to come and take you. And this note was so…I am so sorry, Tim. Please forgive me!"

Blair can't say anything more. She pushes the note and the locket across the patio table to where Tim is sitting in stunned silence. Jewel reaches underneath the table to Blair's other hand and holds it gently. I just sit there waiting for the absolution to come.

Tim waits a second before taking the locket. He opens it slowly and I can see that he is disappointed the little frame is empty. Then he takes the note and opens it slowly. I watch his face as he reads. I can see every line as his eyes move across the small piece of paper. I can tell when he reads the words *I will always love you.*

Tim's lower lip begins to tremble and I can tell he wants it to stop. Instinctively I reach out to him and touch his shoulder.

He doesn't resist but he shakes his head like he can shake the tears back down to his heart where they came from. When he is able to control his quivering lip he says three words.

"I always wondered."

And I want to ask him if he always wondered how old she was, or if he always wondered if she was sorry. Or if he always wondered if she loved him.

"Please, please don't hate me," Blair says, wiping her eyes with the back of her hand. With her other one she is holding tight to Jewel.

Tim fingers the note, touching the words that probably mean the most to him. *Sorry. Love. Always.*

"I don't hate you," he says.

And Blair's soft crying is obviously mingled with a sense of relief.

"So, you forgive me?" she says.

Tim can't bring himself to look at this crying woman across the table. He just shrugs his shoulders.

"Sure, I guess," he says, unable, I think, to see past the wonder of having this note from his mother—the mother who loved him—to the offense that kept him from having it until this moment.

Blair sighs heavily and the flow of tears seems to ebb.

"I am so sorry," she says, one last plea for justice from the boy she wronged.

"I can see that," Tim says instead, not meaning to be comical, but it sounds funny to me and I start to giggle. I cannot stop. Jewel is smiling next to me. Even Tim has a slight grin on his face. Jewel and Tim seem more amused at my reaction than Tim's actual words.

"Why are you people laughing?" Blair says, starting to smile now too, and I notice for the first time she has eye makeup running down her face.

I reach into my canvas bag sitting by my feet and hand her a tissue. I'm a little puzzled that I don't need one myself, that I'm not awash in my own tears. This is not how I expected it to be. I expected my deliverance to come the way Blair's just did, with the grief of thousands of days poured out around me. I expected this to be my Beautiful Gate. I expected to feel an island breeze blowing away my unmet longings and oldest regrets. I should feel like a weight has been lifted. But what I'm feeling right now is simple relief for Blair, compassion for Tim, and nothing out of the ordinary for me. All at once I understand why some people start laughing when they should be crying. It is a defense mechanism.

It didn't work for me.

There is no gate.

CHAPTER 18

Clear as Crystal

We don't stay long after Blair returns the locket and the note to their rightful owner. Before we get ready to leave, Tim shows us his dogs, Bandit and Cosmo, as well as his kennels and the two visiting dogs presently in his care. Patricia and John rejoined us and I'm sure John used the time they were in the house to explain why we had come. I have the impression that Patricia isn't entirely happy about what transpired on her patio.

We exchange e-mail addresses and street addresses, and then we make our way to Blair's car. Tim graciously submits to hugs from Blair, Jewel, and me. Patricia suddenly heads back into the house while all this is happening, but she quickly returns holding a pale yellow baby blanket in her arms. It once belonged to me and seeing it takes my breath away.

"This must belong to one of you," Patricia says, and I'm wondering if she is wishing she had not kept it all these years. Or if she thinks by giving it back it will make Tim that much more hers and less anyone else's.

"It's all right," I say, and my voice sounds strange in my ears. I never expected to get the blanket back. It was my gift to a helpless infant who had nothing of his own. "You can keep it."

"It was yours?" Tim says, and I just nod.

Tim reaches for the blanket and his mother gives it to him. He takes a couple of steps towards me and holds out his hands.

"Seems like a good day for returning things," he says, and he looks at me with those eyes that amaze me with their sameness after all these years. Only the size and shape of the head that holds them has changed.

I reach out and take hold of the blanket, folding my fingers into its softness. As Tim lets go and I take hold, it suddenly occurs to me that this blanket, which is yellow—not blue or pink—was perhaps bought by my mother for me on a happy day when she was simply carrying a child whose gender she did not know. Instinctively I clutch it to my chest.

"Thanks for loaning it to me," Tim says and steps back to stand by his mother.

"My pleasure," I reply.

As we head back into Memphis I'm both grateful and despondent about the blanket that rests on my lap. It's both a reminder of everything I cherish about my mother and everything I wish I could change.

When we get back to Jewel's, and after we tell Corinthia about our amazing afternoon, Blair suggests we cancel our reservation at the Peabody, pick up our things, and head back to St. Louis.

"It's only a five-hour drive from here," she says. It's obvious she wants to go home and start living the rest of her life. Things can only improve for her now. I envy that. But I don't want to stumble into her mansion at midnight. I am tired—in every possible way a person can be tired.

"It might be best to just start your long drive fresh, tomorrow," Corinthia says to Blair, but she is looking at me.

It takes a little convincing but Blair finally agrees, and then she decides to order pizza for all of us and to call her girls. She disappears into a quiet room to make her calls.

Corinthia invites me to step outside onto Jewel's porch and we settle onto a glider for two that is sprinkled with Bob the Builder toys. We move the toys and make ourselves comfortable. She knows something is up. She is going to ask me about it.

"What is it, Tess?" she says, her voice full of compassion.

"It didn't do what I thought it would do," I say honestly, knowing but not caring that this can hardly make any sense.

She studies my face for a moment but I am not looking at her.

"Did you hope to discover something by finding this boy?" she asks.

I pause and she waits.

"It wasn't that I wanted to discover something," I finally say.

"What was it, then?"

I feel like a child sitting here next to her, as if I should gather up the toys we removed from the cushions we are sitting on and put them back in my lap. I feel as young and vulnerable as the child I was when I first met Corinthia.

"I wanted to find a way to make it right," I say, with the voice of a thirteen-year-old.

"Make what right?"

Corinthia leans toward me, intent on understanding. I want to tell her everything but I don't want to feel foolish in front of her. It was bad enough feeling that way in front of Simon.

"I…I thought if I helped Blair find Tim, if I was a part of helping Tim understand why his mother left him, it would somehow compensate for how my mother died."

I peek at Corinthia's face but her eyes and expression reveal nothing. I don't think she is considering how foolish I am.

"How did your mother die, Tess?"

I pause a moment before saying out loud what I hardly ever say.

"She died of an embolism, Corinthia. Amniotic fluid got into her bloodstream while she was in labor. Pieces of my hair and skin were in it. When they reached her lungs, they killed her."

I can't keep my voice steady as I say this.

"And you feel responsible for this?" Corinthia says calmly.

"Well…yes! I've tried to tell myself it was just an accident, that it is something I never would have chosen to have happen, but…" I don't quite finish the sentence.

"But…" Corinthia leads me to continue.

"But the feeling won't go away."

Corinthia's face is a picture of puzzled wonder.

"Why do you suppose you would feel responsible for something you had no control over?" she ponders. "You didn't choose the day you were born. You didn't choose to *be* born. You did not send that fluid into her lungs of your own accord. It happened within her body, a body that is separate from yours."

"Yes, I know, but Corinthia, I can't get past it! I have never been able to get past the idea that if I hadn't been born, my mother would be alive."

Corinthia rests her back against the glider and starts to rock gently. She is deep in thought.

"I wonder why you would feel this way, why you have always felt this way," she murmurs. Then she turns her head to me. "Tess, did you ever talk to your father about this?"

"He didn't like talking about it," I answer, remembering those times I tried and he refused.

"So you've never told him how you feel?"

"Well, no. He doesn't even know that I know it was an embolism that killed her. He would never tell me when I would ask how she died. When I was twelve, I begged a friend of his to tell me. And even this friend wouldn't tell me what an embolism was. I found that out myself five months after we moved to Blytheville when I stumbled across my mother's medical records."

"So your father never told you how your mother died, and you never let on that you knew."

I just nod my head. I can see that Corinthia is working an equation in her head. It frightens me.

"Now why would your father not tell you how your mother died when you asked him?" she says.

"Well, I guess he was protecting me from having to feel this way."

"And why would a reasonable adult who knows that there is no way a helpless infant could kill its mother think that you would feel that way? Why would he think you would need to be protected from feeling responsible?"

Inside, I can feel something within me—something big and wide like a fortress wall—start to crumble. Even as I sense this, I am instantly aware that I've been holding it up for years with the mortar of loyalty to my father. But I try to buttress the collapsing wall with one last brick.

"Because he didn't want me to feel like it was my fault," I say, and my voice trembles like a lost child's would.

"But Tess, why would he think you *would?* The man is a doctor. He knows whose body failed. He knows it was not yours."

The wall is falling to pieces all around me, and the crushing weight of the fallen bricks are heavy on my chest. Corinthia's eyes are misty as she looks at me, as she aches for me.

"I think I know where that feeling came from," she whispers.

I know this is true even before she says it. As each word leaves her lips I hear Simon's voice in my head, telling me he had an argument with my father. I hear Simon telling me that I don't know the source of my pain—that I think I do but that I'm wrong. I hear him telling me not to mention to my dad that there had been an argument between them. *Wait and see if he mentions it first,* Simon is saying in my head.

But my dad didn't mention it. I gave him the bait three times and he did not bite.

I close my eyes as I begin to imagine what Simon's and my father's conversation was probably like.

"Mark, I'm worried about Tess," Simon probably said. "I don't know if you know this, but she has this ridiculous notion that she's responsible for what happened to her mother."

My dad probably paused for a moment to let this sink in.

"What makes you say that?" my dad most likely asked.

"Well, because she has told me. Several times. I've tried to tell her it wasn't her fault but she can't let it go."

"Of course it wasn't her fault," my dad might have said.

"Yes, but she has got it in her head that it *is*."

"Well, surely she knows that things like that just happen sometimes."

"Mark, I'm telling you it is a huge problem for her."

"I appreciate your concern, of course, but don't you think you're perhaps blowing this up a little out of proportion?"

Simon probably started to get very frustrated.

"No, I don't. I don't think you have any idea how much this affects her. I think you should talk to her about it."

"Well, why don't you talk to her about it, Simon?"

"I have! It hasn't done any good. She won't listen to me."

"What makes you think she will listen to me?"

I imagine Simon was on the edge of exploding.

"For one thing, you are her father. She has felt this way since she was a child, Mark. Long before she met me. And for another, you were *there* when it happened. You are also a doctor, for Pete's sake!"

"I don't see any reason to get sarcastic, Simon."

"Mark, don't you get it? This is a huge deal for Tess! It's why she can't bring herself to marry me. She's afraid of starting a family. She's afraid she will die!"

"Look, Simon. I don't think it's fair to lay your relationship problems on me. I'd like to see Tess married and happy, of course, but that's between you and her."

By this time, I can imagine that Simon realized it was useless to try and convince my dad to see what he doesn't want to see.

"Will you please talk to her about it?" he no doubt asked, resigned to my father's blindness.

"About what? What am I supposed to talk to her about?"

"Just tell her it wasn't her fault."

"It wasn't."

"Then tell her."

"I think we're finished talking about this, Simon."

There were maybe a few more words between them—short goodbyes with the thinnest layer of good manners. I can picture them both hanging up in anger.

It's all so achingly clear to me. All of it. And to think that Simon pretty much figured it out before me. The only thing he doesn't know is that it's not the prospect of dying while giving birth to his child that has kept me from marrying him. It's dying and leaving that child to live with what I have had to live with all these years.

I open my eyes and Corinthia is looking at me.

"Tess?"

"Yes."

"Do you know now where this feeling of yours came from?"

Tears that have the weight of many years slip down my cheeks, and I nod as I finally understand.

The guilt I have known every moment of my life did not spring to life inside of me, but from outside of me. It grew and flourished every day of my childhood as I spent it with a man who silently blamed me for the death of his wife.

CHAPTER 19

A Map to Home

Corinthia lets me just sit quietly for several long minutes as I try to readjust the weight of my woes. To realize my father wordlessly blamed me, all these years, for the death of the woman he loved hurts in a different way than having actually felt responsible for it. The ache is as deep, but something is attached to it like a bobber on a fishing line, something that keeps the pain from totally disappearing into the familiar depths of misery. I'm not entirely sure what to call it, but it feels strangely like hope. No...pity. No. It feels like a weird combination of both.

My surprised expression concerns Corinthia, I think. She asks me if I'm angry with my father. But I'm still amazed by the floating bobber, and I don't answer her.

"It's understandable if you are," Corinthia continues. "But there's no sense in getting angry at something you can't change. And you can't change *him*. You can only change you."

"I'm not angry with him," I manage to say. "I don't think I can describe what I feel, but it's not anger."

Corinthia reaches out to touch my hand. She waits for me to make the next move. And there is always a next move. But I don't know how to make it.

"What should I do now?" I say.

"Well, what is your heart telling you?"

I try to imagine living the rest of my life knowing what I now know and never saying a word to my father about it, and I realize that's a nightmare I have already lived. I must talk with him and he must talk with me. I cannot live this way any longer. The fortress is lying in rubble at my feet. I will not rebuild it. I refuse.

"I must go to him," I tell Corinthia. "We have to talk about this. Even if he will not listen."

Corinthia nods her head and strokes my hand.

"I think you're right, but I want to encourage you, Tess, to thoroughly consider why your father did what he did. Why he held you accountable," she says. "If you can understand why he did it, I think maybe it will be easier for you to forgive him. And while he may not deserve your forgiveness, you must offer it or your heart will grow bitter, Tess. I've seen it happen to a hundred hurting people. I don't want to see it happen to you."

I don't want to see that happen to me, either. I'm suddenly aware that fresh tears have formed in my eyes and are now slipping down my cheeks.

"Tess, why do you think your father blamed you? Think hard. Think like someone who has lost something very precious."

I wipe my eyes and try to imagine my father awash in grief. I see the waiting room the way I have always imagined it. I see Joey. I see the pull of the morning outside the windows of the hospital. I see my grieving father. My parents had been married less than two years. They were very much in love. They were going to have a child. Me. They were going to be a family.

Then it was all snatched away from my dad, and it surely seemed horribly unfair. He was angry and hurt and alone.

"Because…because he had to blame somebody," I say.

"I think so too, Tess. He had to blame somebody. Now who do we usually blame for things that happen to us that we can't control?"

The answer comes to me even as she poses the question.

"God," I reply.

"Right. But let's think about this for a moment. What does your father think about God, Tess?"

"I don't think he thinks about God at all," I answer. "I'm not even sure my dad is convinced God exists, or if He does, that He could have saved her."

"So all that bitterness and pain that he wanted to hurl at God, he had to hold back. If he did blame God, he would have to admit not only that God exists, but that He is powerful enough to have saved your mother but chose not to. All that blame had to be shifted elsewhere."

"To me," I whisper.

"I'm not saying he meant to hurt you, Tess," Corinthia says gently. "I'm just suggesting that's what he did with the truth about God he could not live with."

"What…what truth?"

"The truth that God is powerful enough to save but sometimes does not."

I'm starting to feel sorry for my father in a way that surprises me.

"I think there is a lot about God my father does not like."

"A lot of people are that way, Tess. What people don't understand, they usually don't like. And what they don't like, they usually convince themselves they don't need."

Corinthia is talking about my dad, but I think she is also talking about me.

"You know, Tess, all of us are born knowing our need for God. Some of us recognize it from the get-go, but some of us refuse to acknowledge it our whole lives. I've thought about this for a lot of years, and I'm convinced that folks who refuse to surrender to God latch onto one of His wonderful characteristics, an attribute that they really identify with, and they make it their own. That way they can be their own little god."

Corinthia looks toward the house to make sure we are not being overheard and then turns back to me.

"Take Blair, for example. What has she done for herself that God is good at? What does she like to do for others that God is good at?"

"I don't know," I answer, unsure where Corinthia is headed.

"What does she like? What motivates her?"

"She likes having money," I answer. "She likes having things and buying things for other people."

"Good. Can you see how that is like God?"

"Well…" but I don't know where to go with it.

"Tess, God owns *everything*. He has everything. He has limitless resources. And He can meet any material need. That's what Blair likes to do for herself and the people she cares about," Corinthia says quietly but firmly. "What about your friend Simon? What does he do that reminds you of God, of something God would do?"

My mind is starting to ache with the weight of so many thoughts but I try to picture Simon in my head. I picture him at his job at O'Hare, getting travelers safely to the ground. I picture him at home with me, trying to soothe my hidden sorrows. I picture him standing at the wreckage of a little Mazda, bleeding and calling out to paramedics, "Are they okay? Are they okay?" It's starting to make sense.

"He likes to rescue people," I reply.

Corinthia nods. "And your dad?" she says.

An outsider would assume my dad the doctor is motivated by a desire to heal people—as great an attribute as any—but the truth is my dad is not motivated by a desire to ease suffering. If he were, my own troubles would have evaporated years ago. My brilliant father is a problem-solver. He likes the challenge of solving a riddle. When someone needs his skills as a doctor, he says to himself, *Now, what is wrong here?* not *Now, how can I make this person well?* It never really bothered me before and it doesn't now. But it helps me understand him, as Corinthia knew it would.

"He likes to solve problems," I say.

"That explains a lot," she says simply. "He had a big problem. And he found a terrible way to solve it."

I don't mean to bristle at this, but I do. Something about the way she says "terrible" makes me uneasy.

Corinthia squeezes the hand she has been holding. "And what about you, Tess?" Corinthia asks as if she already knows. "What do you do that is like God?"

I don't want to consider this. I'm afraid that there is no holy attribute I have been displaying to fill that God-sized void in my life.

"What do you do?" Corinthia asks again.

Nothing comes to mind.

"Think about why you came to Blair's aid now and why you latched onto her when you first moved to Arkansas even though she was very different from you. Why have you worried so for Simon after his accident? Why did you want to meet that little baby's every need all those years ago? Why is it that your first response to your father's failure is to defend him?"

"Because," I say, slowly realizing what Corinthia has already figured out. "Because I am moved by the pain of others?"

"Yes, I think you are," Corinthia says gently. "And that's one of the most wonderful things about God. It's one of the most wonderful things about you."

I begin to slowly consider this, wondering what it means for me now that it has been spoken.

"And I've found that those things we did so well when we lived apart from God are the same things we do even better, and for His blessing, when we stop running from Him and start walking with Him," Corinthia says, already thinking ahead to some future day.

"But what does this mean right now, for me?" I ask her.

"What I think it means is that you can be sure you will do the right thing when you talk to your father. I think you will say all the right things because you are moved by people's pain, Tess. You have been moved by his. I think that's why it's not anger that you feel, but something kinder."

I lean back in the glider and try to absorb the wealth of knowledge I now possess.

"I think maybe you know now what you need to do to make things right," Corinthia says, leaning back as well. "Not just between you and your dad but between you and God too."

As I rest my back against the gently moving glider, I'm aware that there's much I still do not know about the God Corinthia has been so patient to show me, but I feel that perhaps I'm at last ready to learn, ready to admit He wasn't the one who was far away. It was me. But I also know that there is more to this than just saying to God, "Well, I've decided You're all right after all." I know part of it is realizing *I* am not all right and that in the middle of all of this is the mysterious cross—something I have never contemplated long enough to even begin to understand.

"It may take some time," I say, but in reality I already know I won't wait another minute to set things right between my dad and me. I have already decided I will go to Shelley's party next Friday. I cannot think past anything else.

"Don't wait too long," Corinthia says, eyeing me tenderly. "For either one."

"I won't. I promise," I reply.

"Now, Tess," Corinthia begins as if there is more, and I cannot imagine there being more. "Something has always troubled me. I haven't thought about it in years, but seeing you now brings it back to my mind. And as long as you are making things right, I'm thinking there is one more thing you can do. One more thing that needs to be done."

"There is?" I wonder where Corinthia is headed. I can't imagine what else is unsettled.

She turns her head toward me.

"You told me once, a long time ago, that your mother had a brother," Corinthia begins and then stops, letting me pick up the thought.

"Martin," I say, whispering the name I hardly ever say.

"Do you remember when I asked you about your uncle, not long after you first moved next door to me, and you told me your dad never talks about your mother's family in England?"

"Yes." Simon had asked me the same thing not long after we met.

"Don't you find that a bit odd, Tess?"

I think back to the few times I asked about my mother's side of the family, and I remember my dad's short, nervous answers. My parents had eloped after meeting and falling in love at RAF Upper Heyford near Oxford. My dad was stationed there and it was his first assignment after completing his residency. My mother worked at a flower shop on High Street in Oxford. He had gone to her shop to wire flowers to his mother for her birthday, and they struck up a friendship that quickly blossomed into a romance. My mother's brother, Martin, and her own mother didn't want her to marry an American serviceman who would take her far away from them. So my parents eloped, and eight months later my father was sent to Lajes Field in the Azores, hundreds of miles away from England on a little island in the middle of the Atlantic. My father's relationship with his in-laws was already strained when a year later he called to tell them my mother had died shortly after giving birth. He had been shunned at the funeral.

This is all I know; this is the sum of the information I pieced together from my dad's vague answers and my paternal grandmother's infrequent commentaries on how her son had been mistreated. There were times I had wanted to ask if—before she died—my maternal grandmother ever asked to come to see me. But I was afraid. I was afraid if I asked my father would say, "No, she never did."

My father has said Martin's name maybe twice in my lifetime and never in the context of me being his niece.

"I think the two families parted on rather bad terms," I finally say to Corinthia.

"Now, that sounds to me like something that needs to be made right," she says plainly.

What she is suggesting fills me with all kinds of strange feelings I don't recognize.

"Corinthia, Martin doesn't even know me! And I can't assume he will want to talk to me or see me after all these years."

"Just like you can't assume that he won't."

The thought of contacting my mother's family in England has never been more than a fleeting thought, one I usually chased away with fears of being rejected. But what Corinthia is supposing makes perfect sense. I feel foolish for not having thought of it before.

I suddenly feel as if a map has been placed in my hands, a map that was drawn before my eyes and perhaps even with my own hand—with tremendous help from Corinthia, of course.

This is what I have always wanted to do. To make a map that would lead me home.

"Tess, my girl," Corinthia says, saying my name with emphasis. "I think it's harvest time."

CHAPTER 20

Where All Journeys Begin

When Blair and I arrive back at the Peabody it's nearly nine o'clock at night and I am exhausted. It's hard to believe that when I woke up this morning I thought finding baby Tim would be the answer to all my problems—my Beautiful Gate. How different things look to me now at the close of the day. I'm fairly certain that I can see now where my Beautiful Gate stands. It's up the road far ahead of me, but each step I take from this point on brings me that much closer to it.

I am both anxious and fearful for tomorrow to come. It will mean saying goodbye to Corinthia and Jewel, for at least a while, though I plan on never again allowing thirteen years to pass between us without a visit. But it will also mark the beginning of my journey toward peace and a life free of regrets. I am convinced that at the end of it, regardless of what my dad says or does, and regardless of what Martin says or does, I will have done all that I possibly could to fix what was broken. That is all anyone can do. And when I return to Simon after my travels are over, I am going to marry him.

I have so much to tell Simon. I hardly know where to start. I take my phone out of my canvas bag and pace a few steps in the shared sitting room of our suite before punching in the number. Blair watches me and then announces she is going downstairs for a drink. I wouldn't be surprised if she orders a bottle of champagne to celebrate her little truce with God. When she is gone I punch in the speed dial number and anxiously await to hear Simon's voice.

"Tess!" he exclaims when he answers. "Did you get to see him?"

"Yeah, Simon. We did," I answer as I sink into a thoroughly stuffed sofa. "It was great. I wish you could have seen Tim's face. It was the right thing to do."

"So he's doing okay?"

"Yeah, I think he is. He has some hurdles in his life like we all do, but he seems like a very kind, compassionate person. He has two great parents."

"So, Blair must be feeling pretty good, huh?"

"She has her vindication, you could say. I don't think she's ready to see things any other way."

"I'm glad you found him, Tess."

"Me too," I say, and I take a breath before plunging forward. I will tell him about my plan to go to England first. For some reason I think he will be less shocked by this new development than that I have finally figured out the source of my troubles. "Simon, I have made some other amazing discoveries since I've been here."

"Yeah?"

"Um...yeah. See, I've decided I really need to go to England to meet my mother's family. I know she has a brother there. And there could be cousins too. I think if I do, I will be able to lay to rest some really old ghosts. I'm planning to go right after I get back to Chicago."

Simon is silent for a moment.

"Wow, Tess," he finally says. I can sense that he thinks this is a very positive step for me, but he also knows that it will prolong my absence. "That's...that's great. Do you want me to come with you? If you do, I'll find a way to make it work."

It's not that I don't want Simon with me. It's that I feel I need to do this alone.

"Actually Simon, I want to do this by myself," I tell him. "And...there's something else I've discovered here."

"Yes? What is it?"

"I have a pretty good idea what you and my dad argued about."

"He told you?"

"No, Simon, he didn't. He did just what you said he would do. He never mentioned it. I just finally figured it out—with a lot of help from Corinthia."

"What did you figure out?"

"That even though he probably didn't mean to, my dad has always blamed me for what happened to my mom. It's why I've always felt like it was my fault. All those times he wouldn't talk about her, I assumed he was protecting me from knowing the truth—that if I hadn't been born she would have lived."

"He was protecting himself," Simon says quickly.

"I know it, Simon, but I also know that's what wounded people do. They find a way to insulate themselves from further injury. You and I both know this."

"He's a grown man, Tess. He's had twenty-eight *years* to come to terms with this. He's married another woman!"

"Yes, but it still must hurt, Simon, or he would have asked me about it when you begged him to."

I don't think Simon is convinced. Or maybe he is wondering how I know he *did* beg him.

"I think you're being too easy on him," he says after a pause. "Look at what his choices have done to you."

Simon doesn't add "and what his choices have done to us," but he doesn't have to. I already know it.

"But I don't think he meant for it to be like this. He didn't know any other way to work it out. And Simon, he doesn't have God to lean on. *You* surely remember what that is like."

He knows I am right about this. We are both infants in the cradle of newfound faith, but we at least know this much: Life can be unbearably hard without God.

"So what are you going to do?" he says, and I think he's beginning to understand.

"Well, I've decided to go to Shelley's birthday party this weekend. I will just head there from St. Louis."

"You're going to confront him."

"I'm going to tell him I forgive him."

Simon is silent for a moment. When he speaks again he seems angry.

"Why? He won't ask for forgiveness, Tess. I can almost guarantee it. And I can tell you something else—he doesn't deserve it."

"Maybe he won't ask for it and maybe he doesn't deserve it, but I'm not doing it for him, Simon. I am doing it for me."

There are many long seconds of silence between us.

"Simon, when I get back from England I want to marry you. As soon as I get back. I mean it. If…if you still want to marry me, that is."

"Of course I still do," he says, and his voice is cracking under the weight of so much emotion.

"I love you, Simon," I say, and my own voice sounds weak and raspy.

"I love you too."

"Thanks for coming to my rescue," I add, and he kind of laughs.

"Well, is there anything else I can do for you?"

I laugh too.

"You can find my passport for me."

Blair and I return to Jewel's in the morning to fetch Corinthia and drop her off in Blytheville on our way back to St. Louis. It seems strange that we only spent two days with Jewel, that our long overdue visit is over and done with so quickly. But Blair is anxious to get home to her girls and I can't say as I blame her.

"I promise to call and e-mail more often," I tell Jewel as I hug her goodbye.

"And I will too," she says in response.

We head out of Memphis and are back in Blytheville an hour and a half later. Blair wants to drop Corinthia off and head straight back to the Interstate. But Corinthia wants me to come inside for a moment.

"I'll just be a second," I tell Blair as I get out of the car.

"No hour-long conversation on the porch!" she mumbles, referring to my drawn-out conversation on Jewel's porch yesterday.

"I'll be right back!" I assure her.

I follow Corinthia into her house and am glad to see Samuel in the kitchen making a pot of coffee. I had wanted to say goodbye.

"Take care, now," he says, enfolding me in a warm embrace.

As we part, Corinthia hands me a book—a Bible.

"Don't read it all at once, Tess. Read it a chapter at a time and start with the Gospel of John. I know you will have questions. You *should* have questions. That's normal. You ask this Pastor Jim your Simon knows to help you out, or you call Samuel or me. Anytime. Day or night. All right?"

"Thanks, Corinthia," I say, taking it from her. She had given me a Bible once before when I was fifteen and moving away from Arkansas to Ohio. I wonder how she knows I have no idea what became of it. I suddenly think of Blair waiting for me in the car. I cannot help but think she should be here in Corinthia's kitchen receiving a Bible too.

"What about Blair?" I say, rather absently.

"What about Blair?" Corinthia asks kindly.

"She's going home today thinking she's got God off her back, that He'll leave her alone now to go harass other sinners."

Corinthia smiles at me.

"You know, Tess, I have often prayed for you and Blair since you moved away, and I will continue to do so. But right now Blair isn't looking for the answers to anything important in life.

It's hard to give counsel to someone who hasn't asked for it and who doesn't think she needs it."

"So you're just going to give up on her?" I ask, though I know with Corinthia that can't be possible.

"Of course not, Tess. I just don't think God is going to use me in her life like He did in yours. Whoever is going to tutor Blair on the things of God must be somebody whose opinion she already respects. So my prayer for Blair is that God would speed that person her way."

I think of Blair's friends and colleagues, a mini-society of unchurched, privileged elite, and I am concerned.

"I don't know if there's anyone in her circle of friends capable of doing that," I say.

"Why, Tess! You are so very wrong. There's you!"

"Me!" I exclaim. "But I don't know anything!"

"Not yet," Corinthia says, wrapping her arms around me in a farewell embrace. We part and that easy smile of hers appears, creasing her brown face with beautiful lines.

CHAPTER 21

Small Change

Dayton, Ohio

My flight from St. Louis is early, landing in Dayton's airport fifteen minutes before it is expected. My dad will no doubt be a little late in coming to get me. It's a habit of his to never allow quite enough time to get anywhere. But I don't mind the few extra minutes I will have to collect my luggage and my thoughts.

The past few days have been incredibly meaningful to me in so many ways. On the drive back to St. Louis earlier this week I told Blair more than I thought I would. I didn't tell her everything, though. I knew if I did she would feel differently about my father and I didn't want her to. I did tell her I felt that I needed to visit with my dad about some things that had been bothering me for a long time. When Blair had asked, "What kind of things?" I had told her it had to do with my mother's death and the fact that my father and I never talk about it. She didn't say any more after that. I think it seemed too personal a matter to inquire any more and I was glad for her insight. I didn't want to tell her much more than that anyway.

Then I told her of my plans to go to England to find whoever is left of my mother's family and to resolve that broken relationship.

She was thoughtful for a moment and then turned to me.

"Sort of like returning a note and a locket of your own, huh?" she said.

Yes, I had said. It will be very much like that.

I spent three days with Blair and the girls in St. Louis in their spacious house since I couldn't leave for Dayton until the day of the party. My early presence would have surely given something away, and I didn't want to spoil the surprise Zane had been planning for Shelley. I could have gone home to Chicago for those three days, but as much as I missed Simon, I felt anxious about breaking my momentum with a trip to the place where the rest of my life waits. I wanted to return to Chicago with everything behind me.

They were three very relaxing days—just what I needed to mentally prepare myself for my trip to Dayton. Dad was surprised, I think, when I called him from St. Louis to tell him I had changed my mind about coming to the party. He seemed pleased, though, and we made plans for him to pick me up at the airport in Dayton and then to drop me off at some friends' house until the party.

I had hung up after talking with my dad, and I was sitting in that beautiful sunny room where I had found Blair the morning after Brad had died, that morning that now seems like ages in the past but in reality was only two weeks ago. I had heard the front door open and shut, and then Blair had come into the room and I noticed she was holding a Federal Express envelope in her hand. She had a slim and nervous smile on her lips and she said nothing as she came to me and held out the envelope.

I didn't take it right away because I wasn't expecting anything from Federal Express, and I thought maybe she had just gotten some startling news that she couldn't tell me about in words.

"I want you to have this," Blair said, nodding to the envelope in her hand.

"What is it?" I asked, bewildered, but taking the envelope from her.

"It's my way of saying thanks for helping me put things back where they belong. And my way of helping you do the same."

I had reached into the envelope and pulled out its contents. In my hand I held a round trip, first class airline ticket to London, a British rail pass good for a month, and confirmed reservations for a room at the Randolph Hotel in Oxford for thirty days.

I was very glad to already be sitting at that moment. I felt quite shaken and I could think of nothing to say or do except to just stare at those tickets.

"You can stay longer if you want," Blair said. "Or less. I just thought a month would be about as long as you would want to be gone. We can change it if you want."

"Blair," I say, and my voice sounded breathy and weak. "This is too much! I don't see how I can accept it."

I started to cry about then.

"It's not too much," Blair says, sitting down next to me. "It's nothing compared to what you did for me. You dropped everything for me when I asked you to. And you never complained once. About anything."

I sniffled and gazed at the tickets in my hand.

"Tess, let me do this for you...please?" Blair pleaded.

For a moment I wondered how often Blair has the opportunity to plead for anything. But the thought of her spending thousands of dollars on me quickly re-consumed my thoughts.

"It's so much money," I said, shaking my head.

"That depends on who you talk to, Tess," she said calmly, reminding me gently that she is a rich widow worth millions. "Please take them."

I had turned to her and hugged her tight then, murmuring my thanks.

Even now, two days later, I'm still amazed by Blair's generosity to me. And reminded that this ability of hers to see a material need and meet it is something I never understood or appreciated about Blair until now. I remember how quick she was to spend her allowance on a can of infant formula and a package of diapers that hot July morning that sealed our friendship. I'm awed that she was this way even before she had money.

From the bench in baggage claim where I'm seated I suddenly see my father weaving his way toward me. He looks the same as he did at Christmas, the last time I saw him. He's wearing khaki pants and a buttoned chambray shirt with no collar. His hair is mostly gray these days, and he still wears it cropped close to his head even though he hasn't had to have a regulation haircut in ten years. As he nears me I see he has the beginnings of a goatee. It will look nice on him when it is fully grown out.

I stand and he comes to me, breathless and smiling. A quick embrace, a peck on the cheek, and then he reaches down to grab the handle of my suitcase.

"Sorry I'm late!" he says. "Traffic is already bad at three-thirty. Can you believe it?"

He starts to walk briskly back in the direction he came, toward the short-term parking area.

"It's okay, Dad," I say as I rush to keep up with him.

"Flight okay?"

"Yes. Uneventful. The best kind."

"Good," he says, going through a set of doors that take us to the parking lot. "I'm still so surprised you were able to come after all."

"Yeah. Funny how that worked out," I answer. "Blair and I figured it would take several weeks or even months to find Tim. I never would have guessed it would only take a few days."

"Well, that's amazing really," my dad says. "Must have been very nice for the three of you to see that boy again. And each other too."

We reach his BMW and my dad quickly places my suitcase in his trunk. We get in and make our way out of the parking lot and the airport itself and onto a busy divided highway. My dad asks me if I was able to see the inside of our old house when I was in Blytheville.

"No," I answer. "No one is renting it right now and it's all locked up. Things are kind of different there with the air base gone, Dad. It's not like it was when we lived there."

"Yes. Well, life has a way of throwing surprises at you, doesn't it?" my father says.

Oh, yes. Life indeed has a way of doing that.

We head to his clinic about twenty minutes away so that he can finish some last details before the weekend. I try to sit quietly in his office and stay out of his way. I notice with a twinge of jealousy that there is a picture of my dad, Shelley, and Zane sitting on the credenza behind his desk. It is recent, probably taken within the last year. It shouldn't seem so odd to me. I have been out of the house for nearly ten years, except for those odd times when I moved back home for a time to sort things out in my head. But it vexes me anyway and I'm again reminded that I'm out of place despite being home. I'm closer in age to my stepmother than I am to my half-brother. I look at that picture and it reminds me how abnormal that is. I can feel the courage that I came to Dayton with start to dissolve as I stare at the photo, so I pick up a medical journal sitting on an end table to distract me. I'm reading about new drug therapies for rheumatoid arthritis when my dad breezes in a few minutes after five and announces he's ready to go.

"Okay, I think we can get out of here," he says, turning off his desk lamp and grabbing his keys. "Sorry I can't bring you home right away with me, Tess."

"It's all right, Dad. I don't want to spoil the surprise. Besides, I haven't seen Gerrit and Eva and the boys in a long time. It will be nice to see them again."

Nice is a generous word. Gerrit and Eva are my dad's and Shelley's closest friends in Dayton, and I guess I know them fairly well. But their kids are in Zane's age group, not mine. I used to babysit their boys. I won't mind spending a couple of hours with them until the party, but every hour I spend here in Dayton without doing what I came here to do seems like wasted time.

"Great. They're excited to see you too. We're having the party at Cristobal's. Did I tell you that?"

"Yes."

Shelley's favorite restaurant.

"You and the other guests are supposed to get there by seven-twenty, so make sure Gerrit and Eva get out the door by seven."

"Sure, Dad," I say, mentally moving very fast past the image of me being one of the other guests.

"Shel and Zane and I will get there about seven-thirty. All she is expecting is dinner for three tonight."

I smile wanly, thinking of all the surprises that await debut. We start to walk through the darkened hallways of the clinic, which has been officially closed for half an hour already.

"Bye, Dr. Longren! Nice meeting you, Tess," says Renee, the last front-office worker to leave. She is turning off computer monitors as we walk past her.

"Bye, Renee," my dad calls out. "Have a nice weekend."

"Nice to meet you," I say, making sure our eyes meet.

"Have fun at the party!" she says, smiling broadly.

We step outside into the late afternoon sunshine and again head over to my dad's car.

"So how many people are coming to the party?" I ask, getting into the car and purposely *not* saying how many other guests.

"Well, the guest list was Zane's department. He wanted forty guests for his mom's fortieth birthday. So there you go."

"Oh. But he wasn't expecting me to come. I'll make it forty-one," I say.

"Oh, Zane will be all right. I'm sure he'll just be glad you are here. I haven't had a private moment alone with him to tell him you're coming. I'm sure he will be thrilled you came."

I'm suddenly wishing I could just tell my dad right now, at this moment, what I need to tell him—before the party—and then he could just take me back to the airport. I could then go about the business of rebuilding my life, and he could do whatever he will do with my unrequested forgiveness. I don't want to be the unplanned-for guest, the daughter from the other life, the daughter who is not in the family photo.

But I have already promised myself I will say nothing until after the party tonight, probably not until tomorrow so that my dad can never blame me for ruining Shelley's birthday. And I won't ever be able to blame myself.

When I arrive with Gerrit and Eva and their boys at the restaurant, my first impulse is to just find a quiet corner and wait out the evening. I know only a few of the other people in the room. Most of the guests are friends my Dad and Shelley made after I graduated and moved away. Eva sits by me, sensing my unease.

"It's so wonderful that you were able to come!" she says, and I just smile and nod.

Fifteen minutes later, a guest playing lookout shushes us into silence. A waiter leads my dad and Shelley to the back room of the restaurant where we are all waiting. Shelley's reaction to the room full of people yelling "Surprise!" is probably all that Zane had hoped it would be. He is beaming as he looks at her, measuring her response. When Shelley's eyes meet mine, her face breaks into a wide smile and she makes her way to me. I feel an instant pang of guilt for coming to Dayton this weekend with ulterior motives. I can see that she is touched that I am here. Zane follows her with an equally amazed look on his face.

"Tess, this is so great! I can't believe you're here," she says, hugging me tight.

"Happy birthday, Shelley," I say to her, returning the hug.

She is quickly drawn into another embrace from another guest, and I turn to Zane. He doesn't volunteer a hug—no nearly thirteen-year-old boy probably does—but he warmly accepts one from me.

"I thought you couldn't come!" he whispers to me.

"I didn't think I would be able to. But my plans changed," I reply in a whisper. "Great job on the party, little brother."

He cannot hide his expansive grin.

The evening passes quickly enough. We enjoy a nice meal, dessert, and coffee, and then a few guests put on a skit about growing old. It's funny, I suppose, but a lot of the jokes are ones I don't quite understand since they refer to funny things Shelley has said or done, and I haven't been around to hear or see them.

When we finally leave the restaurant it is nearly ten o'clock. We get home and spend an hour or so chatting in the living room. I give Shelley a pair of summer pajamas I bought for her at the Peabody the morning we left Memphis. Zane tells me about his baseball games so far and lets me know he has a home game tomorrow. I tell everyone about how Blair, Jewel, and I found Tim. Shelley asks about Simon, and I make a concerted effort not to look in my dad's direction as I tell her he's doing much better and has gone back to work.

Zane starts to yawn, and we take the cue from him that it's time to call it a night. We head upstairs, Zane to his bedroom, my dad and Shelley to theirs, and me to my old room, which is now the guest room, and I can't help feeling like nothing has really changed.

I fall asleep wondering who I am to think I can start changing things now.

Chapter 22

Uncovering Secrets

In the morning when I awaken, I lie in the bed that used to be mine and consider when I should talk with my father. The later in the day, the better, I think. I don't want to have to fill the hours between the time I talk with him and the time I leave with ordinary small talk. I have a gnawing suspicion that we will both feel a little uncomfortable afterward. Maybe more than a little. Perhaps I should tell him just before I get on the plane. Maybe we can leave a little early for the airport tomorrow. I can offer to take him out to breakfast. We can find a place that has seating outside, a place with relative privacy, with just enough outside world around it that neither one of us will say or do something we will later wish we had not.

When I come downstairs, Dad is gulping down a glass of orange juice. He has a stubby racquet in his hands and is obviously dressed for a game of racquetball. Shelley is standing next to him, holding out a toasted English muffin.

"Morning, Tess," he says, setting his glass down and taking the muffin from Shelley.

"Sleep well?" Shelley says to me, smiling.

"Yes. Fine," I answer, watching my dad rushing to get out of the kitchen.

"I'll be home in time to take everyone to Zane's baseball

game," he says, giving me a peck on the cheek like he did in the airport. Short, sweet, and obligatory.

"Okay," Shelley says, and I can tell she senses it too. My dad is anxious to get away. I am sure she doesn't know why. She is obviously confused as to why her husband seems leery of being in the same room with his only daughter. I'm not confused. My dad is afraid any prolonged conversation with me will lead to the one he had with Simon. Better to avoid deep conversation altogether. My eyes follow him out the door. And Shelley's eyes are on me.

"Are you going to visit any of your friends today?" she asks, clearing her throat. Clearing the air.

"No, I don't think so," I say, walking to the coffeepot and pouring myself a cup. "Most of my closest friends have all moved away. And I'm only here until tomorrow morning. I'll just spend it here with you guys. If that's okay."

"Of course it's okay," Shelley says. "Why don't you and Zane and I go to the mall this morning? He needs some new summer clothes and we can have lunch out. Sound like fun?"

"Sure," I answer. I am only biding time anyway.

It actually ends up being a very enjoyable morning with Shelley and my brother. Zane doesn't seem to mind shopping for clothes with me and his mom, which surprises me, and he and I have a great time picking out some outrageous summer outfits he has no intention of buying or wearing. The stiff, constricted air that seemed to fill the kitchen is not present as we shop and later enjoy Chinese food in the food court.

As we eat I realize that the older I get, the more I like Shelley. I wish I could think of her as a mother figure, but that feeling has always eluded me. Even when she was planning her wedding, back when I was fourteen and she was twenty-six, I had wanted to see her constant attempts to draw me into the planning—like making me a bridesmaid instead of a junior bridesmaid—as the beginnings of a mother-daughter relationship. But it felt more like the beginnings of a girl-to-girl friendship. And I didn't want another friend. I wanted a mother. No...I wanted *my* mother—the one who bore me, the one whose body sheltered mine, the one whose face resembled my own.

I even tried to manufacture the feeling, but it backfired in my face. About a month after the wedding, after Shelley had moved in and her things began to lie around the house like mine and my dad's, I got caught looking in her purse. I didn't hear my dad and Shelley come into the kitchen from the garage, where they had been staining a dresser. I looked up from my snooping to see them staring at me.

My father was appalled, embarrassed that his fourteen-year-old daughter would invade someone's privacy like that, or worse, that I might actually steal from his new wife. I was merely satisfying my own curiosity about Shelley, trying to clothe her with motherliness by checking out the contents of her purse. Shelley, I think, must have known that I wasn't thinking of stealing anything from her, that I was trying to get to know her better but in a rather tactless way. She looked surprised, but not offended.

"What do you think you are doing?" my dad had demanded, and I remember thinking then, as I still do, that that was a very thoughtless question.

My face was afire with shame and I could not answer him.

"Maybe you were just looking for a tissue or some gum?" Shelley had said, trying to soften the heavy air around us.

I couldn't tell either one of them what I *thought* I was doing. It barely made any sense to me.

"I was just looking for some lip balm," I said, wishing my face didn't feel so hot and that my feelings didn't feel so raw.

"You should have asked first," my father had said, his eyes still shining with anger. Or maybe just ordinary shame. I was *his* daughter after all.

"It's okay, Mark," Shelley had said. "I think I have an extra ChapStick I can give you, Tess. It hasn't even been opened yet. Okay?"

She had motioned for me to follow her into the room she now shared with my dad. And I followed her, walking past my dad and willing him to look upon me with eyes that said *I understand why you did it. It's okay.*

But he didn't look at me at all.

I didn't speak to him the rest of the day. Or maybe it was that he didn't speak to me.

After lunch at the food court, Zane announces he wants to go to a music store, but he tells Shelley and me that he really wants to go in alone. This I can completely understand, and I think Shelley does too. We sit under a fake potted palm to wait for him as he goes inside the store.

"Tess, is there anything I can do for you?" Shelley says as soon as Zane is out of earshot. "You seem like you have a lot on your mind."

I smile weakly as I tell her she's pretty smart. I do have a lot on my mind.

"Tess," she continues. "I know I can never replace your mother, and I have stopped trying to, but if there is anything I can do…"

She stops there because what else can she say?

"It's not your fault, Shelley," I say quickly. My throat feels thick and weighted.

"What's not my fault?"

"You have always been wonderful to me. And you've been wonderful for my dad. He's as happy now as I have ever seen him."

She can see that something is coming and she simply looks at me and waits for it.

"There is something wrong, but it has nothing to do with you," I say. "And no matter what happens, I want you to know that."

A look of alarm splashes across her face.

"What do you mean, 'no matter what happens'?" she says.

I take a big breath to help control my racing thoughts and it occurs to me that she may be able to help me after all.

"Shelley, I need to talk to my dad about something we should have talked about years ago. We should have talked about it before he even met you. He's probably not going to want to and he might even be really angry with me afterward."

Shelley's eyes are wide with concern.

"But I can't live the way I have been living anymore, Shelley. I have to talk to him. Even if he won't listen, I have to talk to him."

"This is about your mother, isn't it?" she whispers, and her eyes look misty. The way mine feel.

"Shelley, I think he blames me for what happened to her," I say. "I don't think he wants to or ever intended to, but he does."

Two tears slip down her cheeks.

"I think he does too," she whispers.

Two tears slip down mine.

"Tess, what are you going to do?"

Despite her empathy for me as the wounded, she is concerned for the man she loves. She is afraid I will wound him back.

"I'm going to tell him I forgive him, Shelley. I won't live with bitterness. Not after seeing what it did to him. What it did to me."

She wipes her eyes and nods.

"All these years I wanted to say something, do something," she says, not looking at me. "And I never did. I thought he hid it so well. If I had known you knew..."

"I didn't, Shelley. I didn't know until a week ago that I felt the way I did because of him. Up until then I really thought it *was* my fault."

"Oh, Tess," Shelley says, shock filling her eyes.

"But it wasn't," I tell her, and I take her hand because her pain moves me, just like Corinthia said was true of me. "It wasn't my fault. I didn't kill my mother. It wasn't my fault."

There are people walking past us in every direction and a few of them can't help but look at the two women crying and talking in quiet voices in the middle of a shopping mall.

We dry our eyes and try to gain back our composure.

"When are you going to talk to him?" Shelley says.

"Tomorrow morning I want to leave early for the airport. I want to take him out to breakfast. I may need your help with this. When I suggest it, he may want you and Zane to come too, and you will have to decline. Can you think of a way to do that?"

Shelley nods her head.

"We'll find a place where we can talk but not so private that it will make him uncomfortable. I'll arrange it so we will only have twenty minutes to talk. If we are both wishing we had more time when it's time to get me to the airport, I'll call the airline and ask for a later flight out. But...I don't think that will happen."

Again Shelley nods her head.

"He might be upset or distracted when he gets home," I continue. "He may not want to talk about it. He may say absolutely nothing at all. I don't know if you can think a certain way for twenty-eight years and then just change your mind about it in twenty minutes. Especially when you've been in the wrong."

Shelley is rubbing her forehead and shaking her head.

"I'm afraid for you, Tess," she finally says. "I mean, I'm incredibly proud of you for not reacting in anger or resentment, but I'm afraid he won't accept it."

"I know," I say. "But that will be his burden to live with if that's what he chooses. I'm done living with it."

"You're very brave," she says, looking at me intently.

But I say nothing to this. I don't feel brave. I feel desperate.

"I wish you could stay a little longer," Shelley continues.

"I think it's better to leave for a while. Besides, I want to mend some other fences. I'm leaving for England on Monday. I am going to try and find my mother's brother and his family."

Shelley looks wide-eyed at me. "You are?"

"I've never even met them, Shelley. It was all a part of that dark bitterness that I grew up with. Dad never talked about my mother's family, never called them or wrote to them, and whenever I would ask about my British relatives he would always tell me to leave lifeless things buried."

"I'm so sorry, Tess," Shelley says. "I should have intervened. I could tell something wasn't right."

"It wasn't your responsibility, Shelley. He probably never wanted to talk with you about it either."

There are a few moments of silence between us.

"So do you have an address for Martin? Do you know where to go?"

"No," I answer, shaking my head. "I am hoping I can get a little information out of Dad before I tell him all that other stuff."

"So he doesn't know you're going?"

"Not yet."

"I know where Martin's address is," Shelley says softly, looking down at her shoes. "I can get it to you later today. It's old—I don't know if Martin still lives there. But I know where in the desk I've seen it. You might want it just in case, Tess. In case he pretends he has no idea where Martin is."

I sit in stunned silence and Shelley raises her head to look at me.

"Thank you," I say, wanting to say more, but unable to.

"You're welcome," she says and the care and concern on her face reminds me very much of what I used to imagine a mother's face would look like, looking down at me. I see her purse resting by her feet and I can't help but remember that long ago day.

"Shelley?"

"Yes?"

"Do you remember that day, after you and Dad were married, and you guys caught me looking in your purse?"

"Yes."

"I wasn't looking for lip balm."

She pauses a moment and then asks, "What were you looking for?"

"I was just looking to see what was important to you. When I was little I used to think a mother's purse was like an extension of her, that it carried all her wonderfully scented secrets and treasures. I just couldn't explain it to you then."

Shelley smiles at me as she understands what I am trying to say. She reaches down, picks up her purse, and places it in my lap. Her eyes say *Have at it!*

I start to giggle and so does she. Zane comes out of the store to find us laughing and wiping our eyes and with his mother's purse on my lap.

"What are guys laughing at?" he asks.

But neither Shelley nor I have a clue how to answer him.

We spend the afternoon at Zane's baseball game. He plays well, earning four RBIs, but his team loses in the final inning. Zane takes the loss well. I think he's just pleased I saw him play and that he didn't make any errors. After the game we go to a pizza restaurant Zane is fond of, and when we return home,

Shelley challenges Zane and me and my dad (who declines) to a game of Monopoly. I have the feeling she's keeping Zane up late on purpose. It's nearly midnight when we all start yawning. Shelley and I declare Zane the winner, and after she sends Zane upstairs to get ready for bed, Shelley asks my dad if he wouldn't mind changing the bulb in the upstairs night-light before we are all settled in

"It went out last night. Tess and I can put the game away," she concludes.

As soon as they're upstairs, Shelley gets to her feet and tells me to keep putting the game pieces away, that she will be right back. When she returns a few minutes later, she hands me a small piece of paper. I glance at it quickly before I put it in my pants pocket. It reads, Martin Bowker, 13 Tanglewood Close, Oxford.

CHAPTER 23

The Face in the Photo

Sunday morning dawns bright and sunny. I wake with the sun, but I do not get up right away. I lie under the covers and contemplate what the day holds for me, and I attempt a prayer for help. Corinthia would think this is the smartest thing I have done in a long time. But I am not seasoned at it and I'm not sure I'm making any sense. I think it must be enough to simply say, *Help me say it, help him hear it,* because that is about all that escapes in whispers off my lips.

At seven-thirty, I get up. The house is quiet. I shower, dress, dry my hair, and head downstairs. Shelley is in the kitchen in her robe, making coffee.

"He's coming downstairs in a few minutes," she says quietly. "He suggested I make pancakes."

Shelley says nothing more and starts to load dishes from the ice cream we ate last night into the dishwasher.

I hear my dad coming down the stairs. He seems startled to see me.

"Well, you're up in plenty of time," he says, smiling. But it's a nervous smile.

Shelley keeps her back to us, fiddling with dishes in the sink.

"I'd like to take you out to breakfast before I have to leave, Dad," I say.

"Oh. You don't have to do that, Tess. We can eat here."

"Yeah, I know we can. But I just thought it would be nice for you and me to do this together. I'm sure Shelley doesn't mind."

"Me?" Shelley says. "Not at all. Sounds like a great idea." She turns back to the sink.

"Well, maybe we should all go," my dad says.

Shelley turns slowly around like she's pretending it might be a good idea, but then she acts like she is quickly changing her mind. It's all part of the ruse.

"Actually, I don't think Zane will want to get up this early. We kept him up pretty late last night. You two go. I'd rather stay here and read the Sunday paper in my pajamas anyway."

She turns again to the sink.

"It's all settled then," I say. "I'll just quickly go and give Zane a kiss goodbye and then tell him to go back to sleep."

"Oh, I'm sure that would mean a lot to him," Shelley says cheerfully. "Mark, do you want to go get Tess's suitcase? I'll put some coffee in a travel mug for you."

Shelley turns to the coffeepot and I leave the room before my dad can say or do anything different. As I take the stairs to go to Zane's room I hear him ask Shelley if she wouldn't like to come also.

I head to Zane's bedroom door and listen for a few seconds. There is no sound. I slowly open the door. He's sound asleep, his face toward me in the bluish light of his room. I walk over to his bed and brush a few stray hairs off his forehead. I cannot think of anything that has happened in his life that would bring him the kind of sadness I have known. And I am glad. It's funny that I've never really been jealous of Zane in a sick kind of way. I have always envied his easy happiness, but I don't wish he didn't have it and I did. I lean down and press my lips to his forehead. He opens one eye.

"Hey," he says sleepily.

"Hey yourself," I say back. "I gotta go. I just wanted to say goodbye."

"What time is it?"

"A little after eight. You should go back to sleep, okay? I just didn't want to leave without saying goodbye."

"Mmmm," he says.

"Bye, Zany Zane."

"Bye, Testy Tess," he says lazily, eyes closed. But his mouth is upturned slightly as we exchange these names we have for each other.

"I love you," I whisper, wondering if I said it loud enough for him to hear.

"Yep," he says back. He heard me. And answered back in his own way that he loves me too.

My dad is waiting impatiently at the door to the garage when I come back into the kitchen. Shelley pretends not to notice and comes to me, folding me into her embrace.

"Thanks for coming to my birthday party!" she says. "And thanks for the Peabody Hotel PJs. I can't wait until it warms up enough so I can wear them."

"You're welcome," I say, returning the hug and whispering in her ear, "Thanks."

I start to follow my dad out to the car.

"Say hi to Simon for us!" Shelley says as she stands at the door and watches us get into my dad's BMW.

"I will! Bye, Shelley," I say, and I give her a look that my father can't see. A look that says *Wish me luck!*

She smiles back at me and nods. Shelley watches as we back out of the garage and make our way onto the street. She waves until I can no longer see her.

"So where do you want to go?" my dad says, looking at the road, not at me.

I suddenly decide I want to be at the airport when I tell him what I came here to tell him. Despite what Shelley thinks, I'm not brave. I want to be able to just walk away when I need to go. I don't want to get back in the car and ride in strained silence to the airport.

"You know what, Dad? Let's just get some doughnuts and coffee to go and eat at the airport. Then we won't have to rush."

"Fine with me," he says.

Traffic is light but we are both quiet as we run through the nearest Dunkin' Donuts and then on to the airport. I make a few comments about Zane's game and Shelley's party. I am tempted to tell him I plan to marry Simon later this summer, but that will lead us too quickly down a road I'm not ready to travel just yet.

We arrive at the airport and my dad finds a parking space in the short-term lot. Inside the terminal, I check my suitcase, and then we walk to a seating area near the security checkpoint. A few other travelers are seated nearby.

We sit down and I open our little bag of doughnuts. I watch as my dad reaches in for the maple Long John he picked out. I have no appetite.

I have forty-five minutes before my flight leaves and there is no line at the security checkpoint. So far so good.

"Tastes pretty good," my dad says, taking a bite and then a sip from his cup.

I fidget in my seat. *Help me say it. Help him hear it.*

"You're not eating," my dad says, his own mouth full.

"I will," I say, attempting a sip of coffee. It is too hot for me. It burns my tongue.

"So you must be anxious to get back to your job," my dad continues.

"Yes," I absently reply. "No. I mean, I'm not going back to work right away."

"Oh?"

"I wanted to share a couple of things with you, Dad, before I left. That's why I wanted to have breakfast with you. Alone."

He just looks at me.

"I am not going back to work right away because I am taking a little trip."

"Another one?"

"Dad, I've decided to go to England. I'm leaving tomorrow. I want to see where Mom grew up, where you and Mom met. I…want to see if she still has family there."

"What are you talking about?" he says, leaning back in his chair. It almost sounds like he is saying "What do you think you are doing?"

"I want to see where Mom grew up, Dad. And I want to see my Uncle Martin."

"This is the craziest thing I have ever heard," he says, half-smiling. "Are you telling me you are just going to get on a plane tomorrow and go to England? Just like that? Have you even *talked* to Martin?"

"No, I haven't…"

"Yeah, and you know why you haven't? Because he wrote you off a long time ago, Tess."

Dad must be angry. Or afraid. I'm sure he can't know how much what he just said hurts me.

"Maybe he did at one time, but people sometimes do things they later regret, Dad."

"Well, why hasn't he tried to contact you then?"

"Why haven't I?" I reply right back.

"I'm telling you right now, Tess, you're setting yourself up for heartache."

I am used to it, I think in my head. But I do not say this.

"Dad, what if he is like me?" I say instead. "What if he is thinking that he has been mistaken all these years? What if he wishes he could go back and do it all over again and this time do it differently? What if he wishes he had stayed in contact with you? With me? What if he wonders all the time what ever became of his sister's child?"

"Well, why hasn't he done anything about it?" my dad shoots back.

"Maybe for the same reason I haven't! I've been afraid to! I let myself think all these years that because he never did try, he never wanted to. I know now you can want something without being brave enough to try to have it."

"You don't even know where he lives."

"Do you?" I ask, giving him the opportunity to help me.

"Tess, I haven't talked to the man in nearly three decades!"

He says nothing about the address I carry in my pocket.

"I'll manage," I say.

"This is absurd," he says, putting his doughnut down on the table next to him and throwing up his hands. "Supposing you *do* find him…what are you going to do if he slams his door in your face?"

"I will try again the next day and the next until I have to come home," I answer. "And there are other things I want to do while I'm there."

"Like what?" my dad says, thoroughly perturbed.

"Like visit her grave."

He says nothing but his face softens a bit like he almost wishes he could come with me and visit my mother's grave too.

"I never got to say hello or goodbye to her, Dad. I want to see the place where she rests. I want to just sit there on the grass and tell her I am there. Tell her what I'm like. Tell her I miss her."

My dad looks away. A vein in his neck is twitching. He looks at his watch. He wants our encounter to be over. But I am not finished.

"Dad…" I begin, but he interrupts me.

"I don't want to talk about this *here*," he says curtly.

"Dad, you *never* want to talk about this! And you don't have to do the talking this time. I will."

"Not *here*," he says evenly.

"Yes, here." I say, matching his tone. "I will make it brief, Dad. I promise you. And when I'm finished saying what I have to say, I'm going to get on the plane and go back to Chicago. You don't have to say anything."

"Simon told you," he says in an almost childlike voice.

"Simon told me nothing! I finally just figured it out, Dad!"

"Figured out what?" he says, and that vein is twitching away like mad.

"Figured out how hurt you were when Mom died. How you needed to blame someone and you didn't mean to, but you blamed me. And still do."

He stiffens and his nostrils flare the tiniest bit. I imagine he must feel a tiny bit like he just got caught—after years of deception—with his hand in the cookie jar.

Or in a purse that doesn't belong to him.

"You don't know what you're talking about," he says, looking away from me.

"C'mon, Dad. Isn't that why you didn't talk to me about it when I called you from St. Louis? Simon begged you to ask me about it, didn't he? He knew the guilt was tearing me up inside. He told you it was destroying me. He begged you to talk to me, to tell me it wasn't my fault, didn't he? But you didn't."

"It's none of Simon's business!"

"But it's *our* business, Dad. It has always been our business. And you refuse to talk to me about it."

He looks at me then, and the pain on his face startles me.

"I never *once* told you it was your fault," he says, his voice breaking on every other word.

O God… This is harder than I thought it would be. He doesn't understand.

"Dad, you didn't have to say it, don't you see? I *felt* it," I say, imploring him with my eyes to search his heart. "With every unspoken word I felt responsible. When you wouldn't tell me how she died I went looking for the answers. I know how she died, Dad! I know it was an embolism. I know pieces of my hair and skin got into her lungs! I know the doctors couldn't save her."

"Stop it!" he whispers, and his voice is raspy and uneven.

"Yes, Dad. I want to stop it. That's exactly what I want to do. I want to stop feeling guilty and I want you to stop feeling bitter. It was no one's fault, Dad. No one's. God could have intervened but for some reason He chose not to. And you and I are just going to have to learn to live with that."

He looks away, blinking back tears that I have never seen my dad shed. One droplet escapes, though, and he reaches up and flicks it away like it's an annoying mosquito.

"Dad, I want you to know that I understand why you did it. And that you didn't mean for it to happen. I'm not angry with you. And I forgive you."

Another tear forms in his eye and I can see him willing it to stay put.

"You're going to miss your flight," he says calmly.

"No, I'm not."

He swallows and looks down at the table. "Tess, can't we *please* be done with this?"

When he says this, I feel a deep longing rise to the surface of my soul. "That's all I have ever wanted, Dad."

I know he will not apologize. I know he will not say something like, "Oh, Tess! I had no idea you felt like this all these years! I'm so sorry. I never meant to hurt you!" But I think the look on his face is communicating something close to this. At least, I can imagine it is. And that gives me the strength I need to rise from the table, gather my things, and say goodbye. I expect him to rise too, but he does not.

"Does Shelley know about this?" he says quietly. His voice sounds like his own again.

"Shelley has always known about this, Dad," I say gently, hoping I have not caused trouble for her.

"I'll call you when I get back from England," I continue. "I'll let you know how it went."

"I still don't think it's a good idea," he says, slowly rising from his chair.

He looks suddenly aged to me, far more than his fifty-four years.

"Dad, I meant what I said. I'm not angry with you. And I do forgive you."

I reach for him and put my arms around his neck. His return embrace is weak and effortless. I wait for the peck on the cheek but it does not come. I give him one instead.

"I love you, Dad," I whisper.

I know how hard it is for him to say the same thing back to me. He doesn't say it very often. So I'm not surprised when the words don't come.

"Sometimes you remind me so much of her," he says instead, and his return embrace is strengthened just for a second. But he quickly breaks away. As do I. He has never said that to me before.

"Bye, Dad," I whisper.

He just nods in a sad kind of way and puts his hands in his pockets.

I walk away toward the security checkpoint, stopping to look back at him. He is watching me with that sad look on his face. I wave and he nods, and I can't help but notice that my doughnut and coffee sit untouched on the chair next to his.

Moments later, as I wait for my plane to begin boarding, I reach into my canvas bag and pull out the photo of my mother that I always carry with me, the one where she is sitting on the steps of their home on Terceira. I have often thought I looked like her, and Blair, Jewel, and Corinthia all said I favored my mother when I showed them this picture. But Dad had never said anything about it before today. As I gaze at the photo I begin to understand a little more about the man who loved my mother, the man who raised their child after she died and who had to look at that child's face every day and pretend it did not move him.

CHAPTER 24

Lace in the Window

Oxford, England

The train I boarded in London is chugging its way through beautiful countryside but I am having a hard time keeping my eyes open. It's one o'clock in the afternoon but it feels like the middle of the night. I want so very much to see everything that rushes past the train but my eyelids are so heavy.

I suppose it's not just jet lag that pulls at me. The last three weeks have been a whirlwind of travel, discovery, and soul-searching. I'm as anxious as ever to finally be at peace. I want to lie down at the end of the day, of every day, and feel like nothing has been left undone.

It was harder than I thought it would be to leave Simon after seeing him again yesterday. As motivated as I am to make this pilgrimage and to make it now, it was still difficult to say goodbye to him. I had clung to him at O'Hare, long enough that it made him worry that I was taking on too much at an already stressful time. But somehow I had managed to assure him that I would be okay.

I had clung to him the day before too, when I arrived in Chicago from Dayton. When I saw him sitting in baggage claim, waiting for me with roses on his lap, I had run to him, crying all the way and causing quite a few stares.

We had spent the rest of the day cuddled on the couch while
I told him about my weekend in Dayton, about Shelley coming
to my aid, about my dad's reaction. Simon, of course, was not
surprised.

"So are you okay?" he had asked when I was finished.

"I will be," I had answered. "It could have gone worse. And
I think in time my dad will come to the same conclusion the
rest of us did. But I know he will have to discover it on his
own. He can't be told it and then just be expected to accept it.
He has to solve it for himself. I can be patient. It's not my burden
to bear anymore."

"You should never have had to bear it at all," Simon said,
stroking my arm.

"Let's not go there," I said. "What's done is done. I don't want
to be burdened with *that* in place of the guilt."

He had smiled then. "You sound like me. I tell myself that
every morning I get up and look in the mirror."

I hadn't given much thought to Simon's healing, being so
concentrated on my own. I asked him if he was doing all right.

"I still have my moments," he had answered. "I still wrestle
with remorse, and maybe I always will. But I'm learning to give
each day over to God as soon as I get up and before I do anything else. I find I can make it through the day when I do."

I had told him then about the conversation with Corinthia
on the way to Jonesboro, how she told me God was not avoiding
me, He was pursuing me. I had asked him if he could understand what that was like because I knew I would have a hard
time describing it. He had nodded.

"I think I know exactly what it's like," he had said. And I was suddenly very glad we were beginning this odyssey toward understanding God at the same time, the same place.

"Tess," he had said next, and his voice was very tender. "I need to tell you something. Something I hope you will understand. I've been thinking about it a lot while you have been gone."

He paused.

"What is it, Simon?"

"I'm going to sleep on the couch tonight, Tess. And when you get back from England, I'm going to move in with my brother until we're married."

My first reaction had been amazement. The only times Simon had ever slept on the couch were when he was sick or I was. I wasn't sure what to say at this point, but strangely enough, I knew where these thoughts came from: a desire to do things right the first time.

"I just think we've been doing everything backward," he continued. "We've been enjoying all the benefits of marriage without the commitment. All this time we've been together we've been saying to each other and to the world that we value our independence more than our love for each other. The more I learn about God and how much He cares for both of us, the more I realize living this way must make Him very sad. I don't want to do that anymore. I could leave you right now and no one could fault me. No one. I can't handle that. I don't want to do things backward anymore."

"I don't either," I had whispered.

And so we stopped.

This morning when I woke up, I came out into the living room to see my beloved Simon, curled up on the couch, clutching a sofa pillow to his chest. As I sat with a cup of coffee in the kitchen and waited for him to wake up, I planned my wedding.

The train's whistle blasts and I realize I have dozed off. We're pulling into the station in Oxford. I sit up straight, trying to see the skyline and the yellow stone steeples and towers of Oxford University, but the train station itself is all that fills my vision.

The train comes to a halt, the passengers arise as one, and we all begin to grab our bags. An older gentleman insists on carrying my suitcase outside to a rank of taxis. I thank him, and a driver in the nearest cab gets quickly out of his vehicle, takes the suitcase, and places it into his trunk. I start to open the back passenger door, but the driver reaches for it first and opens it for me. I get in.

The driver runs around to the front of the car and gets in.

"Where to, love?" he says. His accent is thick and melodic. Like Corinthia's but in an entirely different way.

"The Randolph Hotel," I start to say but then I change my mind. "Wait. Can we just drive around Oxford for a few minutes first? Maybe you could show me where things are?"

"Ah, first time in Oxford, then?" he asks.

"Yes," I say, unable not to smile.

"Right," he says. "I can show you."

He zips away from the curb, sending me tottering toward the passenger door. The streets are narrow and there are lots of people walking around and riding bikes.

"May is a busy time 'ere," he says. "Tourists start to come and they don't stop until November. Are you a tourist then?"

"Sort of," I say. "My mother was born here. And...she's buried here. She died when I was born."

"Och, that's too bad, love. You were born 'ere, then? You sound American."

"I was born in the Azores, actually. My dad was in the Air Force and stationed at RAF Upper Heyford. He met my mother here. When they got married, they left for the Azores."

"Oh, right. You know there's no American base at Upper Heyford anymore?" he says.

"Yes," I answer.

"Okay, right," he says, changing the subject. "'Ere's the Randolph; you can walk to just about anywhere in downtown Oxford from 'ere."

He zips past a multistoried building of stone with flags of every nation on its front.

"Now this is High Street," he says a few seconds later.

"High Street?" I say excitedly.

"You know somebody on High Street?"

"No, no. My mother worked at a flower shop on High Street. She and her mother owned it."

"Oh, well. Could be in there," he says, driving past a little alcove of shops surrounded by towering, ancient storefronts. "There's a little flower shop in there. Now Cornmarket is down that way. Busy street. Lots of stuff down that way."

As I look I see a sea of yellow stone buildings glistening in the sun. I wish he wouldn't drive so fast. He makes a couple of quick turns and starts to go back the way we came. He turns left from High Street.

"Now 'ere's my favorite of all the colleges," he says. "This is Christ Church. It's as old as God Himself. Nice meadows to walk about in. The Cherwell River is right down there. You can get a boat and go for a paddle if you want."

He makes what I am sure is an illegal U-turn so that we again head back up the way we came.

"Oh, the covered market is right down there," he says pointing with his thumb. "And folks like Magdalen Street. Just make sure you say it right, love, okay? Specially since you're 'alf British and all. You don't say the g. Pretend that you are *modelin'* some new fancy fashions. That's 'ow you say it, love. No g."

"I'll try and remember," I say.

"Blackwell's bookstore is there," he says, pointing to a tall corner building. "Nice book shop. 'Ave everything, they do. Wife likes it. Gettin' dizzy yet? Ready to get to your hotel?"

I know I don't want to try and meet Martin today. I'm tired, my eyes are red and droopy, and I'm mentally not quite ready. But I decide I want to see his house. Or at least the house I think is his.

"Actually, do you know where 13 Tanglewood Close is?"

"I do," he says. "You want to go there instead?"

"No, not instead. I just want to see where it is."

"Suit yourself," he says and he zooms away.

We leave the busy downtown district and enter a quieter business section that eventually leads to residential homes. I try to memorize the turns my cabbie takes and gauge the distance. He turns down a street lined with tall, brick homes. He makes two more turns and then we arrive at Tanglewood Close, a quiet cul-de-sac. I am guessing we have driven two miles.

"Thirteen Tanglewood Close," he announces, pulling up to a two-story brick home with a blue door. Tea rose bushes line the walk to the front of the house. The single-car garage is closed. There is a window slightly open upstairs with no screen. There are no screens on any of the windows, and every one is dressed in white lace.

"So you want to see if anyone is 'ome?"

"No," I say, gazing at the house. "I just wanted to see where it was, what it looks like."

"You know who lives here, then?"

"My uncle. I mean, I think he lives here. This is the last address I have for him."

"Not sure, though, huh?"

"No."

"Well, 'ere," he says, reaching under his seat. "I got me a phone directory right 'ere."

He hands it to me.

"You look up 'is name and see if it says this address."

I take the book and eagerly turn to the B's. I can't help smiling. It is there. Martin and Fiona Bowker, 13 Tanglewood Close.

"It's here!" I say. I reach into my bag and yank out my boarding pass and a pen. I jot down Martin's phone number on the back of it and then hand the book back.

"Well, there you go," the cabbie says. "So it's been a while since you've seen your uncle?"

"I've never seen him," I say, looking up at the house and seeing a tiny piece of lace curtain fluttering through the upstairs window, waving to me.

"Never?" the cabbie says, swiveling his head around.

"No. And he's not expecting me. That's why I want to come back tomorrow. When I'm not so tired. Maybe in the early evening after they are both home from work…"

The cabbie says nothing for a second.

"'Ow about if I come around for you at the Randolph at seven tomorrow evening?" he says.

I turn my head to face him.

"That would be nice," I say.

"Back to the Randolph, then?" he says, winking at me.

"I think so," I say, looking back at the house and nearly returning a wave to the fluttering curtain as we pull away.

We soon pull up in front of the Randolph Hotel where attendants scurry out to fetch my suitcase.

"What do I owe you?" I say to the driver.

"Well, let's say the tour was 'alf price, seein' as you are 'alf British, so I'll just charge you ten pounds."

I peel off a ten-pound note from the cash I exchanged at Heathrow. I hand it to the cabbie and notice that he's wearing a name tag that reads "Tony."

"Thank you, Tony," I say. "For everything."

"See you at seven tomorrow, then, love?"

"Yes. Tomorrow at seven."

Tony zooms away and I follow the bellhop into the elegant hotel.

CHAPTER 25

Tears

I awaken several times in the middle of the night, whether from the time change or simple nervousness, I don't know. When my wake-up call comes at nine in the morning, I feel as though I'm being summoned from deep sleep just after midnight. I crawl out of my comfortable bed and try to make my body believe that it's nine in the morning and not the middle of the night.

I feel much better after a hot shower. I am trying to decide what to wear when I hear a knock at my door. Someone calls out, "Room service!"

"Um, I didn't order anything," I say, walking to the door but not opening it.

"Miss, your breakfast was ordered for you," says the voice on the other side of my door.

I open it tentatively, a little embarrassed to still be in my robe at nine-twenty in the morning.

A young man with Indian features is standing there in a starched uniform, bearing a tray with a silver-domed lid, a crystal glass of orange juice, a pot of tea, and a single daisy in a bud vase.

"You have standing orders from the person in charge of your bill to have breakfast served to you twenty minutes after your wake-up call," he says plainly. "May I?"

"Oh. Oh, of course," I say, opening the door and letting him in. I should have guessed Blair would do something like this. I start to reach for my bag to give him a tip but he stops me.

"That's been taken care of too, Miss. Enjoy your day."

He turns and is gone, leaving me in a state of bewilderment. Several seconds pass before I turn to the little table in my room where my breakfast waits.

With a map in hand and pounds in my pocket, I leave the hotel on foot a little after ten. The streets of downtown Oxford are bustling. Buses, bikes, and pedestrians are everywhere. Above my head, hanging baskets of flowers dangle from iron poles. I stop first at Blackwell's bookstore, which is busy, I think, for a Tuesday morning. I wander the aisles with no particular goal in mind. When I come across the section featuring titles on local history, I pick up a book about Oxford, my mother's hometown, and buy it.

I wander down Cornmarket, remembering Tony telling me about the covered market. It is easy to find. Inside the market hall there is the peculiar, combined smell of fresh meat, tanned leather, and handmade soap. At one stall two men are selling rugby shirts with the Oxford University logo. I buy one each for Simon, Dad, and Zane. At another stall, a red-haired woman is selling tablecloths, curtains, and doilies made of Nottingham lace. I pick out a dresser scarf for Shelley and buy it.

Once outside again, I follow my map and the spires of Christ Church to the meadow Tony told me about. The gardens around the college are in full bloom, and several artists are sitting on stools, painting the splendor they see in front of them. I find a quiet spot and sit for I don't know how long. I'm semi-aware that I'm alone in a city where, at the moment, no one knows me. But it's very peaceful here despite the crowds.

Sometime later I walk onto the college grounds and head, almost by impulse, to the cathedral. The air inside the cavernous sanctuary is cool. My steps sound like rocks hitting standing water as I walk slowly the length of the long center aisle. Someone is starting to play the organ, practicing perhaps for Sunday services. There are other people in the sanctuary with me, some studying the intricate stained glass, some gazing at the statues. Some are sitting in the wooden pews, just staring at the altar ahead of them as if God is expected to show up any moment.

I ease into a pew, maneuvering my bags so that I don't sit on them. They make a crackly sound that seems out of place. I don't know how many times in my life I have been inside a church, outside the occasional wedding or funeral. Certainly there were those times as a teenager that I visited the Church of the Beautiful Gate with Jewel. But I never felt like I truly belonged there, and it really had little to do with my skin color.

Sitting here now I am struck by the strangest feeling that I have come home, that I do belong—not just here on this pew in this centuries-old church, but here in a place where it feels like God dwells. I begin to whisper the thoughts that are swirling inside my head. And they sound like prayers.

What if Martin doesn't want to see me? What if he slams the door in my face like my dad thinks he will? What if I came all this way for nothing? In spite of the heaviness of these questions I do not feel panic. I feel hopeful, anxious, nervous. But there is no dread. I feel a sense of presence around me and within me that I can only describe as holy. It would have frightened me a month ago. But at this moment all I feel is peace.

Come with me, I whisper.

And I can't help but imagine God is saying that exact same thing to me.

I have lost track of time. When I start to feel hunger, I leave the quiet sanctuary, stopping to inhale its scented air before I walk outside. I walk back up St. Aldate's to High Street. Strengthened, I want to see inside the little alcove I saw yesterday afternoon. I want to see the little flower shop that Tony told me about.

After a ten-minute walk, I am standing in front of the little shop. It is called the Secret Garden. I open the door and little silver bells announce my arrival. The air inside is sweet and tangy, much more pleasant than the odor of the covered market. A woman behind a counter, arranging lilies in a vase, greets me and asks me if there is anything she can help me find.

"No," I say. "I was just wondering if a lady by the last name of Bowker used to own this shop. It would have been quite a while ago."

"Sorry, I don't know that name," she says. "The owner I work for has had the shop for maybe ten years, but I don't know who owned it before that."

"It's okay," I say. I suddenly think of Fiona Bowker, the aunt I have never met, and whom I hope to meet tonight. "Could you make up a little bouquet for me?"

"Certainly," the woman says, smiling. "Anything special you'd like in it?"

"Just make it look happy," I tell her.

I walk back to the hotel with my "happy" bouquet, tired and ready to get rid of my heavy bags. I am hungry and it is well past noon, but I'm too worn out to go back out and look for a place to get something to eat. I stretch out on my freshly-made bed and close my eyes. Sleep comes quickly.

When I awaken it's nearly four o'clock. I have three more hours before Tony will come back for me. I am starving now, and I head back outside after getting a tip from a hotel employee that a pub a few blocks away from the hotel makes splendid fish and chips.

While I eat, I rehearse in my mind what I will say to Martin. But it is not much of a rehearsal. I keep changing what I will say.

I go back to the room and use the phone card Simon bought for me so that I can keep in touch with him. But of course he isn't home. It is late morning in Chicago and he is at work.

Finally at fifteen minutes before seven, I brush my hair, grab the bouquet and my canvas bag, and head down the stairs to the lobby. It's a warm spring night and I decide to wait for Tony outside. A few minutes before seven, I see a black taxi pull up. His off-duty light is on but it is definitely Tony.

"You're a wee bit anxious!" he says as I open the back door and slide in.

"Yeah, I guess you can say that. Your sign says you're off duty."

"I am. I thought I could 'elp you out this way. Told the wife about you. Can't charge you now or she won't fix me any supper."

"Maybe I should send these flowers home with you," I say, laughing nervously.

"Don't think nothin' of it, love," he says.

A few minutes later, Tony pulls up in front of the brick house at 13 Tanglewood Close. Lights are on in the front windows. The garage door is open and a little red car is parked inside it.

"Tony," I say. "Can you just wait here a second? If they invite me in, then you can go. If...if they don't, I might need a ride back to the hotel."

"No worries," he says, and I assume that means yes.

I gather my things and open the car door. I keep my eyes on the blue front door as I close the car door behind me and start walking past the rose bushes. I feel very, very young. I feel like a child who has been sent to the principal's office, but I don't know what it is I have done that got me into so much trouble. My heart is pounding as I ring the bell. I try to recapture the serenity I felt in Christ Church earlier today. I hear the engine of Tony's cab idling behind me.

The door opens and a woman who looks like she's in her mid-fifties stands there, drying her hands on a dishtowel.

"Hello," she says kindly.

"Fiona?" I say and I sound as young as I feel.

"Yes, I am Fiona."

"I am...I was wondering if I might speak to Martin."

Her eyes grow wide but she politely says, "Well, just a moment." She turns from me and calls to the other room. I can hear the sound of a television and the mew of a cat. "Martin! There's someone at the door for you!"

She backs up but stays within the entry of her home, as I would if a strange woman with an accent came to my house asking to see my husband.

I can sense that Martin is walking toward me. I see his shadow arrive on the wall of the entry before I see him. I wish I could still my pounding heart.

He comes to stand in front of me in the open doorway and I can see that he is tall, taller than my dad, and more solidly built. His hair is mostly silver, but there are tiny streaks of faded reddish-brown. His eyes are a soft gray like mine. Martin is wearing a look on his face that makes me think he is slightly annoyed that someone has come calling on a Tuesday night without phoning ahead first.

I am about to say something when that annoyed, peeved look disappears from his face and is quickly replaced with something like alarm or amazement. I can't tell which. I'm starting to tremble in my shoes as I realize I have seen that amazed look before. John Penney wore it when Blair, Jewel, and I walked into his classroom and he instantly recognized us.

"Good Lord," Martin says, barely audibly.

Martin sees his sister's face. My face. He thinks he knows who I am.

"Martin, it's me. It's Tess," I say, removing all doubt.

For a split-second, we stand there frozen in time, staring at each other as if across the decades. Then Martin finally finds his voice.

"How did you...how...?" But he is unable to finish the sentence.

Behind him, I can see that Fiona has raised a hand to her mouth to cover her shocked expression. She didn't recognize me like Martin did, but she must know my name. She looks utterly bewildered.

"Tess?" she says, behind her fingers and barely above a whisper.

I can't tell if they're happy or appalled to see me. I can almost hear my dad telling me "I told you so."

"I know I should have called first," I manage to squeak out. "But I...I wanted to see you so badly, and I was afraid..." I cannot finish my sentence either. I can't seem to tell them I was afraid they would hang up on me.

"Please, ah...please, won't you come in?" Martin asks, trying to sound polite, but his face has lost its color. He looks as if he has seen a ghost. I suppose to him, that's what I am. I step inside. From behind me I can hear Tony pull away from the curb and drive off.

Martin steps into his living room and shuts off the television. A newspaper is scattered across the sofa and he grabs at the pages. "Please sit down," he says.

I sit on the sofa and he takes the leather chair across from me, staring at me. I hand the bouquet to Fiona.

"They're a bit squished," I say.

"They're beautiful," is all Fiona says in shocked response. She takes them to the kitchen to put them into some water.

"I can't believe you're here," Martin says, staring at me. "How...when did you..." he stammers, but he is still unable to make his mind work in concert with his tongue.

"Let's let her tell us, Martin," Fiona says, coming back to sit by me on the sofa.

Martin stares at me. Perhaps I'm only imagining that his eyes are moist.

"Well," I begin, but despite my rehearsing I struggle to find the right words. "I…I just wanted to see you, Martin. I don't think it's right that we don't see each other or write to each other. You are my uncle. You grew up with my mother. You loved her. I…I just want to know you."

What I have just said sounds rather accusatory, like I'm blaming him for the years of silence. It's as much my and my dad's fault as it is his.

"I'm so sorry I waited so long to find you," I continue. "I was afraid you wouldn't want to see me because…because my mother died after giving birth to me and I know it was very hard for you and your mother…"

Tears have sprung to my eyes and I look down at my empty hands. I'm aware that Fiona has put an arm around me.

When I look up at Martin the tears in his eyes are now unmistakable.

"Oh, Tess," he says and sounds like it hurts to say my name. "It *was* hard losing her. But it was doubly hard losing you too. My mother and I…We didn't treat your father very well when he brought Madeline's body back to be buried…"

"Martin," Fiona says gently.

"No, it's true. You know it's true, Fiona. You said it yourself back then when it happened," Martin says to Fiona, but then he turns to me. "We were awful to him, Tess. We were so angry and sad about losing our Madeline, we took it all out on him. And he must have been hurting like we were. It was awful."

He stops then to chase away those horrible memories.

"When my mother finally got over her grief, she wanted very much to see you, Tess; she did," Martin says when he is able to continue. "She tried to contact your father in the Azores, but he would never return her calls. He sent back her letters unopened. She sent packages to you but they all came back. I tried too. I even got ahold of him by phone one day at the hospital. I begged him to let us come to see you, but he wouldn't agree to it."

Martin stops again and I try to focus on what he is telling me and not how much it is hurting me.

"A couple months after that, your father was reassigned back to the States. We didn't know where he went. No one on the Azores would help us find him because he left orders not to give out his forwarding address. I gave up then, but my mother kept trying. When she died five years later she knew you were both stationed in Maine. She was trying to make arrangements to come see you. She had even written your father, and this time the letter had not come back unopened. She was still trying to convince him to let her come when she died of an aneurysm. I wrote your father when she died. I thought he might come then. But he didn't."

It is more than I can bear. I let my body fall against Fiona's and I just let the tears come. I'm aware that Martin has moved from his chair to sit beside me on my other side and he drapes his strong arm across my back.

It doesn't make any sense. So many wasted years. And for what reason? These three people loved my mother—Martin, my grandmother, and my father. They intensely loved her. In their grief they loved her. And look what their crooked kind of love did to all of them.

To me.

This is not how people—especially family members who are bound by bonds of love and blood—should treat each other.

This is madness. It stops now. I will stop it. I will stop it for all of us.

CHAPTER 26

Words on Stone

Martin, Fiona, and I talk, cry, and look at photo albums for hours. Martin shows me pictures of my mother when she was little, and of he and my mother together, and of the grandmother who died while trying to find me. I have a hard time turning the pages in the photo albums because each picture seems like a part of my own life. The blood of the people in the photographs runs through my veins. I want to memorize each image.

We don't spend much time talking about my dad, although Martin asks about him. I tell him and Fiona that after a long while, my father did find love again. I show them a picture of Zane that I carry in my wallet. I say nothing of the difficult history my dad and I share, but I do remind them—and myself—that my father profoundly loved Madeline, that losing her was too much for him in many ways. Despite my dad's many faults, he did adore my mother.

Martin and Fiona want to hear all about my childhood, of course—where I lived, where I went to school, where I now work. I tell them I am engaged to a wonderful man named Simon Arbareth. And I tell them about my recent trip to Arkansas and Tennessee, how Blair, Jewel, and I had sought and found the little boy whom we discovered on a church doorstep the summer we turned thirteen and how we gave him back the things that belonged to him.

It's long into the night before we finally feel able to rest from filling the space the lost years created. Fiona invites me to stay the night with them. Though I am without so much as a tooth-brush or clean pair of underwear, I accept.

Fiona heads upstairs to turn down a bed for me and I close the last photo album. Martin turns to me.

"Did your father give you my address?" he says, out of the blue.

"He didn't give it to me, but I found it at his house, Martin. He had kept it."

"Did you tell him you were coming here to find me?"

"Yes," I answer.

"What did he say?"

I think carefully for a moment before answering.

"He was worried that I might be disappointed."

"Disappointed?"

"That I might get my feelings hurt, Martin. That you might not want to see me."

"I don't think your dad and I ever really understood each other," he says, shaking his head.

"It's not too late to start."

He looks up at me in awe and surprise.

"That is something your mother would have said," he whispers. "You look so much like her. I knew the second I saw you that you were Madeline's child."

"Martin," I say, after a moment's pause.

"Yes?"

"I want to see where she's buried."

He nods.

"Of course. I'll take you there in the morning."

I sleep in a bed that belonged to my cousin Julia, who is now living in London with her husband, Nigel. They have two children, Max, who is three, and a new baby named Thea. Julia is two years younger than me. I have another cousin too. Colin is a mechanical engineer and lives near Birmingham. He is twenty-three and single.

As for other relatives, the Bowker family is small. Martin and my mother have an aunt who lives in a nursing home near Leeds, and she has three children who are my second cousins. One lives with his family in Liverpool, another with his family in York, and another somewhere in Devonshire.

I am exhausted as I lay my head down and wrap a blanket around me. I close my eyes and see all their faces: my mother's, her parents', Martin and Fiona, Julia and Nigel and Colin, Max, and little Thea.

I fall asleep imagining what these people are like—these strangers, my family.

When I come into the kitchen in the morning, Martin is on the phone with his employer, a telecommunications firm, telling his manager that urgent family business has come up and he needs to take a few days off. Fiona is at the stove, frying eggs. Martin hangs up.

"I hope this won't cause trouble for you at work," I say, taking a chair at the kitchen table.

"It will be fine," Martin assures me. "I've been with the company twenty-five years. I know too much. They won't fire me. How about you, Fiona?"

"Today is good, but I will have to go in tomorrow. I can have Friday off, though. We should have a big to-do here over the weekend so Colin and Julia and Nigel and the wee ones can meet their cousin Tess."

"That would be wonderful," I say.

"Very nice, indeed," Martin says.

"I called them both first thing this morning. They can't wait to meet you," Fiona says happily.

We enjoy our breakfast and then we climb into Martin's little Vauxhall. We stop at the hotel first so I can change into clean clothes. Once back inside the car, I decide I want to bring flowers to my mother's grave. I ask Martin to take me by the little flower shop on High Street.

"You've been to the Secret Garden?" he says, turning his head around to look at me.

"Well, yes. The flowers I brought for Fiona came from there," I answer. "Martin, is that the shop your mother owned?"

"Yes," he says, turning back around. "It was. I sold it when my mother died."

"Do you want to go to a different flower shop?" I offer. "I can find some flowers in the covered market, I'm sure."

"No. It's fine. It's perfect."

There is nowhere to park in front of the little shop, so Martin drops me off and circles the block while I go inside. The woman at the counter recognizes me.

"Well, hello again," she says.

"Good morning. I'd like another one of those bouquets," I say.

A few minutes later I'm standing outside the shop with a familiar bouquet in my hand. Soon, the little red Vauxhall comes into view. When Martin stops in front of me, I quickly get in.

"Wolvercote Cemetery isn't far from here," Martin says as we head down a busy thoroughfare.

We arrive at the grounds of Wolvercote Cemetery in about fifteen minutes. The May sunshine is bright and vibrant and Martin parks his little car under the shade of a tall willow.

I get the feeling as Martin ambles up a path on a little hill that he knows the way very well, but that he does not come here often. Fiona and I follow in silence.

Martin walks by perhaps twenty or so graves and then stops beside a trio of black granite headstones. One belongs to my grandfather, Albert Bowker, who died when Martin and my mother were in their teens. Another belongs to Anna Bowker, Martin's and my mom's mother—my grandmother. The third one bears my mother's name—Madeline Bowker Longren. Underneath her name are the words *Beloved Daughter*.

Martin sighs next to me and I think I know why he doesn't come here often. His parents and his sister, essentially his whole family, lie under the grass at our feet. I kneel down by my mother's headstone and trace my finger across the letters in her name.

"Let her have a few minutes alone," I hear Fiona whisper to Martin, and I am aware of them walking away.

I know my mother isn't really resting in the earth beneath my knees. I know that all that is underneath me is a wooden coffin that holds a mere shell. But I keep my palm against the headstone anyway and I begin to whisper.

"I'm here, Mom. It's me. Tess. I've finally come. I'm sorry it took so long...I saw your baby pictures yesterday. They look sort of like mine. I stayed the night with Martin and Fiona. They were so happy to see me, Mom. And I'm going to see my cousins on Saturday. I bought some flowers for you at your old shop. It looks beautiful and it smells so sweet inside. I love this place where you were born and grew up, Mom. I love Oxford. I sat in the meadow at Christ Church yesterday. It was so peaceful. And I went inside the cathedral too. It was like sitting for a few minutes in heaven. I will have to bring Simon here one day. I'm getting married, Mom! As soon as I get back to Chicago. You would love Simon. He is very gentle and wise. He's my best friend. I wish you could meet him. Mom, I miss you so much. I always have and I always will. I have a mannequin named after you at work. She's my favorite one. She gets to carry the purse...I wish you could come to my wedding...I'm so sorry I waited so long to come. I'm so sorry..."

At some point in my murmurings I begin to weep. I'm not sure when. And I'm not sure when it is that Martin returns to me, but I know that when I can no longer speak, he is crouched beside me, letting me lean on him as he holds me.

We stay like that for quite a while, until my legs and knees are stiff and sore. But I do not want to move from this place. I feel that at last I am sitting, whole and complete, on the other side of my Beautiful Gate. The good side. I don't feel anymore like someone who has been crippled since birth. The crooked things that were in my power to straighten have been straightened. I leave the rest, including my crooked soul, to God to fix. Martin, next to me, makes no move to rise to his feet.

"Thank you for bringing me here," I finally say to him. "Thank you for everything, Martin."

"We never forgot about you, Tess," he says softly.

I lean into his shoulder and rest there for a few more minutes.

"I just want to stay a little bit longer," I say.

"Take all the time you need."

He rises and walks slowly back down the path, leaving me alone, but not alone.

"Thank you," I breathe to the One who has been pursuing me—who, like Martin and Fiona, also never forgot about me.

I lay the flowers at the foot of the stone that bears my mother's name and the tips of the longest petals caress the words below as a gentle breeze stirs them.

Beloved Daughter.

Beloved Daughter.

Beloved Daughter.

Epilogue

Chicago, Illinois

If I concentrate on just one thing, if I block out all other sounds and sights in this room where I lie, I am able to withstand the pain. It is more powerful than I thought it would be. I shift my weight, close my eyes and turn my thoughts toward my happiest moments in the past year and a half.

The best memories begin with the three weeks I spent with my family in England. It still seems odd to me that I can say that about Martin and Fiona and my cousins—that they are my family. I divided my time between staying at the Randolph Hotel and staying with Martin and Fiona. Some nights, if we were up late talking or playing cards, I would just stay the night in Julia's old bed.

After I met my cousins that first Saturday, I couldn't wait to spend more time with them. Julia invited me to stay a few days with her and her family in London. I took the train, and I was able to stay awake while riding this time. Julia and Nigel's kids, Max and Thea, were fun to be with, and Max welcomed me like I was a favorite aunt. Colin came for the weekend. We spent a whole day walking around London, visiting the places I had only ever read about—Big Ben, Westminster Abbey, the Tower Bridge, and Trafalgar Square. We watched the changing of the guard at Buckingham Palace and then had a cream tea in St. James Park while Max fed the ducks. Julia took me to Harrod's, just for fun. All we bought was some tea.

When I got back to Oxford, Martin took a few more days off work and we visited Warwick Castle and Stratford-upon-Avon and Blenheim Palace. He drove me past the air base where my father once worked and took me to some little villages in the picturesque Cotswold region where it seemed time itself has simply stood still.

It was hard to say goodbye when the time finally came, but the nice part was, I knew it wasn't going to be forever.

When I returned to Chicago, Simon moved in with his brother and we began to plan our wedding in earnest. Antonia was hopping mad when I finally showed up for work nearly six weeks after I left her originally thinking I was only going to be in St. Louis for just a couple days. But the temporary help had worked out fine. She really had no reason to complain. She just likes to. Her anger lasted a day. Then she proceeded to deride me daily for deciding on marriage.

My dad seemed quiet and moody on the phone when I returned to the States and called him. If I didn't know better, I'd say he was disappointed I had had such a wonderful time. I think hanging on to his anger all these years made it easy to keep his distance when it came to my mother's family. I could sense disappointment in his tone that the reason for his anger no longer existed.

Simon and I were married the third week in August at the Church of the Beautiful Gate, and Samuel Mayhew performed the ceremony. Dad and Shelley were a little put out that the wedding wasn't held in Dayton, but I could think of no better place to have it. Antonia wouldn't come and pretended that she didn't care that I was marrying the man of my dreams, but she sent two beautiful matching silk dresses for Blair and Jewel to wear as my matrons of honor. Simon's brother, Paul, was the best man. Simon also asked Tim Penney to stand in as groomsman. Tim and Simon had started e-mailing each other after I got back from England and had struck up quite a friend-ship. Chloe and Leah were my flower girls, and Matthias, Jewel's oldest son, was our ring bearer. Despite what anyone might have thought—no one actually said anything derogatory—I had mag-nolia blossoms in my bouquet. I think Corinthia understood why because she was the only one who said it was a beautiful choice.

The wedding itself was rather small since I don't know anyone in Blytheville except for the Mayhews. But with all of them and all their children, plus John and Patricia Penney, Penny Mollet, the Taylors from Paragould, and Carol Ann Marker (all of whom Corinthia wisely invited), all the pews were nearly full. It was amazing to me to see Noble and Rena all grown up. I had never been able to picture them as adults. Noble, his wife, Jocelyn, and his two little girls live in Dyersburg, Tennessee now, but they made the hour-long drive to my wedding, as did Rena, who is engaged and living in Cape Girardeau, Missouri. Shepherd and his young wife, Tabitha, live in Florida and were unable to come.

As thrilling as it was to see Noble and Rena again, I was more enthralled that Martin and Fiona were sitting in the pews that day. My father simply had no choice but to swallow his pride and to talk to his former brother-in-law. By the end of the day I could see that the ice was beginning to thaw. For both of them.

But even that wasn't the most amazing part of the day. Martin had found his mother's wedding dress in the attic of his home a week after I returned to the States. He had it professionally cleaned and then sent it to me. I had nearly fainted when I opened the box and saw the note describing whose dress it had been. It is beautiful, made of creamy colored organza and French lace. I wore it the day I married Simon.

For our honeymoon, I took Simon to England and showed him all the places where I had found healing for my heart, including the grassy knoll where my mother is buried. Blair insisted we use the remaining week she had paid for at the Randolph Hotel. The rest of the time we spent in London, seeing the sights and visiting with Julia and Nigel, and Colin on the weekend. One afternoon back in Oxford, Simon and I loitered around the train station until a familiar-looking taxi driver pulled up into the rank of cabs awaiting fares from the station. Tony was understandably surprised to see me. It took some doing, but he finally agreed to bring his wife over to Martin and Fiona's that night for supper. It was important to me that Tony understand he had been a link in the chain that had brought two hurting families back together.

Two months after we returned from our honeymoon, Simon completed his own pilgrimage to peace by starting to speak at high schools about safe driving habits. By the end of the first semester of school, Simon had spoken to seven different high school driver training classes. I've lost count of how many he has done now. He always starts his presentation by placing a beautiful portrait of Brian Guthrie's wife and daughter on the podium he stands at. The teens always think the same thing—that Simon must have lost his wife and daughter to a drunk driver and the presentation will be just another plea to not drink and drive. They are usually surprised to learn Simon was partially at fault for the deaths of these two people, who were actually the wife and daughter of a now-grieving man. They are surprised that a simple thing like fiddling with a cell phone and not looking over your shoulder when you pass another car can end two lives.

Over the course of the next twelve months, Simon and I studied the Bible together, me using the one Corinthia had given me and he using one Pastor Jim had given him. We have begun attending a church Jim recommended, purposely not attending Jim's church out of respect for Brian Guthrie, and we recently joined a small group that meets weekly. We still have a ways to go to understanding what it means to trust God, but I feel I have a handle on at least one thing. Back when I offered forgiveness to my dad and he not only didn't want it, but also was pretty sure he didn't need it, I began to finally understand the mystery of the cross. Began to. I don't understand it all yet. But does anyone ever really understand all of it?

Blair and I talk more on the phone these days than we did in years past, as do Corinthia and Jewel and I. It seems finding Tim a second time has rekindled the fires of our friendships. Blair is dating a man she met at a struggling art gallery that she has chosen to lift out of near bankruptcy. The man's name is Thomas and he is the owner. He seems like a very nice man, very gifted in the visual arts, which perhaps makes up for his

utter lack of business sense. I met him a couple of months ago
when Blair brought Thomas to Chicago for an art show. Thomas
believes in giving every aspiring artist a place to showcase his
or her work, turning over nearly every penny of profit back to
the artists so they can support their families and their dreams.
Thomas is like Blair in this way. The only difference is Blair gives
from her abundance and Thomas gives of his insufficiency. I
am especially comforted by knowing that Thomas attends a
downtown St. Louis church that meets in an old warehouse,
serves espresso before and after the service, and displays art
tables as a regular part of the worship time. I haven't actually
been to this church; I have only heard Blair describe it to me.
But from what I have gathered, it preaches Christ, honors the
Bible, and embraces grace and truth. Corinthia must be praying.

My relationship with my dad has improved somewhat,
though he still hasn't spoken to me directly about our conversation in the airport a year and a half ago. Maybe he never
will. But I have my peace about the past and the mistakes that
were made. I even have peace about the people who made them.
He will need to find his own peace when he finally decides he
wants it.

As for me, I have turned in my canvas bag and now carry
a purse of my own. I am almost thirty years old, and my life
is about to change in the most wonderful of ways. It was time
to make that transition.

I also convinced Antonia to let me work part-time last fall
so I could go back to school to finish my business degree. It
has changed nothing for my career, but getting my college
diploma eleven years after graduating from high school was very

satisfying. It felt good to finish something I had started such a long time ago. Antonia is afraid I will quit now and start my own business. The thought has crossed my mind. Sometimes I envision a store next to *Linee Belle* paneled in oak and boasting maps and globes of every shape, age, and size on its shelves. I don't think I will ever make maps. But I could happily sell them. I would love to show people there is a way to get from one place to another. There is always a way.

The pain is intensifying now and I cannot simply think about things that have enriched my life these last eighteen months. I can feel my body changing, shifting gears. Something is about to happen.

There is a riot of activity around me. I call Simon's name and he murmurs something to me. I can hear nothing but the sound of my own voice. I am saying something. I am yelling something. The pain is white and hot. It is moving across my body. It is too much. I clench my teeth and wait for it to tear me in two.

But then there is a break in the pain. Something breaks free. It feels like it is me.

"It's a girl!" I hear someone say.

I can hear Simon's voice, but it sounds far away. Then he is leaning down over me, kissing my damp forehead.

"A girl!" he whispers.

I hear the faint sounds of my infant daughter drawing in air and releasing it across her unused vocal cords. She offers a timid yell and the nurses in the room laugh.

"What's her name?" the doctor asks, placing the tiny creature across my chest.

The infant child looks up at me, raises a tiny arm as if to salute me, and then starts to howl.

Simon laughs. I start to laugh too.

"Madeline," I say, gazing in wonder at this child I have borne.

The sound of her name and the vigorous cries from her body fill the air around me, above me, and within in me.

And the air is sweet.

A Note from the Author

Thank you for allowing me to share my love for storytelling with you. My prayer while writing *The Remedy for Regret* was that I would entertain with words but also enlighten with truth. I trust you will be able to sense, after reading this book, that sometimes we are given opportunities to mend the past and we should not waste them. And that sometimes we are asked to accept the part of the past that cannot be changed, that we must entrust it to a wise God who often fashions beauty out of heartache. I love hearing from readers and I encourage you to visit my website at www.susanmeissner.com, where you can follow the link to drop me an e-mail. Discussion starters are available for this book as well as my other two novels, *Why the Sky Is Blue* and *A Window to the World.* You can also write me in care of Harvest House Publishers, 990 Owen Loop North, Eugene OR 97402-9173. God bless you!

Susan Meissner

Susan Meissner is an award winning newspaper columnist, pastor's wife, and high school journalism instructor, and author of one previous novel, *Why the Sky Is Ble*. She lives in rural Minnesota with her husband, Bob, and their four children.

If you enjoyed *The Remedy for Regret,*
you'll want to read Susan Meissner's other novels....

WHY THE SKY IS BLUE

What options does a Christian woman have after she's brutally assaulted by a stranger...and becomes pregnant? Happily married and the mother of two, Claire Holland must learn to trust God "in all things."

A WINDOW TO THE WORLD

Here is the story of two girls—inseparable until one is abducted as the other watches helplessly. Years later, the mystery is solved—and the truth confirmed that God works all things together for good.

Harvest House Publishers
Fiction for Every Taste and Interest

Phil Callaway
The Edge of the World
Wonders Never Cease

Linda Chaikin
Desert Rose
Desert Star

Mindy Starns Clark
THE MILLION DOLLAR MYSTERIES
SERIES
A Penny for Your Thoughts
Don't Take Any Wooden Nickels
Dime a Dozen
A Quarter for a Kiss
The Buck Stops Here

Roxanne Henke
COMING HOME TO
BREWSTER SERIES
After Anne
Finding Ruth
Becoming Olivia
Always Jan

Melanie Jeschke
Inklings
Expectations

Sally John
THE OTHER WAY HOME SERIES
A Journey by Chance
After All These Years
Just to See You Smile
The Winding Road Home

IN A HEARTBEAT SERIES
In a Heartbeat
Flash Point
Moment of Truth

Bette Nordberg
Season of Grace
Detours

Craig Parshall
CHAMBERS OF JUSTICE SERIES
The Resurrection File
Custody of the State
The Accused
Missing Witness
The Last Judgement

Raymond Reid
The Gate Seldom Found

Debra White Smith
THE AUSTEN SERIES
First Impressions
Reason and Romance
Central Park
Northpointe Chalet

Lori Wick
THE TUDOR MILLS TRILOGY
Moonlight on the Millpond
Just Above Whisper

THE ENGLISH GARDEN SERIES
The Proposal   The Visitor
The Rescue   The Pursuit

THE YELLOW ROSE TRILOGY
Every Little Thing About You
A Texas Sky
City Girl

CONTEMPORARY FICTION
Bamboo & Lace
Beyond the Picket Fence
Every Storm
Pretense
The Princess
Sophie's Heart